Advance Praise for

The Ones We Choose

"How could I not love a debut about science, secrets, DNA, and how the traumas of our ancestors still live within our very cells? With gorgeous prose and a deep emotional resonance, *The Ones We Choose* is about the science of love, how our DNA shapes us, and a mother's fierce battle to protect her son while confronting what really makes our identity ours, what and who we choose to let in, and what and who we don't. An absolutely dazzling, profound ruby of a novel."

—Caroline Leavitt, *New York Times* bestselling author of *Pictures of You*

"This chimera of heart and science skillfully produces an extraordinary breakthrough novel. I love smart fiction with a sharp heroine at the core. Julie Clark has perceptively giv⸺ ⸺s that in *The Ones We Choose*. A story of mother and son a⸺ ⸺ that bind, right down to the marrow. Trust me, you⸺ ⸺ to read this."

—Sarah McCoy, *New York Times* and ⸺ ⸺g author of *Marilla of Green Gables* ar⸺ ⸺dren

"An engaging, heartfelt alchemy ⸺ ⸺ion, *The Ones We Choose* is a unique story ⸺ ⸺u thinking about the true meaning of family an⸺ ⸺ritage silently weaves its way into every choice we mak⸺

—Amy Hatvany, author of *Outside the Lines*

"A novel with a wonderfully smart and strong protagonist, Julie Clark's debut, *The Ones We Choose*, is an impressive and surprising combination of hard science and raw emotion. In this absorbing story of friendship, parenting, and the intensity of the sibling bond, Clark reveals how messy family life can be and how the mess itself might be of great value. An engaging read!"

—Amy Poeppel, author of *Small Admissions*

The
Ones
We
Choose

A novel

Julie Clark

GALLERY BOOKS

New York   London   Toronto   Sydney   New Delhi

G

Gallery Books
An Imprint of Simon & Schuster, Inc.
1230 Avenue of the Americas
New York, NY 10020

First Gallery Books trade paperback edition May 2018

For information about special discounts for bulk purchases, please contact Simon & Schuster Special Sales at 1-866-506-1949 or business@simonandschuster.com.

The Simon & Schuster Speakers Bureau can bring authors to your live event. For more information or to book an event, contact the Simon & Schuster Speakers Bureau at 1-866-248-3049 or visit our website at www.simonspeakers.com.

Interior design by Bryden Spevak

Manufactured in the United States of America

10 9 8 7 6 5 4 3 2

Library of Congress Cataloging-in-Publication Data

Names: Clark, Julie A., 1971– author.
Title: The ones we choose / Julie Clark.
Description: First Gallery Books trade paperback edition. | New York : Gallery Books, [2018]
Identifiers: LCCN 2017049736 (print) | LCCN 2017061157 (ebook) | ISBN 9781501184482 (ebook) | ISBN 9781501184475 (paperback)
Subjects: LCSH: Mothers and sons—Fiction. | Paternity—Fiction. | Genetic genealogy—Fiction. | Psychological fiction. | BISAC: FICTION / Psychological. | FICTION / Literary. | FICTION / Family Life.
Classification: LCC PS3603.L36467 (ebook) | LCC PS3603.L36467 O54 2018 (print) | DDC 813/.6—dc23
LC record available at https://lccn.loc.gov/2017049736

ISBN 978-1-5011-8447-5
ISBN 978-1-5011-8448-2 (ebook)

To Alex and Ben, who remind me every day
that I'm braver and stronger than I ever imagined.

And to Sharon, for lighting the way from above.

The Ones We Choose

GENOME

Just as astronomers have mapped the night sky, geneticists have mapped the human genome, the strands of DNA telling your story through every cell in your body. But it's not just your story; the human genome is rich with thousands of years of history, passed down from mothers and fathers to sons and daughters. Those who have come before you live inside you, shaping who you are.

Secrets drift through time, your identity whispering like a feather across your cells. Nearly three billion particles, thirty thousand genes, the microscopic world cracked open as wide as the cosmos, reminding you of who came before and pointing toward who will come next.

Chapter One

If loneliness were a color, it would be the deep purple of my eight-year-old's shirt as he walks solitary laps around the school track. Before opening the car door and letting the playground sounds crash over me, I watch him, wondering how I can fix this, or if my chance had passed long ago.

With the ache of worry that seems to always chase me, I grab my purse and slam the door, hurrying toward the picnic tables where other students are bent over board games.

"Hey, Dr. Robson," the woman in charge of the after-school program says, offering me the sign-out book. It's the third week of school. I should know her name by now, but my brain is stuck in a three-word loop: *Miles is lonely.*

"Please, call me Paige." I sign Miles out, and she looks toward the track. My eyes follow. Miles rounds the far corner, no bigger than a matchstick.

"We set up some games, hoping he'd be interested," she says. "He was very sweet, explaining the periodic table as he played chess. But when the game was over, that was it for him."

I try again to remember her name, this woman who cares enough about my child to help him make friends and settle into his new school. "Thanks anyway," I say. "He takes a long time to warm up to people." His lack of friends shouldn't bother me.

It's how I was as a kid, more interested in books than people. But somehow it's different when it's your child walking alone while other kids play, marking the time with laps, clocking the minutes until he can go home.

The woman smiles, sympathy softening the edges of her mouth.

The weight of her pity bears down on me. "There's hope though. I've convinced him to go on the dads' campout, and we're buying supplies this afternoon."

"That'll be good," she says. "Maybe his dad can do a better job of helping him find friends than I can."

I look back toward the track and watch Miles approach. He sees me now and breaks into a slow jog. He's still far enough away that I could explain, say there is no father, just me, an anonymous sperm donor, and my boyfriend, Liam.

But I don't. Somehow it feels like a betrayal to share the details of Miles's life with a woman whose name I can't even remember.

"I hope so too," I say.

———

I glance at Miles in the rearview mirror as we head toward Camping World. "You looked more excited when we went to the dentist last month."

Miles's eyes meet mine. "You weren't forcing me to spend two nights in a tent with my dentist," he says.

"I'll make sure to add a couple hundred dollars to your therapy fund," I joke.

"Can I start now?" he mutters.

Liam greets us at the entrance. "Looking good, Dr. Robson," he whispers in my ear as he bends to kiss my cheek. Miles's eyes skirt away from us. Even though Liam and I have been together for over a year, there are moments when Miles's resentment crowds everything else out. In some ways I understand. It's only been the two of us for most of his life. In that sense Liam is an intrusion, an unwanted guest, no matter how carefully I try to balance my time between them. But I want Miles to accept Liam. To not fight so hard to shut him out.

"Hey, Miles," he says. "Ready to shop for our trip?"

Miles gives Liam a steady stare but says nothing, and I brace myself. Miles and I have had several arguments about this trip already. I think it will be a great chance for Liam and Miles to bond, away from me. Maybe meet some of the other kids at his new school. However, Miles thinks camping on the beach with Liam is just short of child abuse. But my mind traces his solitary laps around the track, his shoulders braced against the heat of the mid-September sun, and I pray the weekend will give him a friend to walk with. Just one.

The inside of the store is enormous, a cavernous space lit with bright fluorescent lights. We stand next to a display of canteens and try to find our bearings.

"Okay," Liam says. "What's first on the list?"

Miles looks at the crumpled paper in his hand and says, "Tent and guylines."

"They don't waste any time, do they?" Liam says. "Straight to the big-ticket items."

"Why do people say that?" Miles asks, his love of wordplay edging his reluctance aside. "Did they used to pay for things with giant tickets?"

Liam laughs. "The bigger the ticket, the more it's worth. You'd need a ticket the size of a football field just to buy a car. Imagine trying to fit that in your pocket."

But Miles lets the sentence hang in the air and instead studies the list in his hand. "Do you think we could get air mattresses too?"

Liam shifts easily. "I'm not letting my delicate body sleep on the ground, that's for sure." He pauses in the middle of a wide aisle to read the signs suspended above us.

Liam's body is anything but delicate. Though lean and narrow, he's tall, towering over the tops of the aisles, able to survey the store like the captain of a ship.

The briefest hint of a smile outlines Miles's mouth. I collect these moments, like coins in a piggy bank I can pull out and count, evidence that things aren't always so hard between them.

Miles continues, his voice warming as we walk, enthusiasm sneaking in despite his best efforts. "Nick says there's a dirt bike course. Can we do that too?"

I want to ask who Nick is, but Liam speaks first. "I don't know about that, my friend. If you get hurt, your mother will kill me."

Miles's expression shifts, his lips pinching into an angry line as his gaze darts away from Liam. And just like that, the tenuous thaw is over.

"Liam's right," I say. "No dirt biking." I reach out to smooth Miles's hair out of his eyes, but he pulls away.

"There are lots of other things we can do," Liam says. "Like surfing."

"You're the surfer," Miles says, his voice tight and hard. "Not me."

My gaze travels between them, tension heating the air around us.

"I could teach you," Liam continues.

"If you fall off a surfboard, you hit the water," I say. "If you fall off a dirt bike, you might break an arm. Or worse."

Miles stops in the middle of the aisle and crosses his arms over his chest. "I don't even want to go on this trip. The least you can do is let me do the *one thing* I'm actually looking forward to."

"Miles," I warn.

Liam shoves his hands into his pockets, trying to hide his hurt. "That's cool. I totally get it."

"Why do you have to talk like that?" Miles's voice is rising, drawing the attention of other shoppers. To me he says, "He's not even a dad. He says *that's cool* and *no worries*. Dads don't say those things. They have real jobs. They drink coffee. They go to the bank."

"I mostly use the ATM," Liam says, and I want to elbow him in the ribs. He should know joking with Miles right now is not going to help.

"Liam has a job," I say.

"He plays video games."

"No, he programs them. Most kids would think that's cool."

Miles huffs. "Great. Now he's got you saying it too."

I turn to Liam. "Can you find the sleeping bags?"

"No problem," he says, looking both worn out and relieved to escape.

"Don't bother, because I'm not going," Miles calls after him.

I wait until Liam disappears around the corner and then turn to Miles. "Come with me."

I lead him down a row of tents, a small city, set up and empty, and pull him inside a red nylon one where the light is warm and dim and everything takes on a pinkish hue.

Miles looks around the small space. "It's like being inside a bubble," he says. But when he catches the expression on my face, his smile fades, realizing we're not in here for fun.

"What's going on with you?" I ask.

Miles shrugs, looking out the tent's window, which opens onto a cinder block wall.

"Miles." I stare at him, waiting for him to look at me. When he does, I say, "This isn't about dirt bikes or Liam saying *cool*. For whatever reason, you've decided you don't like him, though I can't imagine why. He's always gone out of his way to show how much he cares about you." My sister's husband, Henry, went to college with Liam, and when Liam moved to Los Angeles from New York five years ago, he instantly became part of the family. But looking back, Miles never really interacted with him. Times when we'd all be together, Miles would step around him, rendering Liam irrelevant with his silence. And when I started dating him, Miles was forced to be more obvious with his contempt. "Why won't you give him a chance?"

Miles doesn't answer.

I wait.

Finally, he crumbles, his anger falling away. In a small voice he says, "Why did you do this to me?"

"Do what?" I brace myself, expecting him to rail on Liam and blame me for making them take this trip together.

"At school, everyone talks about their dads and all the things they've done." Tears shine in his eyes, and he swipes at them. "I'm the only person who doesn't even know who his dad is."

I sink to the ground, pulling him onto my lap. All his sharp edges dangle over the sides, but he curls into me, fitting into the space that has always belonged to him. I wrap my arms around him.

This is what they don't tell you at the sperm bank, as you sit in a small office with your genetic counselor, thinking you can pick a donor and then forget about him. That someday, you might find yourself hiding inside a tent at a camping warehouse, trying to explain to your son why you dropped him into a fatherless life. I think of my own father and wish I could tell Miles that even when you know who your dad is, there are still thousands of ways he can fail you.

"We've talked about this, Miles. So many times. I wanted to be *your* mom, and that was the only way." I squeeze him tight and breathe in the scent of him—sweat and shampoo and something that's uniquely Miles. I can feel the tremor of tears he's trying to hold back. "Hey now," I say. "It's us against the world, remember?"

"Right," he says, though his voice is flat and heavy.

I think back to the year I turned thirty-eight, to the yearning that pushed me to find my way to motherhood on my own terms. I knew Miles was out there waiting for me. How I got to him was just a detail. "I know it's hard," I finally say, because I have to say something.

"No, you don't!" he says. "I shouldn't have to make up stories about who my dad is or take other people on dad campouts because I don't have one."

"Honey." I pull back and smooth the hair off his forehead. "There are lots of different families. Remember Nina from your old school, who has two moms? Or Reggie, who lives with his grandparents? No one is going to care that Liam isn't your dad. What matters is that Liam wants to do this stuff with you."

Miles presses his lips together, gearing up for what he wants to say next. "I have a dad. Why can't I know who he is?" His voice carries the weight of his tears, the words thick and wobbly.

I exhale. "Because those are the rules, and I agreed to follow them."

"I never agreed," he whispers, his soft words slicing through me.

I didn't see this coming. I expected questions, not blame. I expected curiosity, not this ragged pain that seems to be coming from Miles's deepest place. I did everything the donor websites told me. I met all of Miles's questions with accurate and age-appropriate answers, never hiding the truth and revealing more as he got older and his questions clarified. I felt righteous in my honesty, as if I were paving the way for the more evolved adult I imagined Miles would grow into. He changed the boundaries of my life. Being his mother has pushed me to be less selfish, to take myself less seriously. To have fun; to be silly. He's all I ever wanted. It never occurred to me that I might not be enough for him.

"I love you," I say, and wait. When he doesn't pick up the line, I tug his ear.

He sighs. "I love you more."

I give him a final squeeze and finish it off. "Not possible."

—

We find Liam standing in front of a wall of sleeping bags hung like curtains, about fifty choices that all look the same to me.

"What do you think?" Liam asks. "What kind of filling do we need? It gets cold out there at night."

A salesperson with a red polo shirt, black polyester pants, and a name tag that reads *Eric* zeroes in on us. "Hey," Liam says, drawing Eric closer. "Which of these bags would work best for a beach campout?"

Miles has wandered to the far end of the row, to a display of lanyards, and is letting them cascade through his fingers. I tune out Liam and Eric and watch my son. Sometimes it shocks me, to see this version of myself from the outside. Apart from his green eyes and untamable cowlick that sticks out over his left ear, Miles is a carbon copy of me, from my brown hair and lean frame all the way down to the sprinkle of freckles across his nose. If I blur my vision, I might be looking at my younger self. The only thing missing is the Shaun Cassidy T-shirt.

"Hey, you guys." Liam yanks my attention back. "This guy went to college in New Hampshire and hiked the entire Appalachian Trail alone. I think we're in good hands."

Only Liam would befriend this kid—not to be polite, but because he's interested.

Eric rubs his hands together. "I can outfit you guys, no problem."

"Don't forget the bear repellant," Liam says, winking at me.

Miles rolls his eyes. "We're going camping in Malibu, not the Rockies."

———

We wander down a wide aisle of lanterns and flashlights, and I look at the list, overwhelmed and silent. I should make Miles apologize to Liam, but it's easier to drop it for now. Liam grabs a torch and turns to me, his expression serious. "I'm sorry, Paige. The tribe has spoken."

"You're ruining my reputation as a serious scientist and scholar," I say, taking the torch and returning it to the others.

"Oops," he says, though he doesn't look sorry. He wraps his arms around me, and I sink into him. I've never let anyone love me the way Liam does. I was perfectly happy keeping the important things—my career, my son, my family—separate from the men I dated. But Liam snuck in the back door. I never imagined I'd fall for a guy who surfs, whose job requires him to be up on the latest video game trends. But I'd never met one with such a whip-smart sense of humor, who somehow knew how to balance the seriousness of his job with the playfulness of life. Liam loosens my strings and loves me despite the fact that sometimes I get too wrapped up in work, or with Miles. He's thoughtful, remembering details about me that he pulls out months or years later, like a magic trick just for me. Several years before we began dating, I mentioned in passing a preference for rainbow-sprinkled cupcakes from a bakery downtown. The morning after our first date, while I sat at my desk fuzzy from lack of sleep and the warm tickle of new love heating my chest, a box of cupcakes with rainbow sprinkles arrived at the lab—one for me, one for my lab partner, Bruno, and one to take home to Miles. *For the girl who loves rainbow sprinkles.*

It's a side I wish Miles would acknowledge. I give Liam a gentle squeeze and pull away, watching Miles in front of a display of lanterns designed like old-fashioned oil lamps.

"I thought I had him with my riff on big-ticket items," Liam whispers. "But I'm running low on material. By the end of the trip, I'll only have *got your nose* left."

Liam's words carry an edge of defeat. This trip is doomed to fail. There will never be room for Liam, because apparently Miles is saving himself for someone else.

"Hey, Miles." We turn to see a boy walking toward us, his father following behind. I don't recognize them, but it's still early in the year. I wonder if this is who Miles mentioned earlier, but the boy's smug expression tells me it's not.

He points at Liam. "Is that your dad?"

It's an innocent question, but his voice carries a hint of menace beneath the surface, as if he already knows the answer.

Miles stares straight ahead. "No."

Before I can say anything, Liam steps in. He reaches out to the father and shakes his hand. "Hey there. I'm Liam. You guys going on the campout too?"

The boy turns to Miles. "You have to go with a dad. It's a *dads'* campout."

Outraged, I turn on the boy's father, waiting for him to discipline his child. But he only gives an uncomfortable chuckle and says, "No need to be so literal, Ethan."

I step in front of Miles, as if to shield him. "Not all families are alike."

Liam reaches a hand out to steady me, but Miles is already pushing past us, his small face twisted in anger and humiliation. "You see? People *do* care. You're the only one who doesn't get it." He tosses the flashlight he was holding into our cart and runs down the aisle, disappearing around the corner.

Ethan's dad shifts from one foot to the other, his eyes darting around the store, looking for an escape. "Sorry about that," he says.

"It's a little late for sorry." I turn away from them and go after my son.

———

I find Miles waiting by the car. He's not crying, but wet tracks line his cheeks. My sister, Rose, always says, *There's no way to raise a child without a few broken pieces.*

"I'm not going on the trip," he says.

"Okay." I watch him, waiting to see what he'll say next.

"Can we go home now?" he asks.

"Sure."

I think of Liam, still somewhere inside the store, carrying with him the weight of Miles's words, along with hundreds of dollars' worth of camping gear they'll never use. We're supposed to go to dinner, but the thought of dragging Miles through that charade seems pointless. I dig my phone out of my purse and dial Liam's number.

He answers on the first ring. "Is he okay?"

I glance at Miles, who stares out across the parking lot. "I think we're going to take a rain check on dinner."

"Come on, Paige. Seriously? What about all this camping gear?"

"I know. I'm sorry," I say, feeling terrible. "But I don't think either of us would be very good company."

Liam sighs. "No, I get it. It's fine. Should I call you later?"

"Sure," I say.

After I hang up, I stare at the phone in my hand, the pressure of always having to choose sitting on my chest like a pile of bricks. There is no right decision. One of them will always lose.

———

Liam calls as I'm getting into bed. I love when he calls late at night, when his voice can be the last I hear before I drift off to sleep. We don't get too many nights together, instead having to find stolen moments during the week when Miles is at school or at Rose's. But these late-night calls bridge the gap and connect us even when we can't be in the same room together.

"Sorry about bailing on dinner," I apologize again.

"How's Miles?"

I think about our silent drive home, the way he'd stared out the window, lost somewhere inside his head where I couldn't reach him. "Quiet," I say. "Sorry about the trip."

Liam sighs, and I can feel his frustration through the phone. "I don't know how to get through to him. No matter what I try, it doesn't work."

"It was wrong of me to push it." But that's not the whole truth. It was wrong of me to force Liam into a space Miles wants to hold for someone else.

"Don't blame yourself. It was a good idea," he says. "Hey, on my way home tonight, I passed a Mazda Protégé broken down on the side of the road. So of course, I thought of you."

I laugh. Two years ago, before we were together, I was at a wedding downtown for one of my colleagues, and at the end of the night, my car wouldn't start. I was exhausted and didn't want to deal with a tow truck, so I'd called Rose and Henry to come get me. Liam had been over and was getting ready to leave for the night, so he volunteered to pick me up.

"That was the best detour I ever made," Liam says.

I close my eyes, thinking back to a time when I was satisfied with all parts of my life—leading an important study on a national stage, raising a smart and engaged son—I thought I could do it all.

"When I drove up and saw you standing out front in that green dress looking so beautiful and so pissed off . . . I still owe Mazda a thank-you note for making such shitty cars."

I remember my panic and then the relief when Liam pulled up, giving me a smile that lodged itself inside my heart, where it slowly grew into something more.

"I still want to be the one you count on," he says.

"You are."

His voice is like velvet, and all I want to do is let it carry me to sleep.

"I love you, P," he whispers. I roll over on my side, the door to my room open so I have a clear view down the hall and into Miles's room. He's nothing more than a shapeless lump under the covers.

"I love you too."

OXYTOCIN AND FATHERS

Oxytocin, "the bonding hormone," is well documented in mothers, helping them through labor and in forming an attachment to their babies. A recent study has found that oxytocin levels in new fathers are nearly identical to those in mothers—even several weeks postpartum—proving that fathers are as biologically programmed to care for their offspring as mothers.

Chapter Two

As I walk up the hill to my office Monday morning, I take a moment to enjoy the silent campus. Behind me, Malibu is buried under a thick layer of fog, but Annesley College is situated in the Santa Monica Mountains, and the sky is clear above me. A small, private university hidden in the shadows of UCLA and USC, the ivy-covered brick buildings are reminiscent of an upper-crust East Coast school and remind me of my undergraduate days at Princeton, without the frigid winter temperatures. I pass beneath an arbor that's just beginning to turn orange and into the main quad. It's deserted at this early hour, students still sleeping after a long weekend of partying.

As a researcher, I live on the fringes of campus life, but I'm required to teach one section of freshman biology every semester. I pretend to be annoyed, but secretly, I love it. Researchers tend to lock themselves away in their labs and lose touch with the real world, but it's there that I find inspiration for the puzzles that consume me.

I'm leading a study on paternal bonding, which is nearing the end of its first phase, and I'm readying myself for the onslaught of attention our discovery will generate. It's never been easy, being a woman in a male-dominated field. I didn't get here by questioning myself or falling into self-doubt. I've had to work harder, push harder, and fake confidence I didn't always have. That Miles gets to see his mom accomplish something this important makes me feel as if I'm doing something right.

As I move deeper into campus, I leave behind the turmoil of the weekend—Miles's revelation, the canceled camping trip—one piece at a time. I pick up the pace and see a light burning through the second-floor leaded-glass windows of my office, and I know that Bruno, my research partner, is already there, checking email and entering data.

"What's the day look like?" I ask as I enter. Our office is tiny, just two desks face-to-face and edged up against the windows overlooking the quad.

Bruno doesn't look up. "Typical."

We met in grad school. It quickly became clear he wasn't cut out for peer review when he lit his critiqued thesis on fire in front of our stunned adviser. I was the only one who laughed, and our friendship was sealed. I went on to get my PhD, and he moved to Boston, where he made a name for himself working as a lab assistant at one of the top genetics labs in the country. When I landed at Annesley, Bruno was the only one I wanted by my side. Even though it's my name on the papers, it's Bruno's work as much as mine, and I never forget it.

I toss my bag in a corner, slump into my chair, boot up my computer, and lean back, waiting.

Bruno glances at me, then at my bag on the floor, and back at me without speaking. I sigh and pick it up, placing it in my bottom desk drawer, making my motions exaggerated and slow. Bruno is responsible for the organized state of our office and lab, which is ironic because he dresses as if he's rolled out of a dirty laundry basket—mismatched socks and wrinkled madras shorts in obscene color combinations. Luckily for him, we don't have a department dress code. Today he looks like an Easter egg on ecstasy: pink pants paired with a pale yellow T-shirt that reads *RAD*.

I slam the drawer closed and notice he's still looking at me.

"What?" I glance around for something I missed.

"You look like shit."

"Thanks."

"Did you see the email from Jorgensen?"

"I did." I swivel back to my computer, now awake, and open the message.

Dr. Jorgensen is the dean supervising our study. He's been making noise about our shrinking numbers, and Bruno and I have been scrambling to reassure him that our data set is still substantial and will show significant results.

Our study focuses on oxytocin production in fathers. The recent discovery of it in men has led us to look more closely at its correlation to paternal engagement. My team has discovered an inhibitor gene in 63 percent of the men in our study that prevents the release of oxytocin. In other words, we've found a genetic reason to explain why some men aren't good fathers.

The next phase—the clinical trial phase—is critical. We hope to test a synthetic version of oxytocin, but none of that matters if Dr. Jorgensen doesn't approve it.

I scroll through my in-box and locate the email, titled *Meeting ASAP*.

"What do you think?" I ask, scanning Dr. Jorgensen's short note.

Bruno shrugs. "Could be nothing. Could be the beginning of the end. We need to finish this next round of tests so we can compile the data before we meet."

I rub my forehead. "Okay. Can you get the new lab reports on my desk by the time I get back from teaching?"

Before he can answer, my cell phone buzzes with a call from Liam. I silence it, wanting to slip into the science, like a warm bath, and let the real world fall away for the next eight hours.

Bruno notices the missed call and says, "How'd the shopping trip go? Are Liam and Miles ready for campfires, s'mores, and 'Kumbaya'?"

When I hesitate, Bruno says, "Uh-oh. Tell me."

I fill him in on what happened, and he pushes himself away from his desk to look at me, raising an eyebrow. "So you ditch him in a camping store on Friday and now you're ignoring his calls. Excellent strategy. Guys love that."

"Shut up," I say. "It's fine. I'll handle it."

Bruno smirks, as if he expected me to say that. "How?"

I sigh and lean back in my chair. "Honestly? No clue." Bruno is one of very few people I will admit that to. I rearrange pencils and some Post-its on my desk, wishing we could drop it.

"You should tell Liam that it's not him. Put the man out of his misery."

"I will."

"When?" he presses.

"Jesus, Bruno. Let me take a breath first." I pick up a paper clip and trace its edges with my finger.

"Of course," he says. "You'll want it all figured out before you talk to him, lest he see that you might not always have one hundred percent control of a situation."

I look up. "That's not true."

"Let's review," he says, and I groan. He leans back in his chair and starts firing off names. "Simon Matthews. Greg What's-his-name. Guy-you-met-at-the-Dodgers-game. What do all these men have in common?" I don't bother answering his question. It's best to let Bruno burn himself out. "None of them could get past the brilliant Dr. Robson facade," he continues. "You never let any of them *do* anything for you."

"Like what?" I say, tossing the paper clip onto my desk. "Take care of me? I've managed just fine on my own."

Bruno's expression softens. "Not all men are like your father, Paige. They're not all out to disappoint you."

I look out the window, avoiding his stare. My father was a serial leaver, abandoning us for the first time when I was seven. Over the years, he'd return for brief periods of time, filling my sister, Rose, and me with high tension and even higher hopes. We worked so hard to hang on to him, filtering every conversation and measuring every interaction so as not to do anything that would make him bolt. I know now there wasn't anything we could have done or said that would have kept him with us, but I never stopped trying.

I gesture to the neat stacks of lab reports and anecdotal data surrounding us that prove there are plenty of men like my father. "Forgive me if I disagree."

He leans his elbows on his desk and says, "Honestly, I thought with Liam, we were past this. Finally, someone who's as smart— if not smarter—than you. Someone who won't put up with your bullshit."

I look out the window again and see students leaving their dorms, on their way to class. I have to leave too, if I want to make it to my lecture on time. "Your point?"

Bruno's eyes lock on to mine, and I force myself to hold his gaze. "If you keep treating him like an acquaintance, pretty soon that's all he'll be." His expression softens. "Don't try to fix this problem on your own. Let Liam help you. It's not a weakness to tell him you don't know what to do. You don't always have to be Dr. Robson-with-all-the-answers."

I'm not the kind of person who can make adjustments easily. I'm still trying to figure out exactly what Miles wants, and to do that I need more time to think about it. Analyze the possible solutions. I'm not ready to admit there isn't one.

"I need to get to class. Can you get me the lab reports by the time I get back?"

"Sure."

As I'm passing through the door, he calls, "And stop being an asshole, Paige. Take the damn call."

———

When I get back from class an hour later, I settle in to read the reports. The data looks good, and I'm spinning it into a compelling argument for Dr. Jorgensen when my office phone rings. I'm surprised to hear Scott Sullivan, one of our subjects, on the other end.

"Hey, Dr. Robson." His voice is rough, as if he's got a sore throat.

I first met Scott and his wife, Mara, at the beginning of our study five years ago. Mara was propped up in a hospital bed begging Scott to hold a screaming newborn so she could go to the bathroom.

I'd been a mom for a few years by then and recognized the exhausted desperation of a mother on her own. But Mara had a husband, a careless man who ignored their daughter, Sophie, as if she were no more than a shadow, reminding me of the many years I had tried to love a father who didn't love me back.

"Hi, Scott. How are you?" I quickly check my visit log to see if we missed a meeting with the Sullivans, but there's nothing.

"I have some bad—" Scott starts but then chokes up. He clears his throat and tries again. "I have some bad news. A few weeks ago, Mara passed away suddenly."

"Oh my god, I'm so sorry." I gesture to Bruno, trying to pull his attention from his computer. "Scott, can I put you on speaker? Bruno's here too."

"Sure." Scott's voice rasps into our office. Bruno leans forward, and we exchange a silent look of worry.

"What happened?" I picture Sophie's face and try to hold myself steady. "How is Sophie?"

"She's okay," he says, his voice cracking over the words. "The doctors think Mara had an aneurism, but we won't know for sure for several more weeks. She fell asleep on the couch watching TV one night—she did that when she had trouble sleeping. Sophie found her the next morning and tried to wake her up and—" He takes a ragged breath and blows it out into the silence of our office, unable or unwilling to finish his sentence.

In the background, I hear soft crying that soon grows to a louder sob, and five-year-old Sophie's voice says, "Daddy, please stop talking about it. Please stop telling it."

Bruno and I exchange concerned glances, and I lean forward in my seat, as if to see what's happening on the other end. "Scott," I say, fighting to keep my voice steady. "Is Sophie in the room with you?"

"She won't leave my side," he says, not bothering to hide his impatience.

I think again of my early appointments with Scott and Mara. Whenever Sophie cried or fussed, Scott bolted from the room. He would take calls, find work on his computer, or ignore the sobbing baby, forcing Mara to deal with her. Biologically, Scott should have been producing massive amounts of oxytocin directly following the birth of his child. But faced with his crying daughter, Scott exhibited a flight response.

And now Sophie is left with a man irritated by her presence. I think of Miles and what would happen if he were to lose me.

Scott interrupts my thoughts. "I think we need to drop out."

Bruno shakes his head. This definitely can't happen.

"I can only imagine how hard things are for you right now, Scott," I say, trying to make my voice soothing and supportive. "Maybe I could come over and talk in person? See if there's anything I can do to help you and Sophie?"

"We're not really up for company right now."

I stare at Bruno, worried. We need Scott in the study, but more important, I want to make sure his daughter is okay. Knowing Sophie's only caretaker is a man who—based on our results and his current state of mind—has no natural affinity for parenting leaves a knot in my chest.

Bruno speaks before I can. "I understand why you'd feel that way, and if that's the decision you ultimately make, we'll respect it. But why don't we give it some time and revisit in a few weeks? Nothing needs to happen now."

"I appreciate that," Scott says. "I'm just really overwhelmed." I can hear him gulp, and I know what he's probably thinking: *This will never get better.* "The study was important to Mara," he whispers.

I try to get my bearings. "Well then, let's put a pin in it and see where we are in a few weeks," I finally say.

"Okay," Scott replies. Then in a harsher tone, "Jesus, Soph. A little space, please."

I'm eager to get off the phone, not just because I don't want to give Scott any more time to withdraw from the study, but also to run from my own ghosts. I lower my voice, trying to keep it from cracking. "We're so sorry about Mara, Scott. She'll be missed."

We say our goodbyes, and I disconnect the call, Bruno and I staring at each other across our desks.

"Holy shit," he says. "That poor kid."

People will call this a tragedy, say *poor kid*, and then get on with their lives—order a cup of coffee, go to work, eat dinner, and fall asleep at night. But Sophie's loss resonates with me on a deeper level. This is why I need our study to succeed. For kids like me. For kids like Sophie. Because her life has just taken a sharp left turn into my biggest fear as a child: something happening to my mother, leaving Rose and me alone in the world with a man who was only consistent in putting himself first.

CELLS

My interest in science was sparked with a lie: *Every seven years, the cells in our body are replaced with completely new cells. Biologically, no part of your old self exists.*

My high school biology teacher delivered this information, not knowing the hope his words would ignite in me. I latched on to the idea that after enough time, there would be no part of me that had firsthand knowledge of my father or the pain he caused. That all the way down to my cells, he would eventually become a stranger.

Even though that turned out to be a myth—some arbitrary math to make shiny the otherwise rudimentary concept of cell regeneration and death—there is some truth to it. All cells have a life cycle.

Our bodies are made up of approximately seventy-five trillion living cells, each one toiling away at a specific job for the entirety of its life. They self-replicate through mitosis, splitting in half to create an exact copy. Every minute, we create one hundred million new red blood cells, which will live for four months before dying. White blood cells last longer—about a year. Skin cells only live two to three weeks. So if you've broken up with your boyfriend, in a few months, there will be no part of you he's touched. That much is true.

But there are some cells that last a lifetime. Brain cells in the cerebral cortex start recording from conception and don't stop until death. This is where your memory lives. Your thoughts. Your awareness. These cells carry with them every moment of your life—even the ones you'd rather leave behind.

Chapter Three

When I pull up to Rose's that night, I park a few cars away from Liam's and sit for a second, letting the events of the day wash over me. I wish I could go home and climb into bed. Instead, I've got to suck it up for family dinner night.

We let ourselves in, and Miles disappears upstairs to find his cousins while I pass through the narrow central hall and into the family room and kitchen that comprises the entire back half of their house.

Liam sits, arm slung across the back of the couch, a beer nestled between his knees. "Hey there." He stands to give me a kiss, and I let my lips linger on his for a few extra seconds, wishing I could stay there indefinitely.

Rose hands me a full glass of wine. "I called you earlier," she says. "Did you get my message?"

"Once she's at work, she's in another dimension," Liam says.

"What's wrong with that?" I take a big sip, hoping to calm my jagged nerves. To Rose I say, "I'm sure you've already heard the camping trip is off." I give Liam an apologetic smile.

Rose's eyes travel between Liam and me. "It's not too late. Maybe you can still talk him into it," she says.

I stare into my wineglass. I know that's not going to happen.

From somewhere above us, Hannah, my eleven-year-old niece, yells, "Mom!" in a tone that indicates Rose has about three seconds before things upstairs get ugly.

"Tweens." Rose grabs the glass out of my hand and takes a deep drink.

"Hey," I say, taking it back.

"I need it more than you do." She pushes through the swinging door that connects the kitchen to the formal dining room, leaving me and Liam alone.

"How was your day?" he asks, leaning against the counter.

I think of Mara and Sophie. What I need is a dark room and Liam's arms around me, erasing all my worries. What I have are fifteen minutes to get a salad made before four kids clatter down the stairs, demanding to be fed.

"Busy," I say. I grab the carrots Rose left on the counter and wash them, letting the cold water run over my hands.

Liam points to the carrots and knife. "Better practice before *A Night of Asian Fusion*," he says in his game-show-host voice. We religiously watch *Iron Chef* together—in person if we can manage it, or over the phone when we can't—and the Asian fusion cooking class I signed us up for next spring seemed like the perfect outlet for our obsession.

I laugh. "You might want to do some practice yourself. I almost broke a tooth on the salad you made the other day."

As I slice the carrots, he comes up behind me and peers over my shoulder. "I really think you should julienne them."

I give him a skeptical look. "Do you even know what that means?"

"*I've* been studying. Of course I know what it means."

I offer him the knife. "Go for it."

He holds his hands up and says, "I choose not to chop. At least not today."

I laugh and resume my work. "That's what I thought." The sound of Miles and Josh arguing floats downstairs.

Liam glances at the ceiling and says, "How was his day? Any issues with that kid Ethan?"

I dump the carrots into a bowl. "He seemed fine when I picked him up."

"Did you ask?"

"With Miles, sometimes it's better to let things rest for a little while. But I'll check in with him tonight. I had a lot going on today."

"Like what?"

I grab a cucumber, glad to have something to do with my hands. "One of our test subjects is thinking of pulling out."

I glance at Liam, who takes a sip of beer. "Is that going to be a problem?"

I think of Sophie. All day, memories of my father have been popping up unexpectedly, leaving me unsteady. I know my father can't hurt me anymore, but it's unsettling to be drawn so easily back to my own childhood.

I hear Henry's car pull into the driveway, so I keep it simple. "His wife died unexpectedly. To be honest, I'm more worried about his daughter than the study."

I scoop the cucumber chunks into the bowl and face Liam, drying my hands on a towel. He sets his beer on the counter and wraps his arms around me. My cheek presses against his chest, and I listen to his steady heartbeat, savoring the warm space he's created before slipping out of his arms and turning back to my salad.

In the dining room, Rose badgers Hannah to set the table. I

finish the salad and wipe the counter just as Henry comes through the kitchen, depositing several large bags on the counter. "Ribs are here," he announces.

Liam grabs a stack of plates from the counter and follows Henry into the dining room. I rinse off the knife and set it aside to dry as I stare out the window into the dark yard, my shadowy reflection looking back at me.

"Are you okay?" Rose asks. I didn't hear her come into the kitchen.

"Of course." I hand her the salad bowl and smile, willing it to be true.

——

Dinner is noisy, with the kids talking over one another and the adults trying to be heard above it all. At one point, Rose's youngest, Josh, says, "Aunt Paige, is it true that when you were little, you locked Mom in the bathroom by taking the doorknob off and turning it around so it could be locked from the outside?"

I laugh and give Rose an incredulous look. "Did your mom also tell you that she'd been in the bathroom for two hours?"

"Forty-five minutes," Rose says.

"Two hours," I repeat, and Miles grins. He loves to hear stories about me and Rose growing up. "Don't get any ideas," I say to him before turning back to Josh. "I thought since she loved looking in the mirror so much, she should spend the night in there."

Liam laughs and reaches for more corn. "How'd you get out?"

"Mom came home around eleven and unlocked the door," Rose says. "Paige was asleep. Not a care in the world."

I shrug. "I would have let her out if there was a fire."

"Thanks a lot." Rose laughs.

The kids finish and tear into the backyard to play night tag, and Rose and I rinse the dishes while Henry and Liam begin putting the leftovers away.

"We've got this," Rose tells them. "Go outside and referee."

"I need to go," Liam says. "We've got a deadline, and I'm headed back to work for the night."

"I'll walk you out," I say.

He claps Henry on the shoulder and says, "Thanks for dinner."

"See you next week," Rose says.

"If I don't see you sooner," he tells her.

I dry my hands on a towel and follow him to his car. The cool night air caresses my arms, and the smell of wood smoke and damp leaves hint at the coming fall.

Liam rubs my bare arms before hugging me. "Sorry about your test subject," he says. "Do you want me to call you later?"

My skin tingles under his touch. "No. I'm probably going to fall asleep the minute my head hits the pillow."

"All right. I'll call you tomorrow." He gives me a kiss and says, "And answer your phone."

I watch him drive away before returning inside, where Rose is busy putting leftovers in containers.

"How is Miles liking the new school?" she asks.

We'd been wait-listed for the school Rose's kids attend— a science and math magnet for gifted students. When we got the letter offering him a spot for third grade, I'd let myself believe a fresh start with kids more similar to him might draw him out. But so far, it's been more of the same. Plus Ethan. I sigh and slide the potatoes pan into a sink filled with soapy water. "I thought he'd find more friends here."

Rose glances at me. "Give it time."

I nod. "He loves the work. This is the first time I think he's ever been challenged. His teacher seems a bit rigid though."

Rose laughs. "Yep. Ms. Denny is a taskmaster, but Mikey loved her by the end of the year." She turns to face me. "I promised Mom I'd talk to you about something."

Dread pools inside of me. "What?"

"Dad's back."

As if I conjured him out of thin air. I pinch my eyes closed, battered by this day.

That my father has returned is nothing new. He's come and gone more times than I can count. I'd done my best to make peace with who he is years ago—a man intent on pleasing only himself. But for Rose, it's different. I don't think she's ever accepted his inability to love us, choosing instead to hope—despite all evidence—that each time he came back, he'd be different. Better.

"How long has it been this time?"

"She knew you'd react this way, which is why she wanted me to tell you."

"React what way? Skeptical?" I submerge my hands in the hot water and scrub hard.

Rose waits a few seconds before saying, "They want us to come for lunch."

"No, thanks."

I attack the burnt potato edges in the corner of the pan, wishing I could scrape our father from our lives as easily. "It's been ten years since we've seen him. I honestly thought we might be done with the charade."

"Paige," she warns.

"No. I don't play this game anymore. Dad is free to come and go, and you and Mom are free to have a relationship with him if you want. I don't have to."

"He's almost seventy-five."

"I can do the math as well as you can."

Rose grabs my arm, forcing me to drop the pan and look at her. Her voice is sharp, the words brittle. "He's getting older, and while you're so busy punishing him for not being the father you wanted, you're missing the opportunity to know him now. Yeah, he wasn't around back then. Get over it."

I yank my arm away and resume my scrubbing. "I am over it."

"I'm just afraid you're going to regret it if you don't allow yourself to have some kind of relationship with him."

"I think Dad should be the one worried about regrets." I turn the faucet on, hoping to end the conversation.

"It's lunch," she says over the sound of the running water.

I slam it off again and turn on her. "It's more than he deserves." Rose believes in unlimited second chances. I believe in natural consequences.

"Dad's made a lot of mistakes. He's hurt all of us. But he's the only father you've got. Miles's only grandfather. You need to stop locking him out of your life for fear of what might happen."

I set the clean pan on the counter, trying to subdue my anger.

"He's moved back in with Mom." Rose's voice is quiet.

"He always moves in with her." Dad would pull up, unload a suitcase from his trunk, and fill his dresser drawers, as if he were returning from a business trip. "That's not news."

"This time he brought everything with him," she says. "Furniture. Books. More than a single suitcase."

I dry the pan with a dish towel and put it away, uneasy.

"Mom says he has something important to talk to us about." Her voice softens. "It's one lunch, and then you can retreat. If you don't say you'll come, Mom will badger you until you give in. Think about it."

Rose is right. Our mother never accepts no for an answer, and she'll launch an elaborate campaign of phone calls, emails, and drop-ins to change my mind. It's not worth it.

"I'm not bringing Miles," I tell her.

"Fine. We'll have Henry watch the kids."

I sigh. "Okay. But this is it. I don't care how long he stays this time. I'll do the lunch and then I'm out."

"Fair enough," she says. "Thank you."

We work in silence for a few minutes.

"So what else is bothering you?" Rose asks, wiping down the counter.

"Dad coming back isn't enough?"

She shakes her head and starts the dishwasher. "No. This is something else."

"What are you, a mind reader?"

"You're my big sister. I've spent my whole life studying you. I know when you're worried about something."

I sigh and lean against the counter, spinning the stem of my nearly empty wineglass between my fingers. In a low voice, so Miles won't overhear, I tell her about his meltdown in the tent and how he wants to know his donor.

"Shit," Rose says. "Did you have any idea?"

"We've talked about how he was conceived, lots of times. But he's never said anything like this before." I gesture around us. "This is all he's ever needed. What's changed?"

Rose tosses the towel onto the counter and faces me. "Kids change. How many times have I caught myself parenting the kid who existed yesterday, only to realize they've woken up as someone entirely new today?"

"I suppose," I say. "Though that doesn't help me know what to do now."

"Did you tell Liam?" she asks. "It might make him feel better, knowing it didn't have anything to do with him."

"Between you and Bruno, it's like an episode of *Dr. Phil*." I catch her look and say, "You're right. I'll tell him."

I finish my wine, the dregs burning my throat as I swallow them, and steal a glance at the photograph on the fridge: Henry and a six-year-old Mikey, sitting on the edge of a lake fishing. The set of their shoulders, the slight tilt of their heads to the left, even the way they're holding their fishing poles is identical. Miles will never have a moment like that with a father. Not with Liam. Not with anyone.

Rose should understand this, but I think it's buried beneath layers of good fortune. She met Henry, fell in love, then married him. She wanted a family, tried for children, then had three in neat succession. Perfectly planned and executed. It's always been that way for her, perfect beginnings, middles, and ends, always what she wants, always when she wants it. I gave up resenting her a long time ago, but it still sneaks up on me when she assumes everyone has it as easy as she does.

She's forgotten how isolating it is to grow up without a father, like missing a limb—a faint memory that something should be there. Despite everything I swore I'd give my child, it turns out none of it mattered. Miles is no different than I was at that age, watching the kids with dads and wondering what it's like to ride on top of a father's shoulders.

Later that night, I pour a glass of wine and carry the bottle into my bedroom. My bare feet sink into the soft carpet I had installed shortly after I bought the place—a small two-bedroom bungalow in West LA. Enough room for Miles and me and not much else. I painstakingly restored it over the course of two years—putting in hardwood floors, painting the walls a rich, buttery yellow. Even though it's small, it's mine, and aside from the lab, it's the place where I feel most like myself.

My closet, however, is tiny, crammed with clothes and shoes and a shelf that buckles under the weight of sweaters and jeans. But tucked behind all of that, in a plain manila folder, is the file from ACB, American Cryogenic Bank, containing the paperwork from my journey through intrauterine insemination.

Sperm banks are businesses, set up to use cookie-cutter science. They run a series of blood tests and basic genetic screening panels that most first-year grad students could do. They're blind to the newest developments in genetics, unaware of how much more our cells know than our minds.

When I decided to use a donor, I knew I would have to do more, *be* more, than someone who had a partner. I was okay with that. I relished the idea of handpicking Miles's father based on science and facts. I never wanted my child to suffer the way I had, so I eliminated the risk. I crossed it off, like an item on a list—*father*—relieved to have spared my child that kind of pain.

I honestly believed that between me, my mother, and Rose and her family, Miles would have everything he needed. I made it my job, my mission in life, to make sure that no hole was left unfilled. But so much of parenting is guessing, then second-guessing, never seeing your mistakes until long after you've made them. You think it will be simple—*if my kid struggles, I'll find a way to help him*. But the reality is that you never imagine your child might push back on that help or that what your child needs is something you can't give.

Miles first started asking questions, as I knew he would, when he was four. *Why don't I have a dad like Mikey does?* I was ready, keeping my explanation simple. *Sometimes people need extra help to make a baby, and thanks to the kindness of strangers who donate sperm or eggs in a doctor's office, now they can.* Miles knew about blood banks, and this seemed to fit in with his narrative of *people helping people.* But now I wonder if I should have told him more about who I chose and why.

I take the folder to my bed and spread the documents before me—my donor's profile, the baby picture I paid extra to view, a well-read printout of all of his genetic stats and tests, his personal statement, and the staff reflection. I skim the personal statement, read so many times I have it memorized: *I'm an engineer who loves the outdoors—skiing, windsurfing, and hiking. The only child of two loving parents, I'm especially close with my father and grandfather.*

I loved the idea of a man who was close to his father and grandfather, as if they might pass down something deficient in my own genes to my child. And I loved the simplicity of it—none of the emotional baggage or misplaced expectations of the relationships I'd known.

I finger the baby photo, the edges curling and color fading. Somewhere I have an almost identical photo of Miles, and I'm struck again by the similarities—the shape of their eyes, the dimple in one cheek, the thread of genetics weaving its way through time and linking the past to this moment. It's not just me who lives beneath Miles's surface. I've let myself forget that. But Miles has never forgotten.

I finish my glass of wine and pour another, taking a healthy sip for courage. I open my laptop and google *Donor Sibling Registry*.

I'd first heard of it when Miles was an infant, when I was still reading the various donor boards on the Internet shortly after he was born. They talked about how important it is to give your child a sense of identity. The DSR connects donor-conceived children with biological siblings and their donors. At the time I thought it might be something Miles would do in his twenties or thirties, spurred on by a friend or partner, curious about his past. I never imagined I'd be hiding in my room with a bottle of wine, searching for Miles's father while he slept.

I enter the information I have—our sperm bank, donor number, and state—into the appropriate fields, and my finger hovers over the submit button.

What will I do if Miles's donor is there, looking for him? Or if he has half brothers and sisters who want to know him? *This is what he wants.* But he's eight. Does he really understand what this will open up for him—for us? And what will it do to Liam, who wants a permanent place in our lives? If I do this, all of that will be derailed.

And yet.

How can I not at least look? I don't have to do anything with the information. I can tuck it away with everything else, and it'll be there if I need it.

I click submit and wait, feeling as if I'm free-falling and I'm not entirely sure my parachute will open in time. A new screen pops up. *Your search has generated <zero> results.*

I let out a breath I didn't realize I was holding. Okay.

When the adrenaline has faded, I'm surprised to find I'm disappointed. And worried that I've gotten it all wrong. That it isn't enough to be loved unconditionally if you have no idea who you are.

DONOR PROFILE

Donor #: AF39742

Personal Statement: I love talking to others, whether with a stranger in line at the movies or over drinks with my oldest friends. I'm an engineer who loves the outdoors—skiing, windsurfing, and hiking. The only child of two loving parents, I'm especially close with my father and grandfather. We have a unique bond that transcends most of my other relationships. They inspire me to be a better person, a better man. I'm most proud of my career. I've worked hard to get where I am, and I've conducted myself with integrity. I chose to be a donor because I wanted to do something for someone else—without the accolades or recognition—just one pure, good thing. I can't think of a better way to change someone's life than to be able to help them have a child.

Donor Type: Anonymous

Height: 6'2"

Weight: 185

Hair Color: Light brown

Eye Color: Hazel

Complexion: Fair

Ancestry: German, Irish

Ethnic Origin: Caucasian

Religion: None

Education Level: Master's

Area(s) of Study: Engineering

Occupation: Engineer

Blood Type: A+

CMV Total Antibody: Negative

Chapter Four

"I brought ice cream!" My mother pushes past me, carrying a reusable grocery bag from the ninety-nine-cent store. "Liam," she says, catching sight of him in the kitchen. "Be a love and put this in the freezer."

"No problem, Beth." Liam takes the bag and disappears into the kitchen, where I can hear him trying to rearrange my crammed freezer to make room for the gallon of ice cream.

My mother zeroes in on a basket of Miles's laundry sitting in the hallway, waiting to be folded. She picks it up and moves it to the couch, where she starts to make neat stacks of shirts and underwear.

"Mom," I say. "Go play with Miles. I don't need you to fold my laundry."

She smiles, apologetic, holding a sock in one hand and searching the basket for its partner. "Sorry. Nerves."

She glances at me quickly, waiting to see if I'll ask her why she's so nervous. But I don't, because I don't want to leave any opening for her to launch into my dad's return.

"Thanks for babysitting tonight," I say over my shoulder. "We won't be late."

"I'm happy to," she says. "Miles and I need to work on his

Halloween costume. Besides, your father has a poker game, so I was at loose ends anyways."

I let her words hang in the air, refusing to engage. My relationship with my mother is complicated. She's one of the strongest women I know, often sacrificing what she wanted to give Rose and me what we needed. And yet, I've never understood what it was about my father that left her unable to move on.

Equally confusing to her was that I preferred to stay home and study rather than go out with friends. Rose made more sense to her. But even though Rose grew up to live the life my mother wanted for herself, I think she resents how easy it is for Rose, often making snippy comments to me about how Rose *just doesn't understand how difficult it can be*, as if the two of us are in some kind of hardship club.

"Grandma!" Miles flies out of his room and crashes into her.

She folds him into a tight hug and says, "What's it going to be this year? Pirate? Dinosaur?"

He wiggles away and says, "I made a list. But I need you to help me narrow it down." He dashes off to his room again.

"A list." My mother laughs, her eyes catching mine.

And just like that, my annoyance melts away. I couldn't do any of this without her. I can't imagine what it was like, raising Rose and me by herself. No one helped her with babysitting or Halloween costumes. She did it all on her own, with only my father's intermittent attention.

She deserves so much more.

I move forward and wrap my arms around her. "Thanks, Mom."

"It's just a costume," she says. "You know I love to do it."

"It's not just the costume," I say. "It's everything."

She cups my chin in her hand. "I know."

Liam returns from the kitchen. "We'd better leave if we're going to make our reservation."

I step away from my mom and grab my sweater.

As we walk out the door, she calls, "Drive carefully."

I smile despite myself. Since we each turned sixteen, our mother has always said this when we walk out the door. I think she is terrified that if she doesn't say it, something will happen and it will be her fault. Rose calls it Beth's Blessing.

I follow Liam to the car, hoping a night out will wipe away all thoughts of my father's return and the worry that he'll hurt my mother and Rose once again.

—

Liam has me laughing throughout dinner as he catches me up on his week. One of his programmers inadvertently designed a character that looked like an enormous penis, and the CEO, in front of a conference room full of investors, asked why the main character looked like a giant prick.

"Want to go for a walk on the beach?" Liam says after paying the bill.

"Sure." That seems as good a time as any to drop Miles's revelation on him.

Liam takes my hand and leads me down a side street that arcs onto the beach. The Santa Monica Pier rises in front of us like a carnival on a postcard.

"I wish you'd let me teach you how to surf," he says.

I lean into him. "And risk getting bitten by a shark? No, thanks."

He chuckles. "I don't know what it is with you and sharks."

"*Jaws* ruined the ocean for me. Sorry."

We walk toward our favorite lifeguard station in silence. Finally I say, "I think I've figured out why Miles is so hard on you. He told me he wants to know his donor. That I *ruined his life.*" I give a shaky laugh, hoping the sound of the ocean covers the uncertainty slipping through.

"You haven't ruined his life," Liam says. "But no wonder he lost it on you in the camping store."

I sneak a glance at him, trying to gauge his reaction. He catches me and lifts my hand, kissing my knuckles and easing the tension I've been carrying around since last Friday. We slow our pace and sit in the faint shadow of the lifeguard station.

Liam shakes his head. "So all this time, we've been forcing the issue, sliding me into the spot he thinks belongs to someone else."

"The problem isn't you. But I don't know how to help him."

Since last Friday, things I never really thought about have come into sharp focus, like the way Miles will watch Henry and the kids when they're playing in the backyard. A part of Miles runs around with them, but another part soaks it in, absorbing Henry's *fatherness* like his body might absorb a cold glass of water. Tears prick my eyes, and I swipe them away with the tips of my fingers, frustrated. I don't want to cry about this. Liam places his hands on my knees. Over his shoulder, the Ferris wheel begins its slow rotation, lights twinkling in the night.

"He wants to know his father, which is impossible," I continue. "I should have seen this coming, should have prepared better for the inevitability."

"Maybe you can find a support group for him. He's probably not the only kid who struggles with this," Liam suggests.

"We were in one for a little while when he was younger," I say.

"Why'd you stop going?"

I sigh. "I don't know." I look beyond the crashing waves to the moon reflecting on the ocean's surface. "Meetings were in West Hollywood. Traffic was a beast there and back. He didn't seem to get much out of it, and it was just one more thing we had to do every week." I take a deep breath. "I'll figure it out."

I hope I sound more confident than I feel. I have no idea what *figure it out* means. Searching for Miles's donor? Calling the clinic? Bribery? I'm up against a wall, with no way to give my son what he desires and no clear path to the life I want with Liam.

Liam turns so he's sitting behind me and pulls me back into him, wrapping his arms around me. We stare at the ocean glowing in the moonlight. After a little while he says, "Henry tells me your dad is back and wants to see you."

"Same story, different day," I say. "As regular as a leap year."

"Are you going to see him?"

"Mom wants us to come for lunch." I try to maintain an even tone and suppress my resentment at being pressured into going.

He rests his chin on top of my head. "Maybe he'll surprise you."

"I don't need any more surprises from him."

Liam sighs into my hair. "I only meant maybe you might want to reevaluate, considering what Miles is going through. It might help him."

"You can't be serious, knowing how he's treated us."

"It was just a suggestion."

We sit in silence for a few minutes, and I try to match my breath with the slow roll and tumble of the waves.

"What about you?" he asks softly.

I turn to look at him. "What do you mean?"

"Therapy for you," he says. "To help sort out your feelings about your dad."

"My feelings are pretty simple," I say. "Not a lot of sorting to be done."

"That's not what I mean." He looks away, toward the bright lights of the pier. "It affected you. To be left like that as a little girl. Did you ever think about seeing someone, to help process it all?"

I shrug. "My mom took me to see someone when I was sixteen. She was worried I was closing myself off from people, because I didn't want to go to pep rallies or bonfires like everyone else my age."

"And?"

"And it was a waste of time. My therapist was a middle-aged man who wore brown knit vests and had a comb-over. He was a cliché, all the way down to the fern hanging in a macramé plant holder. He had me write a letter to my father, telling him all the ways he disappointed us."

"Did you send it?"

I look at Liam, surprised. "No."

I think back to those stuffy afternoons in that dark office, saying all the things I'd rehearsed earlier to convince the therapist I didn't need to see him anymore: *I'm fine. No, I'm not angry with my father. No, I don't miss him. Sure, I have friends.* It never occurred to me that my answers were wrong. That by denying my pain, I was confirming it. What child wouldn't feel those things?

"Therapy wasn't for me. I've accepted my father's failures, and I've moved on."

Liam says, "Just because you've accepted it doesn't mean you're not still scared of it."

"I don't think sitting for fifty minutes and rehashing all those feelings would serve a purpose now."

Liam nods, though I can tell he doesn't agree. "Fair enough."

I feel a silent shift in the air between us, and it surprises me that it wasn't the revelation about Miles that did it but rather the discussion about my dad.

"It's late," I say, hoping to move on. "We should let my mom get home to Prince Charming."

Liam stands and pulls me up. I brush the sand from my pants and reach up, wrapping my arms around his neck. "I love you," I say, letting my unease slide back to the ground where it belongs.

"I loved you first," he says, giving me a soft kiss, and then leading me back to the car.

BIOLOGY

A father's abandonment can imprint itself on you, shaping how you see the world and every decision you make. Rose grew up to create the perfect family. I grew up to pull apart the science of our father's choices, to find a genetic reason to explain why some men leave while others stay.

We can now look at your DNA and know where your family came from thousands of years ago. What they ate. How they lived. It can reveal secrets you never imagined possible. Your ancestors' long-ago choices influence who you are, just as the decisions you make today might be the beginning of a genetic response that will manifest itself generations from now.

No pressure.

Biology matters. It links you—definitively—to your family. No matter how hard we try, we can't erase what's already written inside.

Chapter Five

I'm running late for parents' night at Miles's school. I'd gotten waylaid on my way out by a student asking for a makeup quiz, and by the time I got there, the lot was full and I had to park three blocks away and walk. I'd hoped to go home and change, but there wasn't time, so I'm still wearing the blue jeans, blouse, and boots I wore to work this morning. At least I ran a brush through my hair, though the evening air is causing it to frizz. I remind myself that I'm doing important work, that it doesn't matter that I look wrinkled and worn out from the lab. But there's something about PTA mothers that makes me momentarily forget that I'm the one with a PhD, that my work will improve lives all over the world. Those women make me feel inadequate, with their Pinterest-inspired bento box lunches and their commitment to Mandarin lessons, reminding me I will always be two steps behind.

A tiny woman with sleek black hair and a pencil skirt stands outside the door to Miles's classroom, having a loud conversation with her husband, who for some reason felt the need to wear a bow tie to tonight's presentation. When I get closer, I recognize him. Ethan's dad, from the camping store fiasco.

"I just wish people would arrive on time," the woman says. "The email clearly said *arrive early to sign up for volunteer slots*." This must be Ethan's mother.

I walk past them into Miles's classroom. The walls are papered, floor to ceiling, family tree projects crowding every inch of space. I look around for Miles's project and spot it, tucked into a corner in the back. The flower design stands out—if only because it looks different from everyone else's.

This project has been a source of stress since it was assigned. Create a family tree with pictures and names going back at least three generations. I'd emailed Ms. Denny, who seemed sympathetic but inflexible. *I can't start making exceptions, so just do the best you can!* I scoured the insemination message boards and found a modification, displaying our heritage as a flower, with Miles's picture at the center and the rest of us surrounding him as petals. Miles insisted Ms. Denny would never allow it. But the alternative was to have half a tree, and that was unacceptable to him as well.

"All right, moms and dads!" Ms. Denny stands in front of the classroom, her cropped gray hair matching her gray suit, making her look like a dirty snowball, round and uneven. "If everyone will take a seat, we can start."

I slide into a chair in the back corner, letting the other chattering parents take the front seats. I tug my phone from my purse to make sure it's on vibrate when Ms. Denny's voice silences everyone.

"Please make sure you put your phones away, moms and dads." When I look up, she's glaring at me. "The information I've got for you tonight is critical to your child's success in my classroom."

It's the third grade. I look around. The room is a study in organized chaos. Tubs and bins in bright colors crowd the shelves. A multicolored rug and fat pillows dominate the one area that's clear of tables and chairs. In a corner, a giant tree made from twisted brown bags and green construction paper leaves climbs the wall and hangs from the ceiling.

"Homework is critical to success," Ms. Denny is saying. "If your child misses an assignment, he or she will be kept in at recess. If we don't start teaching responsible study habits now and holding children accountable, we do them no favors later in life."

I glance around the room, curious to see the other parents' reactions. As a college professor, I'd much rather hear about critical thinking and self-advocacy, not blind adherence to a homework policy.

Ethan's mother sits in front, nodding vigorously. I already know most of what I need to about Ms. Denny from Rose's kids. As long as Miles behaves and does his work, he'll be fine. So I have no concerns. He was reading well before kindergarten and taught himself multiplication last year, *just for fun*. He loves homework and learning. I just wish it wasn't such a solitary endeavor.

My phone vibrates with a text from Bruno. *Please don't forget we have a staff meeting tomorrow at nine.*

I scowl. We have a staff meeting every week. This is a passive-aggressive way to remind me of my earlier mistake and how I need to keep a clear head as we transition into phase two.

Bruno had walked into the office this afternoon and dumped a stack of files onto his desk. "I would have appreciated knowing ahead of time that you were planning to skip the meeting with Jorgensen," he said.

My eyes shot to the clock and then down at my calendar, where it read *2:00—grant renewal meeting*, circled in red.

"Bruno, I'm so sorry." I pushed my hair off my forehead and rubbed my eyes. "I don't know where my head is."

He looked me up and down. "We tabled most of the issues, and I told him you had an emergency with Miles."

Relief flooded me. Dr. Jorgensen was not someone we could afford to anger.

"Thank you."

"What's going on with you?"

The last thing I needed was another lecture, so I kept it vague. "I don't know. Distracted, I guess." But the truth was, I'd been unsettled since my conversation the other night with Liam, at his suggestion that Miles might benefit from time with his grand-father.

"It's not like you to forget something like this," he said.

"I'm sorry. I'm just tired, that's all."

He stared at me a moment longer, and I could tell he didn't believe me. "Go home and get a good night's sleep."

"I don't know what I would do without you."

"I don't know either," he said.

Ms. Denny's voice yanks me back. "And now we'll hear from Nan, Ethan's mom, about the exciting volunteer opportunities you can look forward to this year."

Nan stands and glances around the room, waiting for every-one to look at her before beginning. "Thanks, Ms. Denny." Her voice is sugary sweet.

"We are *so* lucky to be in this class." I look to see if anyone is agreeing with her, but all I can see are the backs of the par-ents in front of me. "Ms. Denny is *the best* third-grade teacher at this school. It's important we support her in every way we can, and there are *so many* ways to help. Ms. Denny needs volunteers to run her learning centers—word sorts, number tiles, reading groups—they're really fun because you can come into the class-room and see your kids in action." Nan consults her clipboard.

"That's daily, between nine thirty and noon. We also need parents to help with dismissal at three and snack at ten twenty-five. There are school-wide ways you can volunteer as well, running the book fairs in the fall and spring or coordinating our after-school enrichment classes from three to four."

A hand goes up in front—a woman with wild dark hair and gold bangles on her wrists. "What about parents who work? Are there ways they can get involved? It sounds like most of the opportunities to volunteer happen during the school day."

"Um . . ." Nan frowns, looking to Ms. Denny for help. "Well, maybe they could take a day off to chaperone a field trip. Or go in late one day a week and help out in the morning. I'm sure something can be arranged."

Before anyone can ask any of the obvious follow-up questions to such a ridiculous suggestion, Nan says, "I almost forgot! Our back-to-school picnic is next week on the big yard. Food trucks, games, dessert. Bring your blankets and make some new friends!"

Her enthusiasm makes my head hurt. She can't be that excited about a picnic at a school playground. But I file the information away, though I'm doubtful Miles will be interested.

Nan's still talking. "And now please enjoy the beautiful family tree projects and have some refreshments. I'll be coming around with the volunteer sign-ups, so please see me before you leave. It's going to be a great year!"

Parents stand and stretch, so I do too. They gather in groups, friends since their kids were in kindergarten. No one seems interested in meeting the new mom. I take a deep breath, steeling myself. When I decided to have Miles, my mother warned me it would be like this—single parenting sets you apart. People don't know how to include you, so they avoid you. I didn't believe her.

Maybe that was what it was like in the seventies, I told her. *But it's the twenty-first century. Things have changed.*

But nothing has changed. Even though there are several other mothers on their own, I feel the separateness that's been my constant companion since Miles was born. I swallow my discomfort and study some of the projects near me. An elaborate three-dimensional oak tree looks like it has ancestors going all the way back to the *Mayflower*. I worry about Miles's simple, inadequate flower and wonder if I should just leave. Then I hear Nan's low voice.

"I mean, it's a *flower*. How hard is it to follow the directions?"

Her husband mumbles something I can't hear.

I freeze, but a different voice says, "Wow. That's a shitty thing to say."

I sneak a peek. It's the woman who asked about working parents. She's tall and wears a colorful caftan belted around her waist over tights and boots, stylish and funky in a way I wish I could pull off.

Nan's cheeks flush. "I only meant—"

"Has it ever occurred to you that maybe not every family looks like yours?" The wild-haired woman gestures toward the fancy 3-D tree I was admiring a few minutes earlier. I look closer. *Of course. Ethan.*

"I have a lot of sympathy for families less fortunate than mine. I'm a Christian," Nan huffs.

"Here's something to pray on," the stylish woman says. "Just because a family looks different doesn't make it *less fortunate*."

The crowd has thinned, parents unwilling to get caught in the crossfire, so it's just the three of us standing there, with Nan's mute husband looking on. I think back to the camping store, when he was unable to string together a sentence in the face of his son's cruelty. We move away, leaving Nan sputtering to her husband behind us.

"Sorry about that," she says. "I'm sure you're capable of speaking up for yourself. But Nan has been pissing me off since kindergarten."

She holds out her hand, and I shake it. "I'm Jackie," she says. "Nick's mom."

I smile, recognizing the name. "Paige," I say, releasing her hand.

Jackie grins. "Apparently, our boys enjoy doing word puzzles together at recess."

Miles has a friend. Relief and joy fizz through me, and I have to hold back from hugging her.

"So how are you guys settling in to Elmwood Elementary?" she asks.

"Pretty well," I tell her.

"What was your old school?"

"Iverson. It was fine, but they didn't have much of a gifted program. We were so happy when a spot opened up this year."

Jackie nods. "We've been here since kindergarten. At first, we worried Nick would get lost in such a big school. My husband went to a small private school in the Valley, and we heard no end of criticism from his mother. But I grew up on Long Island when everyone went to the local public school. So far it's been great."

Her eyes—brown and sparkling—light her from within, and her smile is wide and engaging.

"Ms. Denny seems to have quite a system here," I say, gesturing toward the labeled tubs and elaborate charts on the walls.

Jackie leans in closer. "The woman is a fucking drill sergeant."

I laugh at her unexpected word choice.

In a high-pitched voice that almost perfectly mimics Ms.

Denny, she says, "*Students must line up in alphabetical order. Homework is to be turned in on the right and backpacks hung on the left.* It's like a work camp." She holds up her plastic cup. "Do you want anything? Organic, fair-trade coffee? Cardboard cookie? They're gluten free."

I laugh. "I'll pass, thanks. I'm allergic to anything that doesn't have high-fructose corn syrup in it."

Jackie grins. "Finally. A living soul among the zombies." She gestures around, lowering her voice. "Most of the parents here are nice, if a little bland. Have you met anyone yet?"

"Not really. I don't linger too long at drop-off since I have to work."

"What do you do?"

"I'm a geneticist."

Jackie's face registers surprise, like most who discover a female scientist. "Fascinating. Tell me, what does a geneticist do?"

"Lots of things. Some work on cures for diseases like Parkinson's. Others focus on the sociological side, studying human behavior and the genetic reasons for it. Then you have forensics—crime-scene stuff you hear about in the news."

"And what's your area?" she asks.

"I run a small research lab at Annesley. We're studying the link between a genetic marker and paternal bonding. And I do a little teaching as well."

"Wow." Jackie swipes the hair out of her eyes. "That sounds like fun."

I think of Mara and Sophie. My job is interesting and challenging. But I've surrounded myself with men like my father, and there's nothing fun about watching kids struggle to make sense of a disengaged parent.

A man approaches us from across the room. "I signed you

up for helping with morning snack every Tuesday and Thursday," he says to Jackie, grinning. "And gate duty on Mondays, Wednesdays, and Fridays."

His face isn't extraordinary, but his hazel eyes are gentle, with laugh lines framing them like fans.

"This is my husband, Aaron," Jackie says to me. "He thinks he's a comedian." To him she says, "This is Miles's mom, Paige."

Aaron's eyes brighten in recognition. "Miles! We hear a lot about him at home. His library on outer space is on Nick's must-see list."

I smile. "It's a work in progress."

The room has cleared significantly, with only a few parents lingering by the snacks. Nan, clutching her volunteer clipboard, is one of them. She's looking our way, and I want to escape before she can pin me down to wash paintbrushes every week.

"I should go," I tell Jackie and Aaron.

"Us too. But let's get the boys together soon," Jackie says.

"We'd like that," I say, desperately hoping Miles is as interested in being friends with Nick as Nick seems to be with him. "It was nice to meet you both," I tell them.

Aaron holds up his hand in a silent farewell. Jackie offers a warm smile. "You too. See you soon."

I exit onto a dark and empty playground. The night air smells like wisteria, and I walk to my car, buoyed by the fact that Miles has a new friend, and maybe I do too.

ENTANGLEMENT THEORY

Entanglement theory is based on quantum physics. Physicists have learned that two particles—like electrons—that have interacted in the past but moved on will still behave as if they're the same entity. Meaning, if you change one, the other changes instantly and to the same degree. They're always connected. Always in tune with each other, no matter where they are. Obviously, entanglement theory doesn't apply to humans or genetics, but I think of the way a mother's heartbeat rises and falls, always in sync with her child's, and I wonder if there isn't something we don't know yet.

Chapter Six

S ince parents' night, Miles keeps mentioning Nick, telling me about his tree house or showing me a rock Nick loaned him. It seems like a real friendship, and I feel weightless with relief.

"And then," Miles says, finishing a story from the back seat, "Nick gave me the rest of his cookies."

We're on our way home, but stopping at the grocery store for our weekly shopping trip. "That's pretty generous," I say, putting the car in park. "Maybe we can buy some cookies for your lunch tomorrow to share with him."

I lock the car and we make our way through the crowded parking lot toward the bright lights of the store. As we approach the doors, Miles says, "Do you have the list?"

I pull it out of my purse and rip it in half, holding the two pieces behind my back.

Miles taps my left hand, and I hand him his half. He looks at it, and his face falls. "I got produce. *Again.*"

"Fate does not smile kindly on you," I say as we enter the market and each grab a cart. "Time?" I ask, and he looks at his watch.

"Five minutes after five," he says.

"Okay. Same rules as always. Fifteen minutes. We meet in the bakery, and the person who has the most items on their list wins." We start to move away from each other, and I call over my shoulder, "No running."

He calls back, "No cheating."

I widen my eyes in mock offense. Miles and I have been playing this game for a little over a year. It was the only way I could squeeze in the grocery shopping without constant complaining. He has fun racing the clock, I get food for the week, and I pretend I don't notice the two or three snack items he sneaks into his cart until we're home.

I zip around, gathering the things from my list as fast as I can. We pass each other near the canned goods. I glance in his cart and say, "You're slow tonight."

He rolls his eyes. "Nice try." He heads toward the paper goods, and I move toward the pasta sauce.

When the fifteen minutes are up, we meet in the bakery, where we tally the results. This time, Miles wins by two items, and he does a victory dance around the doughnuts.

I pretend to be disappointed, but I actually love it when he wins. The joy on his face is worth it, every time.

"I'm going to get Starbursts." He quickly transfers his groceries into my cart before heading toward the candy aisle, and I realize he's going for one of those mega bags. I want to stop him, but the rules for this game were set a long time ago. *The winner gets to pick anything, any size, no veto.* So I settle for stealing several every night until they're gone.

As I make my way toward the checkout lines, I hook my finger around a bottle of wine as I pass a display. Miles isn't the only one who sneaks treats into his cart.

He finds me in line and tosses the bag of candy in with the rest of our groceries. Next to the tabloids, on a low rack where kids can see them, is a display of children's books. Miles pulls

one off the rack—*Chemistry for Kids*—and begins reading immediately. As I unload our cart onto the conveyor belt, the man in
front of us turns. It's Aaron.

His eyes brighten. "Paige, right?" He looks over my shoulder
at Miles, who doesn't look up from the chemistry book.

"Yeah—"

"Hey, Mom, do you know the chemical formula for calcium
chloride?"

Before I can answer, Aaron says, "$CaCl_2$."

Miles looks up, his eyes full of questions flashing between me
and this stranger.

Aaron gives him an easy smile and says, "I'm Nick's dad."

I brace myself for Miles's usual greeting of a silent nod or,
worse, a silent stare. But Miles looks around and asks, "Is Nick
here too?"

"No, he's home with his mom." Aaron points to an enormous package of toilet paper on the conveyor belt. "Emergency
situation," he whispers, widening his eyes dramatically. He looks
ahead and grimaces at an old woman counting out coupons. "I
hope I'm not too late."

Miles stifles a giggle.

Aaron points to the book in Miles's hands. "I know that
book. There's a great experiment on page 127 where you can
make calcium carbonate."

I look at him sideways. "You know the page?"

"Jackie takes a three-hour yoga class on Saturdays. That's a
lot of time to fill."

Miles flips through the book. "Chalk," he says, a smile opening his face. "Chemical formula?"

Aaron rattles it off.

"Reactants?" Miles quizzes him.

"Calcium chloride, baking soda, water."

And they're off, talking about chemistry as if it's the most natural thing in the world. As if my child has struck up conversations with strangers a million times.

As Aaron takes his receipt from the cashier and hoists the toilet paper under his arm, he says, "Obviously, I'm needed at home." He winks at Miles, who grins back at him. "Will I see you guys at the school picnic this week?"

Before I can answer, Miles says, "Sure!"

Aaron smiles and says, "Great. See you then."

I offer a small wave and turn to Miles, whose eyes follow Aaron out the door.

As the cashier tallies up our groceries, I say, "The picnic? You want to go?"

"Definitely," he says. "Hey, can I get this book?"

"Sure." I put it on the conveyor belt with everything else. "Aunt Rose has been asking whether we'd go to the picnic, but I didn't think you'd be into it," I say, trying to figure out what's gotten into my child. "You've never wanted to go to anything like that before. Why now?"

He looks toward the door Aaron just exited. "Nick's going to be there. And his dad. So can we go?"

"Of course."

Miles does a shorter version of his victory dance, which makes me laugh.

After our groceries have been paid for and bagged, I push the full cart into the parking lot, Miles trailing after me. When we're settled in the car, Miles says, "Nick's dad is pretty cool."

It's taken him over a year to answer Liam's questions with more than one-word answers, yet he just had an open and animated conversation with a man he's never met before, and agreed to go to the picnic, which never would have happened at his old school. I feel as if someone has blindfolded me and spun me around twenty times, the world I thought I knew suddenly topsy-turvy.

Miles's voice jolts me. "Mom? Are we going or what?"

—

The following day, I'm delivering a lecture about genes to an auditorium filled with freshmen who haven't figured out how to skip class yet. As I step from behind the podium, my eyes travel across the faces of my students, a diverse group, most of whom are here only to fulfill a science requirement. I don't know all their names yet, but I will.

"You inherit traits from your parents, through your chromosomes, which contain about thirty thousand protein-coding genes. Some traits are simple, only involving one or two genes. Others are more complex, depending on multiple genes and even the environment. For example, being left-handed is the result of several genes, but if your teacher hits you with a ruler often enough," I say, smacking my hand onto the podium in front of me, "you can be forced into right-handedness."

A quiet murmur of laughter trickles through the room. I pause, letting them catch up on their notes. In the front row sits Rebecca. She has a strong handle on the material, and I want to encourage her to stick with science. She writes furiously, only looking up when she's ready for me to continue.

"Genes control how your body functions." I walk to the center of the dais and bring up a graphic of a chromosome and gene on the screen behind me. "Methylation is a process that controls when a gene is—or is not—expressed. It is why you ended up with your mother's brown eyes instead of your father's blue ones. You inherited both genes, but only one is expressed. But as with anything, errors can occur. We're learning that faulty DNA methylation can be triggered by outside factors, such as famine.

"The most well-known example of this is the Netherlands famine of 1944–45, which affected nearly four and a half million million people. Because this was a developed country, scientists were able to study the aftereffects on the human genome and found that survivors had a change in their DNA that resulted in smaller offspring—not just that first generation, but the one after it as well."

Rebecca's hand shoots up. "Can methylation turn off genes that might cause disease?"

"For acquired mutations, yes. But if it's a hereditary mutation, such as the BRCA gene, it's unlikely, which is why we encourage people who have family members with genetic mutations to undergo genetic testing themselves."

"What if you don't know that information?" Rebecca asks. Her eyes challenge me. "What if you're adopted? Then what? Hope for a methylation? You're screwed."

A few students snicker. I close my laptop, since we're nearing the end of class and sit on the edge of the dais, facing her.

"Actually, Rebecca, this is the perfect time to be alive for those people."

I look up into the lecture hall. A few students are quietly gathering their things, hoping to make a quick exit. I direct my voice toward the back to halt them. "How many of you have heard of 23andMe?"

Several hands go up.

I look at Rebecca. "You're eighteen, right?"

She nods.

"You can run a DNA test that will give you a medical background more comprehensive than anything your parents might be able to tell you." In a softer voice I say, "You don't need to know your biological parents to know your genetic history anymore."

I think of Miles and wonder if a medical background is really what Rebecca's after.

I hear louder rustling and check the clock on the wall.

"See you next week. Be ready for a quiz on chapter seven."

I stand and begin to pack up my things. When I turn around, Rebecca's waiting for me.

As we walk up the stairs to the back of the hall together, I say, "You know, there have been a few stories about people who've used companies like 23andMe and found biological relatives."

Rebecca looks at me, hope in her eyes. "Really?"

"Keep your expectations realistic," I warn. "That's not what they're set up to do. But there are a lot of ways for you to get the information you want."

I think about what databases and genetic tests might be available when Miles turns eighteen and if any of them will give him the information he craves.

23ANDME

23andMe is a genomics and biotechnology company that provides saliva-based direct-to-consumer genetic testing. Clients can access detailed genetic reports that outline their risk for genetic diseases, identify their ancestry from out of thirty-one populations worldwide, and learn how their genes might be affected through lifestyle choices. The name is derived from the twenty-three pairs of chromosomes found in a normal human cell.

Chapter Seven

MICHAEL

Music blares from speakers tucked into the corner of the playground as kids weave in and out of the crowd, hopscotching over blankets and playing an indecipherable game of tag that only makes sense to them. Dressed in layers, I stand on the edge of the field holding our blanket and chairs, a knot of apprehension in my stomach. While Miles is excited to be spending the evening with his new best friend, I'm worried about who I'll hang out with, since Rose is busy making change and folding paper around funnel cakes in the dessert booth. I'm hoping to sit with Jackie, but what if she's in the middle of an existing friend group? Will I be able to sidle up and join them? Making friends as an adult takes a lot more extroversion than I've got.

Liam wanted to come, but I held him off.

"Why not?" he asked. "I'd like to check out Miles's new school, maybe get some ideas for new things to talk about. Or more things he can ignore."

"Very funny," I say.

"Seriously, I want to go."

I was tempted to say yes. It would be nice to have him here, but I imagined the impression that would make on the other parents, saying *I'd like you to meet my boyfriend, Liam.* It was one thing to send him on a dads-only camping trip. But I didn't want to seem like one of those moms who had to drag her boyfriend to every school event just to prove she could get a man. And Liam's presence would make Miles feel even more different from his peers. But of course, I couldn't say any of that to him.

"I know. And I love you for that. But I think it's better if it's just me this time, okay?"

I tried not to register the look of resignation that crossed his face.

Miles dashes forward, and a boy who must be Nick rushes toward him. They immediately begin talking at the same time. Before, Miles would have come to this grudgingly and sat on the blanket with a book. But tonight he's glowing with happiness as he laughs at something Nick says. They lean into each other as they catch up on the few hours it's been since school.

Jackie approaches from behind them, waving. I smile, my anxiety easing, and walk toward her.

"I'm so glad you made it!"

"I'm surprised to be here. This isn't really Miles's thing, so I was shocked when he said he wanted to come."

She smiles over her shoulder and spreads her blanket on the grass. I follow suit.

Before I can worry about what we should talk about, she says, "Let me fill you in on some of the key players here." She points toward the food trucks. "The woman in the purple sweatshirt and jogging tights is Myra Guthry. She's run seventeen marathons. She was seven months pregnant for the first one."

"Yikes," I say.

"Exactly. And see the guy working the game booth?" I follow her finger. A handsome man with an intentionally rumpled look gives change and a wink to a giggling mom. "His name is Rex Butler."

When I glance at her, she says, "You heard me right."

"Oh my god," I murmur, stifling a laugh. "How do you keep a straight face?"

"You should see him in an orange vest doing gate duty. You won't be laughing then." Jackie gives me a meaningful look and then cracks into a smile.

I lean back, letting the last of the setting sun warm my shoulders. "This is nice," I say.

Jackie's gaze catches on something behind me.

Rose plops down next to me. "Remind me next year to plan a trip to Aruba during the back-to-school picnic."

"Jackie, this is my sister, Rose. She's got a fourth grader and a fifth grader. And a seventh grader at home."

Rose smiles. "Nice to meet you. Which one belongs to you?"

"Nick," Jackie says, pointing at the two boys across the yard near the handball courts. "He and Miles have bonded over chemistry and robotics."

Rose's smile widens. "Miles is his mother's son."

We duck as a Frisbee flies toward us, and a girl wearing yellow ribbons in her hair dashes by, throwing an apology over her shoulder.

Jackie turns to Rose and asks, "What about you? Do you work?"

Rose feigns horror. "Who has the time? I spend my days planning the bake sale for the back-to-school picnic. Tomorrow I'll go over my notes, make some color-coded charts and graphs to figure out our top-grossing desserts, and start planning for next year."

I snort. "She'll throw her receipts in a shoe box that'll sit on the kitchen counter until Valentine's Day."

Rose turns on me. "This, coming from a woman who prepares for her tax accountant by handing him a banker's box filled with receipts and a bottle of tequila."

Jackie laughs, and I shrug. "I think it's rude to show up empty-handed."

"How about you?" Rose asks Jackie.

Jackie looks toward the food trucks, their long lines winding out of the parking lot. "I stay home," she says in an offhand way that betrays more emotion than she intends. "I take care of Nick. Plan meals. Vacations. You know."

I'm surprised. I assumed she worked, based on her question in Ms. Denny's classroom. "Staying home is hard," I say. "My eight weeks of maternity leave nearly killed me."

"For God's sake, you spent every day of those eight weeks parked on my couch," Rose says.

Jackie offers a sad smile. "I used to work in marketing, before I got married. I was pretty good too." She pulls her sunglasses down, covering her eyes again, and lowers her voice. "Aaron will kill me, but I've actually been looking for a job. I have an interview coming up next week with a Santa Monica firm. He'd rather I stay home, like his mother did. But I'm not Beverly, and I sure as hell am not like that fucking Nan."

Rose makes a disgusted sound.

"You know Nan?" I ask her.

"Everyone knows Nan," Rose says. She turns to Jackie. "The worst thing that can happen is that they'll say no."

Jackie shrugs, apparently done with the topic. "I'm not going to worry about it until there's an offer on the table. But, God, what I wouldn't give to get dressed every morning in something other than yoga pants."

I look across the playground at Miles and Nick, hunched over something next to one of the classrooms. I check my watch and see it's six o'clock. The lines at the food trucks are finally shorter, so I stand up and say, "I'm going to get us some food while the lines are good. You want anything?"

Jackie checks her phone. "Aaron's supposed to be here soon, so I'll wait for him."

Rose says, "I ate too many desserts, and both Josh and Hannah have money. They're on their own."

I cross the blacktop, skirting around a kickball game, over to where Miles and Nick are looking into a rain gutter. Their backs are arched, feet tucked under them, motionless.

"Hey, Miles?" I say.

The boys turn to face me. "We found a grasshopper." Nick's smile splits his face open in the same way Jackie's does, his eyes dancing with excitement. "We think it's a female," he says.

"Cool. I'm going to get dinner. Are you hungry yet?" I ask.

The boys shake their heads and turn back to their specimen.

"Do you think we should find a container for her?" Miles asks. "Maybe one of us could take her home."

"Ten minutes and then come back to the blanket for dinner," I say, trying to catch Miles's eyes so I know he's heard me. "Miles?"

"Okay, Mom. Ten minutes." I can't remember the last time I've seen him so happy, so at ease with someone who wasn't related to him. I smile and head toward the food trucks, my chest expanding, as if one hundred butterflies have just taken flight.

⸺

I return to our blanket with burgers and fries and plop down, ravenous.

Jackie and Rose are talking about husbands. Jackie turns to me. "What's Miles's dad like? Is he involved?"

Rose looks at me, her eyebrows raised, waiting for me to respond.

"Shit," Jackie says, clearly embarrassed by whatever look has crossed my face. "I've pushed too far. I have a tendency to do that. I'm sorry."

I put my hand on her arm and shake my head. "It's okay. I conceived Miles via sperm donor. So no, his dad isn't involved at all."

Rose steals a french fry from my plate, and I swat her hand away.

"Really?" Jackie says. "I've always wondered how that works."

I give her a brief explanation, searching donor profiles, making a selection, and going through the procedure.

Rose laughs. "We used to joke that it felt a lot like online dating, except better because in the end you get a baby instead of a bad date."

Just then, Jackie's phone buzzes. She reads the text and sighs. "Looks like Aaron isn't going to make it after all. He's got to work late again."

"What does he do?" Rose asks.

"He's an environmental engineer. Eco-friendly building." She looks at her phone again. "They're bidding on a project soon, and it's a big one."

"That's too bad," I say. "Miles was excited to see him again."

Rose looks at me, surprised. "Really?" To Jackie she says, "Miles doesn't exactly get excited about new people."

"Well, it'll have to be another time." Jackie stands. "If Nick comes looking for me, tell him I've gone to get food."

"She seems nice," Rose says when Jackie is out of earshot. She bumps her shoulder into mine and steals another french fry. "It's nice to see you and Miles out socializing."

I hand her the rest of my fries, since I know she's going to eat them anyway. "You make us sound like a pair of shut-ins."

Rose raises an eyebrow and pops another fry in her mouth. "Not at all. It's just that you've never been very good at the give-and-take. She tells you about her job interview. You tell her about how your kid doesn't like people. You know. *Sharing*. It's what most of us do with friends and family."

"Thanks for the citizenship lesson."

Just then, Jackie returns with three slices of pizza. "In case you change your mind, Rose," she says, holding one of them up.

Rose grimaces. "I don't want to eat again for a week," she says and stands. "I'd better get back to the dessert booth. I left Marty Pendoza in charge, and she's a soft touch for kids who didn't bring any money. Last year she gave away thirty dollars' worth of mini cupcakes. Jackie, it was nice to meet you."

"You too," Jackie says.

To me, Rose says, "Can you have Liam call me later? I need him to take a look at the faucet in the downstairs bathroom."

"Sure," I say.

With a smile, Rose walks off.

"Who's Liam?" Jackie asks. "Your plumber?"

I laugh. "No, Liam is my boyfriend, who just happens to know how to fix leaky faucets. He's really a video game programmer." I think of how much Liam would have enjoyed the picnic, and I wish I'd let him come.

Jackie looks interested. "How long have you been dating?"

"A little over a year, but I've known him forever. He was college roommates with Rose's husband."

Jackie smiles and looks across the yard. "Those are the best kind of relationships, I think. The ones that start from a friendship."

"How did you and Aaron meet?"

Jackie shrugs. "Oh, it's not very interesting. Colleagues of mine were going out for drinks with colleagues of his. So basically, we met in a bar." She lowers her voice. "How do Miles and Liam get along?"

I hesitate. "Liam adores Miles. And Miles . . . sometimes needs a little convincing."

"It's got to be hard," she says. "To find someone you like, who your kid likes too. I can't even imagine dating with a child."

"I never really did, until Liam. And then it just sort of happened. I wasn't looking for it. Having a kid saps all my energy. I don't even know how people with more than one manage."

"So you never thought about having another?" she asks.

"I had the option to conceive a genetic sibling to Miles," I say. "But he's enough for me. We're incredibly close, and I didn't want to mess with that. Besides, I'm too old now."

I wonder if that would have helped Miles. To have a brother or sister who understood.

Miles and Nick approach us, consumed in their conversation, walking across other people's blankets.

"Miles," I say. "Watch where you're walking."

He looks down and then up at me, baffled. "I'm walking on the ground," he says.

Jackie and I laugh, and she says, "Yep. One and done."

DNA

DNA is the hereditary material found in a cell's nucleus. It's a unique code made up of four bases—A, G, C, and T—which pair up: A with T, and C with G. Like letters form words and words form sentences, the sequence of the bases builds an organism. Humans have about three billion bases. What's incredible is that 99 percent of those bases are the same in all people. It's the 1 percent that makes us unique. How can DNA be different in every human who has ever lived, and yet still be 99 percent the same? It's the infiniteness of that 1 percent, the endless combinations and recombinations, that makes us who we are.

Variations in our DNA help us trace how closely two individuals are related. These variations can occur through transcription errors—when a cell divides and the DNA code is copied incorrectly—or through environmental factors such as diet or exposure to carcinogens. Our DNA is constantly changing, undergoing tiny modifications as we go about our lives unaware—shopping for shoes or fighting with a spouse. So the DNA we're born with isn't the DNA we'll die with. Even identical twins, born with the same genetic code, will accumulate environmentally triggered variations, growing more unique as they age.

Chapter Eight

"So what do you think Dad wants to tell us?"

It's a question Rose has asked me a dozen times since I agreed to this lunch and one I still don't have a good answer for. Before we could tell my mother the kids wouldn't be coming, she'd called to tell us not to bring them. And now we're in Rose's minivan, heading up the 405 Freeway toward the valley. Traffic is light, and we're making good time. Where is LA traffic when you need it?

"No idea," I reply, just like every other time she's asked it. I don't want to hypothesize about Dad. I've felt on edge since I woke up this morning, preparing for a confrontation I don't want to have.

"Guess," Rose says.

"Why?"

"I don't know. I want to be prepared."

I turn on Rose, annoyed. "Maybe they want to tell us that Dad's signed up for that manned mission to Mars, where people are sent to colonize the planet and can never come back"

She pauses. "I think they're getting remarried."

I laugh, sharp and without humor. "Don't even joke about that."

"Think about it. They asked us to come alone because they

know you'll pitch a fit. No one wants to see that." She grows more serious. "Mom seems different this time."

"How?"

Rose shrugs. "I don't know. Distracted. Flustered. I called her the other day to ask her what temperature she roasts her lemon chicken at, and she got mad at me and said, *For God's sake, Rose. Google it.*"

That is strange.

Rose taps the steering wheel with her thumbs in a rhythm-less tempo. She's nervous. If I were to ask, she'd say she's ex-cited. But years of disappointment are written inside of her, and I can see the evidence in the rigid set of her shoulders, the stiffness of her determination. Despite her hope, her body is folding in on itself, remembering past rejections and preparing for the next one.

I try to ease my anxiety by thinking about how happy Miles was at the picnic and how much he's changed in the past couple of weeks. As we crest the hill and descend into the valley, I hold on to the idea of Nick and Miles, like a warm pebble, solid and smooth, fitting perfectly into the palm of my hand.

———

Rose and I approach the front door silently. It's been at least ten years since we've seen our father. He's never met Miles.

Our mom opens the door before I have a chance to knock or ring the bell, and I wonder if she's been watching through the peephole.

"Girls!" She flings her arms wide. She wears one of her usual tracksuits—today it's bright pink velour that makes her look like a giant puff of cotton candy. Every movement has the weight of a performance, as if an audience is behind her, watching. She seems high-strung, almost manic in her greeting. Dad must be sending her over the edge. I give her a brief hug, pulling away first. I can't stand to see my mother flit around like this.

I walk past her into a white, gleaming foyer, frigid air blowing out of the ceiling vent. Rose untangles herself and follows.

My mother closes the door and ushers us down the hall. "I have tea set up in the breakfast nook."

The "breakfast nook" is a tiny table shoved up against a small window overlooking a barren patio. After she sold the house, my mother decided she wanted nothing more to do with gardening or yard care of any kind. She chose her condo based on the large amount of outdoor concrete and its proximity to Target. I sit on a rickety chair that wobbles on the uneven tile floor, and Rose settles in next to me. As we wait for Mom to bring over the teapot, mugs, and an assortment of bagged teas, we raise our eyebrows and shrug. Dad is nowhere to be seen.

Mom sits across from us and pokes through the teabags. "I've just discovered dandelion tea." She flaps a pack and rips it open. "It tastes like dirt, but its effect on digestion is incredible. The first day I drank it, I had three bowel movements."

I groan inwardly and look around again. "I thought we were having lunch. Where's Dad?" My stomach grumbles in agreement.

"He'll be here any minute." Mom looks sideways at the clock, busying herself with her tea. "So how have you girls been?"

"Fine," Rose answers for both of us. "So what's Dad's big news?"

Mom looks down, stirring her tea, a slight tremor in her hand. Then she looks out the window, a blinding concrete oasis of statues and cinder block. "I'm going to let your father tell you," she says, a stiff smile pasted to her face.

I breathe a little easier. That isn't the smile of a woman who's about to remarry the love of her life.

"So where is he?" I ask. I'd like to get this over with. It wouldn't surprise me if he were hiding in the back bedroom, waiting for the perfect moment to make his grand entrance.

"We ran out of sugar, and your father offered to pick up more." She fluffs up like a bird, smug and pleased that she's got a man who will jump to make her life easier. A part of me understands what a big deal that can be for someone who's been on her own for so many years. How something so simple can mean so much. This is the kind of stuff Liam wants to do for me.

As Rose and Mom make small talk, I grow edgy. How long does it take to buy sugar? My leg starts jiggling, and Rose reaches over to steady it, pressing her hand down on my thigh.

"Remember when your father drove all the way to Hollywood to get that bubble gum ice cream you wanted for your birthday, Rose?" Mom stirs her tea, a nostalgic smile playing around the corners of her mouth. "That was the year you had your party at the ice rink."

Rose nods, taking a sip from her cup. "I remember he got there right before cake and presents. He dumped the ice cream on the table and spent the rest of the party on the pay phone in the lobby."

Mom doesn't reply, her smile frozen, trying to hold on to her version of the memory instead of Rose's. She sets her teacup on the table and says, "Let's go ahead and eat. Your father won't mind if we start without him."

She goes into the kitchen and returns with a platter of small sandwiches. It looks like something from a hotel, but when she gets closer, I can see slices of Velveeta pressed into Wonder Bread and a plastic tray made to look like crystal from far away. I know she's trying as hard as she can. I just don't know if it's for us or our father, who can't seem to find the sugar at the supermarket.

I help myself to a sandwich, noting she's used both mayonnaise and butter, making the bread stick to the roof of my mouth. Rose grimaces as she sets hers down on the small plate our mother placed in front of each of us and takes a sip of tea. We sit, chewing, sipping, and listening to the clock tick on the wall behind us.

"This is ridiculous. I'm going to call his cell." Mom hurries into the kitchen, just an open doorway away, and soon we hear her half of the conversation.

"But the girls are here already. We didn't want to start without you, but they can't sit here all afternoon waiting." She pauses. "I *know* Peter. Well, when can you get here? . . . Really?" Then her tone shifts, interested. "Charlie? Well, I suppose so. Okay, I'll tell them." She whispers something into the phone we can't hear and hangs up.

Mom comes back into the room, a bright smile on her face. "Well, your father's been waylaid." She fixes more dandelion tea for herself, avoiding our eyes. "Do you remember his friend Charlie?"

"No." I abandon the small sandwich on my plate and wipe my mouth. Of course. Our father returns after ten years of silence, and he can't even be bothered to keep a lunch date with his daughters. I swallow a seed of anger, but it takes root inside of me.

"Of course you do," Mom insists. "He and your dad traveled

through Australia together after college." She says this like it's something I used to know but have carelessly forgotten. "Well, he ran into Charlie outside the store and they stopped to chat—it's been fifteen years since they've seen each other!"

I feel pressure from Rose's knee on mine, urging me not to shout that it's been nearly that long since he's seen us. "You know how much your father loves to talk, and Charlie is leaving tomorrow for some kind of job." Mom's babbling now, trying to fill up as much time as possible because she knows as soon as she stops talking, I'm going to explode.

"You forget, Mom. We don't actually *know* Dad very well," I say. Then I shake my head. "No, wait. That's not true. I know he'd get this hunted look on his face when he was alone in a room with us, terrified we'd want him to play. I know he never showed up when he said he would. Remember my fifth grade musical? He swore up and down he'd be there. But he rolled in for the last five minutes and completely missed my performance. Or what about the time he volunteered to help Rose sell Girl Scout cookies? He dropped her outside of the Safeway and left her there for seven hours. When I had my tonsils out, he sent me a balloon. One. It read *Happy Birthday*."

"That was the gift shop's mistake, not your father's," my mother says.

I stare at her, incredulous that she'd make another excuse for him. Yet, this is what she always does—tries to rationalize the many ways our father failed us, as if she could rewrite his good intentions over our heartbreak.

There's more, but Rose silences me with a hand on my arm. "So Dad's not coming," she says.

A statement, not a question. Her tone sends me back forty years, when we would wake up and find him gone again, disappeared during the night without a goodbye, our mother blathering another empty excuse about why he had to go. And me, trying to hold together the pieces of my sister's broken heart.

"We can reschedule." Mom looks between us, measuring who might be the safer person to direct her explanation toward.

"I don't think so," I say.

I pull Rose's arm to leave, and our napkins tumble to the floor.

My mother's face is stricken as I yank open the door, the heat of the Valley afternoon hitting me full in the face.

"Paige, Rose, wait." She struggles to find words. "He has some things he needs to talk about. Please."

Rose's voice is strong, but I can hear it crack beneath the surface. "He can email us."

As we make our way down the path, Mom stands in the doorway, torn between making excuses for Dad and begging us to stay. And once again, because she can't choose, she stays silent.

Rose rolls the windows down and blasts the air conditioner to dispel the heavy heat that's settled into the car. As we pull away from the curb, I steal one last look at Mom, standing in front of her anonymous condo in a row of others just like hers, bland and barren.

"Drive carefully," she calls, her blessing falling flat on the concrete that surrounds her.

I take deep breaths, angry that I opened myself up to disappointment again. I'm forty-seven years old, for God's sake. And like the little girl I used to be, I feel punched in the gut when he doesn't show up.

Rose navigates lunchtime traffic carefully, and soon we're traveling back over the hill toward the west side. Rose's face is pinched—the same face I remember from when we were little, when she was trying not to cry. I'm angry with my father for disappointing me, but I hate him for hurting Rose.

GENES

When I was a little girl, I secretly loved that I'd inherited my father's eyes, identical down to the shade and shape. I'd lock myself in the bathroom and wrap a towel around my head so I could only see my eyes, and stare at myself in the mirror, trying desperately to conjure my father from thin air.

My blue eyes are the only obvious physical trait I inherited from him—approximately sixteen genes found on chromosome fifteen. But genes do more than just determine what we look like. They are a series of switches, allowing us to change and adapt, to grow, and eventually die.

Scientists are learning that it's not just environmental triggers that activate or silence genes, but emotional ones too. Stress triggers cortisol and adrenaline, which travel through our bodies, delivering information that can impact cell function—positively or negatively—and forever alter our gene function.

Stress can also be activated by a memory. Your body can't tell if you're living through a physical attack or simply recalling one. All those times, when I'd stare in the mirror, I'd feel the sharp pain of rejection, no matter how long it had been since my father left.

It doesn't matter that you don't want me. You're here with me even when you're gone.

Chapter Nine

By Monday morning I've managed to banish my father to the far corners of my mind where he can't disappoint me. I'm on my way to the lab when I run into Jenna, the doctoral student in charge of Scott Sullivan's case, who had managed to convince him to let us do a home visit after all.

"Hey, Dr. Robson, I was just looking for you. I wanted to check in with you about the Sullivan visit."

"How were they?"

"They seemed okay," Jenna says. "The house was a mess. Scott was all over the place. He kept jumping up while we were talking—that was new. He used to just sit there, letting Mara do all the work."

She tucks a piece of hair behind her ear and looks down the hall. "To be honest, he seemed overwhelmed. Putting something in the oven for dinner, helping Sophie unwrap a piece of string cheese." Jenna shakes her head. "He was totally out of his element."

I imagine Scott bumbling around, trying to perform the lead role of *parent* when all he's ever been is a very ineffective understudy. "How was Sophie?"

"She was quiet, so it's hard to tell. I convinced him to stick around until the end of this phase, but it wasn't easy."

"Great. Any chance he'll change his mind and join phase two?"

Jenna blows out a stream of air that lifts her bangs off her forehead. "Doubtful."

I'm torn on what to do next. Jenna isn't supposed to go back for another four months. But I'd like her to keep an eye on things. Scott isn't negligent, but he's the kind of man who would want to put on a good face for outsiders. Sophie can only benefit from that.

"Do me a favor," I say. "I want you to visit monthly for the remainder of phase one."

Her eyes widen. To step up our visits with just one subject could jeopardize our entire study.

I hurry to clarify. "No blood draws, just anecdotal visits. I want to keep an eye on the situation."

"What are you looking for?"

I can't explain that the father Sophie's stuck with is uncomfortably familiar and that I need to make sure she'll be okay. That I'm haunted by the sound of Sophie, crying, and Scott's cold dismissal of her. I worry about all the children in our study, growing up with men who view them as appendages instead of people. But the rest of them have mothers to stand between them and the rejection of their fathers. Sophie has no one, just Scott.

"I don't know," I say. "But don't log it, okay?"

She hesitates before saying, "Sure."

"Thanks."

I swipe my keycard and enter the lab, ending the conversation.

—

That afternoon, Miles is silent and morose on the ride home from school. When we arrive, he dumps his backpack in the entryway and says, "I'm hungry."

He unzips his sweatshirt, revealing a green stain cascading down the front of his shirt.

"What's that?"

He looks down and shrugs. "I don't know. What can I have for a snack?"

"Why don't you go change your shirt first?"

"What for?"

To be fair, my request is unusual. I only ever make him change for my mother.

"Because Liam is coming over for dinner, and you shouldn't look like a slob."

Miles rolls his eyes but knows better than to say anything. He slams down the hall and into his room. I leave him be, losing myself in dinner preparation. But it's not until we're seated around the dinner table that I notice his face, pinched and blotchy as if he's been crying.

"How was school today?" Liam asks.

Miles shrugs, pushing peas across his plate.

"Miles," I prompt.

"Fine," he says, sinking lower into his seat.

"You don't sound fine," I say.

Miles's expression is closed off. "I don't want to talk about it."

"We can't help you if you don't tell us," Liam says.

"*You* can't help me at all," Miles says to him.

"Miles, what happened?" I ask gently.

Miles stares down at his plate and says, "Some of the kids are saying stuff. Calling me *flower* because of my family tree project."

I fight to keep my voice calm, though I feel as if a firecracker has exploded in my chest. "Who?"

Miles rolls a pea back across his plate with his finger. "Just some kids from class."

"Ethan?" I ask, his smug voice from the camping store still echoing in my mind.

"He's one of them."

"How many?" Liam asks. He puts his fork down and glances at me, concern spread across his face.

Visions of Miles being teased—at the drinking fountain, in the bathroom—dance in my head, and I have to hold on to the edge of the table to keep from leaping out of my seat and grabbing the class roster, making angry phone calls, one after another.

"Three," Miles finally replies. "Ethan, Jasper, and Rory."

"Have you told Ms. Denny?"

"If I told on them, it would just get worse."

"Do you want me to call their parents?" I imagine calling Nan and unloading all of my rage onto her, demanding she fix this somehow. At the very least, hold her child accountable.

"No." His voice is panicked.

I take a sip of water, trying to put some space between my anger and what comes next. "It's just a word," I tell him, not believing myself. "It doesn't mean anything. If you ignore it, they'll stop."

I wince, knowing this advice, which is shoveled out by every parent across the globe, won't help my child feel any better. And it won't stop it either.

He shrugs. "I guess."

"Are they doing anything else?" Liam asks. His gaze travels between Miles and me.

"Not really."

"What does that mean?" I ask.

He sighs. "They're saying other stuff too. That I wasn't allowed to go to the dads' campout because I don't have a dad."

Electric rage pounds through me. How dare those kids make up such cruel lies to hurt my son. He's never done anything to them, and yet they've singled him out as a target for ridicule.

"That's it. I'm calling Ms. Denny."

Miles shoots up, his voice bouncing against the walls of the small dining room. "That won't fix anything! She'll keep them in at recess one time, and then they'll be back outside, saying the same things."

"I have to do something, Miles," I say.

"Please, Mom," he begs. "Besides, it's not like it isn't true."

"What do you mean? You chose not to go. The school didn't say you couldn't."

He shakes his head, impatient with me. "I didn't go because I *don't* have a dad. It's the same thing."

Fat tears drip from his cheeks to his napkin, wadded up on top of his unfinished dinner.

"Lots of kids don't have a dad, Miles," Liam says gently. "Your mom and aunt Rose didn't. It's not as unusual as these kids are trying to make it sound."

"Don't even try to tell me it's the same," Miles says, still only speaking to me. "You knew who your dad was. You knew his name and had pictures of him. I have nothing."

Miles pushes himself away from the table and disappears into his room, the soft click of his door echoing louder than if he'd slammed it.

I start to follow him, but Liam puts a hand on my arm. "Let him have a minute."

Don't tell me how to parent my child, I want to say, but I bite back the words and sink into my chair, knowing he's probably right.

"He's angry," Liam says. "That isn't a bad thing."

I give Liam an incredulous look.

"He doesn't want you racing in and fixing everything all the time. He wants to solve the problem himself. So give him the tools to do that."

I push my unfinished dinner away. "And what tools are those?"

"He needs to feel confident to stand up to them. He should learn how to defend himself."

"You're suggesting he fight them?"

"No." Liam shakes his head. "I'm suggesting you enroll him in a boxing class."

He leans across the table and takes my hand.

"Look, Paige, I know what it's like to be the one everyone picks on. I know how powerless Miles is feeling. My dad taught me to box when I was Miles's age to help me stand up to the kids who called me *string bean* and made fun of me because I always knew the answers in math but could never kick a ball more than a couple of feet. All it took was one bully—and one well-placed punch—and my problems were solved."

I yank my hand away from him. "Are you crazy? I am not going to tell my son to solve his problems by fighting."

Liam holds up his hands.

"Okay. Karate then. At least let him learn how to defend himself. Even if he never has to use it, the other kids will think twice about messing with him if they know he can kick their asses."

I pinch the bridge of my nose. All Miles wants is to read about chemistry and mind his own business.

"Do you hear yourself? *Kick their asses?* No, Liam. Just let me handle this."

His face hardens. "Got it. Your kid, your problem. As usual."

"What's that supposed to mean?"

He stands and picks up the plates. "It means you're going to solve this all by yourself. You don't need any help from me. Message received."

He carries the plates into the kitchen, an angry clatter of cutlery and glass that makes it clear he doesn't want to continue the conversation.

I close my eyes, but I can't stop thinking about my child in his room, believing he deserves to be bullied because he doesn't have a father. And it leaves me wondering if changing schools was a mistake. Even though Miles was lonely and bored at his old school, at least he was safe.

CHROMOSOMES

The most significant scientific discovery of the twenty-first century was the mapping of the human genome—the twenty-three pairs of chromosomes that live inside the nucleus of every single cell in your body. We inherit twenty-three chromosomes from our mother and twenty-three from our father, which then filter through the process of recombination, shifting and churning those genes to create something completely new.

We like to think we have some control over who our children will grow into, simply by the way we raise them. But the truth is, we don't know which traits will emerge or be discarded until our kids are living stories, unfolding before our eyes. Genetics is a lottery. Every time chromosomes recombine, you spin the wheel and cross your fingers. It helps to start with a good partner, with traits you'd want to replicate, but that's no guarantee.

Miles is a unique combination of genetic material that's never occurred before, and never will again. Unlike parents who know exactly where each half of their child's chromosomes came from, I've had to study Miles as he's grown. I know exactly where he got his flat feet and his allergy to cats. But so much more remains a mystery. I wonder what it's like, to have a stranger living beneath your skin.

But Miles isn't interested in the individual pieces. If he were, I could run tests when he's old enough that would tell him he'll be tall or that he should lay off red meat after age thirty. Miles wants to know the living, breathing person who made him—a man who is so much more than an accumulation of chromosomes and traits. It's a biological itch he can't scratch, and it chases him, no matter how hard he runs.

Chapter Ten

School pickup has become an exercise in scanning the yard for enemies. I find myself studying groups of kids lingering outside classrooms and in the hallway, wondering if they are the ones teasing Miles. I've just located Ethan, throwing a football, when I hear Jackie calling my name.

"Thank God I caught you." She's dressed conservatively. A small, silver watch replaces her bangles, and the large hoops are gone, tiny diamond studs in her ears instead. Her unruly hair is gathered in a low bun at the base of her neck.

"You look nice," I say.

She swipes my words away. "I need a huge favor," she says, lowering her voice. "Remember that interview I told you about? My babysitter double-booked and canceled at the last minute. I don't want to tell Aaron until after I know if I'm even in the running, but I can't find anyone to watch Nick. Can he go home with you guys? I could pick him up in a couple of hours. Maybe we could all go for pizza afterward. My treat."

"We'd love that."

"Thank you," she breathes in relief. "I really owe you."

"You don't owe me anything. I'm happy to help."

She envelops me in a tight hug. "You're different than the other moms here," she whispers. "They'd smile and wish me luck, and then the minute my back was turned, they'd start talking about how sad it was that I had to *work outside of the home.* As if that's some kind of terminal disease."

I pull away and smile. "I'm sure you'll do great."

"Thanks." She walks over to Nick and gives him a quick hug, then trots off with a wave.

"Who wants frozen yogurt?" I ask the boys.

They both shout, "We do!" and sprint toward the car.

———

Later that evening, Jackie and I sit across from each other at Pitfire Pizza while the boys grab the booth behind us, deep in a discussion about *Star Wars.*

"So how did it go?" I ask Jackie.

She drinks her beer. "Pretty well, I think. I swear, Paige, walking through the doors of that office made me feel alive again."

I smile. "It's nice to have something to think about other than your kid's next meal or whether they're getting enough sleep. When I'm in the lab, I have to set two alarms, just to make sure I remember to pick up Miles from school."

She smiles at the waitress who deposits our pizzas and tops off our water. "I miss that. It doesn't make me a bad mother to want something for myself."

"Absolutely not. In fact, I think I'm a better mother because Miles sees me following my passion. He watches me set goals and achieve them." I take a sip of beer. "So tell me more about the interview. When will you find out?"

"The second round is after the CEO gets back from a trip to Thailand." She leans toward me, resting her elbows on the table. "I don't want to let myself think too much about it, in case I jinx it. So let's talk about something else. Tell me more about the study you're running at the university. What's it about?"

"My team has discovered a genetic marker on the Y chromosome that inhibits paternal bonding."

Jackie smiles. "Now tell me in English."

I laugh. "Sorry. Basically, we've always believed in nurture theory—that people will parent their children much the same way they were parented. But what we're discovering now is that some aspects of parenting are actually genetic."

I tell her what we've discovered about oxytocin and its role in fathers. "We're studying a specific genetic marker on the Y chromosome that we now know inhibits the release of oxytocin in fathers."

"So it's inherited?"

"Yes," I say. "Instead of assuming these men are just assholes, we've figured out a genetic explanation for their apathy."

The boys' laughter floats up from behind us, and we turn, making sure they're not getting into trouble.

"What are the men in your study like?" she asks, turning back to me.

I think about Scott Sullivan. "Broken," I say. "Though they'd describe their lives as good. They don't know what they're missing. It's their kids who suffer the most."

"That's got to be really hard to watch."

I think of Mara Sullivan's laughing face. "I've got a test subject whose wife just unexpectedly died," I tell her. "Their daughter is five. They were one of the first families to sign up, so they've been with me from the beginning."

"Oh no," Jackie breathes. "And the father is . . ."

"His oxytocin is some of the lowest in the entire study," I say.

"So now what?"

Mara should be raising her daughter, and Sophie should grow up to have more than just a few fuzzy memories of the kind woman her mother was. "I guess he'll do the best he can, but it's not going to be easy for either of them."

I think about my father, about his inability to show up for even the basic events in our lives. Or even a simple lunch. I shudder at the idea of him raising Rose and me by himself.

Jackie plays with the silverware, trying to balance her knife on top of the fork. "Can I ask what made you decide to use a sperm donor?"

I shrug. "I used to date men who weren't interested in more than a casual relationship, and for a while, that worked for me. I was chasing my own dreams and didn't have time for drama. But as I got older, my priorities shifted. I'd watch Rose with her kids and ache to hold my own baby."

Jackie nods. "I remember that. It felt like everyone in the world had a baby except for me."

"Right. But I worked all the time. I didn't have time or energy to put into falling in love." I decide not to expand on all the underlying reasons behind that thinking, the ones that are too complicated for an evening of pizza and beer. "So one night my lab partner had a dinner party, and there was a lesbian couple there—very pregnant—and the dinner conversation was all about how they used a sperm bank to conceive. Something just clicked for me. I had a great job with great benefits. I was financially secure and I really didn't need to wait. I could jump right to the baby. So that's what I did."

"That must have taken a lot of courage."

"Not really. I knew what I wanted, and I knew I could be a good mother. And I am. But—" The image of Miles crying over dinner pops into my head. "Miles has been struggling lately."

I tell Jackie about the bullying, how his conception makes him feel different, and that I don't know how to help him. It's a relief to lay it all down, and the sympathy in Jackie's eyes makes it almost bearable.

"That must be so hard," she says. "There's really nothing about his donor you can tell him?"

"I have a profile," I say. "But it's pretty generic. They structure it so that it's impossible to get any identifying information."

"Maybe it would help him to have it anyways."

"I don't know. Maybe. It's just . . . where would we go from there? He still wouldn't know who his donor was. What if that makes it worse?"

Jackie tilts her head to the side, thinking. "Maybe he just needs a touchstone. Something he can claim for himself." She shrugs. "Think about it. You'll know if it's the right thing to do."

We sit in silence for a few minutes. Behind us, Miles laughs, and Jackie's eyes meet mine. "How does Liam feel about the donor?" she asks.

"It's kind of a nonissue. I knew Liam long before we ever started dating, so the fact that I used a donor was always something he knew about me," I tell her. "It wasn't something I ever needed to disclose."

Jackie lowers her voice. "So how often do you get to see Liam? Do you guys get any alone time?"

I pull a piece of pepperoni off my pizza and nibble it. "Not a lot," I say. "We grab nights together when we can. The occasional weekend away. And a lot of late-night phone calls."

"How does Liam feel about *that*?"

"He'd like more," I say. "We both would. But Miles doesn't want to let him in, no matter how hard Liam tries."

I push my plate away and look out the window. The sun has set, and cars sweep by, their headlights illuminating the dingy tire store across the street. "The hardest part is balancing the two of them, finding ways to include Liam without making it seem like I'm trying to push my boyfriend on my kid."

"I think you have to let Miles lead," Jackie says. "And hopefully Liam can hang in there. Eventually, Miles will come around." She tosses her used napkin on top of her plate and looks at me. "How about I invite the three of you over for dinner in a couple of weeks?"

"That would be great. Thanks."

Behind us, the boys' conversation heats up.

"Obi-Wan says it himself," Nick argues. "'Only Imperial Stormtroopers are so precise.'"

"Well, if that's true, why is it that every time they're shooting at someone, they miss?" Miles asks.

"Because then the movie would be over."

"Well, they should at least hit *something*. Otherwise, what's the point?" Miles says, making Jackie and me grin.

—

The following afternoon, Bruno and I are seated in Dr. Jorgensen's office. Sometimes, I wonder what it would be like to sit in his seat, supervising the science department and overseeing publications and research projects. But I love being on the frontlines of research. There's more risk, but more reward.

Bruno has been silent since we left our office. He's dressed up for today's meeting—khakis and a bright green button-down that's pinching him in all the wrong places. As a clock in the corner ticks away the seconds, I turn to him. "Everything okay?"

He glances at the door and then at me. "You asked Jenna to visit Scott Sullivan every month. What were you thinking?"

"Just anecdotal stuff. Nothing on the books," I explain, though I know he's right to be worried.

"That's the problem," he hisses. "It's not on the books. It's also not in the IRB."

The Institutional Review Board is required prior to any human research study, and IRB documents are inviolable. Even a slight deviation could revoke our funding and possibly ban us from future human research.

"I'm worried about Sophie."

Bruno sighs. "She's in a shitty situation, but we can't risk everything for her."

Just then, Dr. Jorgensen enters behind us, closing the door and circling around to sit behind his desk. "Good to see you finally."

I take a deep breath, funneling my attention toward the task at hand. "Thanks for understanding about last time," I say.

Dr. Jorgensen smiles. "Let's get started. I read over the materials Bruno left, so I'm caught up on what you've done so far." He flips though a few pages. "It's very impressive. Now tell me what you need."

"We need a bridge grant to tide us over until our funding from NIH kicks in next fall."

Dr. Jorgensen nods. The National Institutes of Health is a slow-moving organization. Bridge grants are often given by universities when there's a funding gap between phases of an ongoing project. "What's next?"

I hand over our proposal and charts representing our two hundred remaining men. "Sixty-three percent of the men in our study have the inhibitor and qualify for the phase two trial, where we'll administer synthetic oxytocin. Some will get the synthetic drug; others will get a placebo. Our protocol will remain the same for another two years—quarterly blood draws and anecdotal data."

Dr. Jorgensen slips his glasses off and thumbs through our proposal. "Safety trials?"

"Already done five years ago by a team in Rochester studying a link between oxytocin and stress." I slide another folder toward him. "Their trial failed, and the drug company is eager to find a use for the synthetic oxytocin they're stuck with."

Dr. Jorgensen leafs through the report, making a couple of notations, then looks at me. "And these men, how are you going to inform them of this next phase?"

"That's the tricky part," I say. "To those who qualify, we'll send out a letter announcing the end of phase one and set up one-on-one meetings to offer the opportunity to participate in the phase two trials. We'll outline the body's use for oxytocin, focusing on the importance of the hormone in relaxation, trust, and psychological stability. We'll end with a focus on relationships—specifically the paternal relationship. We'll include their individual oxytocin levels and all the waivers needed for them to opt in for phase two. We'll have the same compensation schedule—one hundred dollars for every blood draw—but because we'll only be working with men who carry the gene, overall costs will be lower than in phase one."

"How many do you think will sign up?" Dr. Jorgensen asks.

Bruno shifts in his seat. "We estimate about one hundred men," he says.

Dr. Jorgensen nods. "Where are we on publication?"

I pull out a draft of an article I've been working on about the oxytocin inhibitor gene and our phase one findings and hand it to Dr. Jorgensen. "I'm hoping to get this published by next summer, in time for the phase two trials to begin."

Dr. Jorgensen sets it aside. "All of this sounds terrific. I don't have to tell you how pleased we are with how well this has gone and the attention Annesley could get from it. I'll take your proposal to the board and get back to you soon."

"Thank you," Bruno and I both say. We stand, and Bruno gestures for me to lead the way out. He doesn't speak until we're alone in the elevator. "Helping Sophie isn't going to fix what happened to you, Paige." His voice is soft, absent his usual edge, which brings tears to my eyes.

Over the twenty-five years we've known each other, Bruno has witnessed several of my father's returns and departures and has seen the toll it takes on me. He understands better than most what it's cost me and why I need our study to succeed.

"I know," I say, staring at the numbers above the doors, blinking our descent toward the lobby.

"Jenna could show up every day, and Scott will still be Scott. You can't protect that little girl. And it's not your place to. The best thing you can do for Sophie is to finish up this phase and get Scott into phase two. But that won't happen if we're brought up on IRB violations."

The elevator doors open into the lobby, and a few students step aside to let us off before boarding. We push past them, and Bruno glances at me. "Oh God. You're not going to cry, are you? You know I need a thirty-second warning if you're going to cry—that's also in the IRB."

"Shut up."

"Just fix this thing with Jenna," he says, before tipping his sunglasses over his eyes and stepping into the bright sun.

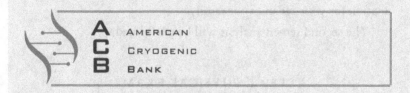

DONOR RECRUITMENT

Congratulations on deciding to become a donor for American Cryogenic Bank! You should be aware that we conduct one of the most rigorous screening panels in the world, and fewer than 1 percent of applicants go on to become donors.

The following are the steps you will need to complete in order to be considered an ACB donor. Be aware that disqualification can happen at any time.

STEP 1: ONLINE APPLICATION

This will give ACB basic information from which to work. It will ask you for your age, height, weight, ethnicity, education level, and family medical history. It might be a good time to talk to your immediate family and personal doctors so you have all the information you need.

STEP 2: FIRST OFFICE VISIT

The first semen analysis and test freeze will be performed, as well as a formal collection of personal information.

STEP 3: SECOND OFFICE VISIT

This orientation comprises a preview of the donor profile, consent forms, and more than fifty pages of social and medical information for yourself and your family.

The second semen analysis will be performed.

STEP 4: PHYSICAL EXAM

One of ACB's preapproved doctors will run a full medical panel.

STEP 5: ADDITIONAL TESTING

Tests are run for infectious diseases and STDs. Urinalysis, blood work, and the third semen analysis will also be done.

STEP 6: GENETIC EVALUATION AND MEETING WITH GENETIC COUNSELOR

We run a full panel of genetic tests on all applicants.* You will review your results with an ACB genetic counselor.

STEP 7: FINAL REVIEW

All directors—medical, genetics, and donor liaison—must sign off on your application before you are approved.

---

* *Testing performed on all donor applicants includes chromosome analysis and carrier screening for conditions such as cystic fibrosis, sickle cell anemia, spinal muscular atrophy, and thalassemia. For a complete list of genetic screening panels, please refer to our website.*

ONCE QUALIFIED

Every donation will be subject to a semen analysis, and you will be required to update us on any change in health or sexual partners. Further, we require monthly STD tests and infectious disease testing every three months. Every six months we require you to return for a full physical exam and to have your application renewed by our director.

Chapter Eleven

I see them from a block away. A group of boys, gathered in a clump. As I pull up next to the playground, I see Miles in the middle with his fists clenched at his sides and his cheeks flushed with anger. The circle tightens around him, and he yells something at them, though his words are lost in the distance.

One of the boys laughs.

I slip into a parking space haphazardly, leaving the tail of my car sticking out into the street and hurry toward the playground entrance. Every inch of me is frantic to get between my child and those boys.

I'm practically running by the time I reach them. As I draw nearer, I can hear their words. "Poor Flower, crying because he doesn't have a dad."

"I'm not," Miles says, his voice wobbling with unshed tears.

"He probably ran off when he saw how ugly you were." One of the boys laughs but then catches sight of me and the smile falls off his face.

"What's going on?" I ask.

Miles turns, eyes brimming with tears, and says, "Nothing."

The boys step back—there are four of them, including Ethan. "I met your parents the other night, Ethan. I'm sure they'd be interested to hear about this."

"Mom," Miles says. "Don't."

But the boys are already backpedaling, getting swallowed by the yard.

I turn toward Miles. "Let's go."

Miles hesitates a moment and then grabs his backpack, trailing behind me, silent.

We approach the picnic tables, where a new supervisor sits. This one is young—no more than a college student.

"Hi," I say, struggling to keep my voice steady. "Are you new? Where's the other supervisor?"

"Gloria?" the girl asks. "She's sick. I'm filling in."

"Four kids had my son cornered over there, taunting him."

"Mom," Miles pleads again.

The girl looks across the yard to where I'm pointing. "Which boys?"

"I don't know. Ethan was one of them."

She doesn't seem surprised Ethan was involved. Maybe she's more aware than I thought.

"This isn't their first incident," she says. "Do you want to file a report? That would go through the director, and she'd follow up with you, the other kids, and their parents."

"Mom, *please*," Miles's voice is an urgent hiss behind me.

I pause. "Just keep an eye out," I say. "Maybe you could speak to them today and let them know if it happens again we'll be contacting the director and their parents."

The girl nods as if that's what she would do. "Sounds good." She turns to Miles. "Are you okay, Miles?"

He nods but doesn't look at her.

The girl waits a moment longer before saying, "It won't happen again. I'll make sure I'm watching."

"Thanks," he whispers, and I want to hug her.

As we leave, my eyes scan the yard for the boys, though the only one I'd recognize is Ethan. But they've disappeared somewhere to regroup and probably plan their next attack on my child.

When we get back to the car, I sit for a moment. The image of Miles, surrounded and upset, burns behind my eyes, and I blink hard to erase it. I turn so I'm facing him. "Are you okay?"

He stares out the window, already buckled in, ready to leave. "I'm fine."

I don't believe him for a minute, but I don't know what to do, other than push on. I turn forward and start the car. "We can't keep letting this happen," I say, pulling away from the curb and joining the stream of cars heading toward the freeway.

Miles's voice is small and accusing. "It wouldn't be a problem if I had *something* to tell them about my dad. Anything, just to prove I have one."

Miles exists. That should be proof enough that a man was involved at some point. But I know it's not.

I turn up the air conditioner and glance over my shoulder, pretending to check traffic behind us. But what I'm really doing is getting a good look at Miles, measuring how much damage those boys have done.

What if I hadn't left work early and things had gotten physical? I hate the thought of Miles throwing a punch, but maybe Liam is right. Maybe karate isn't the worst idea.

—

After some much-needed food and a heated game of Scrabble, Miles seems more himself. As we stack the letter tiles back in the box, I say, "I'm going to sign you up for karate classes."

Miles gives me a confused look. "What for?"

"I don't think those boys would have gone any further than they did today, but you should know how to defend yourself if you have to." His eyes widen, and I hurry to clarify. "I'm not saying fight them. I'm saying karate might give you the tools to prevent that."

Miles folds the board and puts the lid on the box. "What kind of tools?" he asks. "Like a ninja star or nunchakus?" His eyes sparkle at the thought of using weapons he's seen in Jackie Chan movies.

"No. Like how to diffuse a situation so that you *don't* have to fight."

"Oh," he says, his enthusiasm fading.

Miles's words from earlier tug at me. *If I had something to tell them about my dad.* I think about what Jackie said, that maybe he just needs something he can claim for himself. "Come with me," I say, before I can change my mind. "I want to show you something."

He follows me into my room and sits on my bed while I pull the ACB file from the closet. I dig around and hand him the baby picture. "This is your father."

Miles hesitates, wiping his hand on his pants before taking it. "How did you get this?"

"It was part of the package the clinic gave me when I picked him."

Miles stares at it for a minute, the clock in the kitchen ticking away the seconds. "Why haven't you shown it to me before?"

I sit down on the bed next to him. "I should have." I blink back tears, imagining my child alone at night, wondering who his father is and wishing he were anyone but himself. "Why did you wait so long to tell me how much you were hurting?"

He shrugs, not meeting my eyes. "You really want Liam to be my dad. I thought you'd be mad at me."

"Honey, I want Liam to be a part of our lives. I would love it if you wanted that too. But if you don't, that's okay. I'd never be mad at you for something like that. Never." I sweep his hair off his forehead. "Letting Liam in won't take anything away from this." I gesture toward the file.

He nods once, acknowledging what I've said, and asks, "What else is in there?"

I pull out the rest of the documents, explaining each one to him. The profile with the donor's height, hair color and eye color, the staff impressions about what kind of a person he is, and his personal statement about why he chose to be a donor. Miles handles each one like an ancient artifact, delicate and precious.

When I reach the end, he asks, "Is there anything else?"

I pause. "There's a website where donors can enter their information and their children can find them."

Miles's eyes light up. "Can we look him up? Maybe he's there, looking for me."

"He's not on there, honey. I've looked."

His enthusiasm wilts, and he stares at the photo again. "So all we know is he's tall, has brown hair and hazel eyes, and that he doesn't want to know me."

This is why I've never shown him the file. It's like giving a starving man a cracker. Just enough to awaken the hunger, not nearly enough to satisfy it.

"This is the man who helped create you. But that's not the same thing as a dad. A dad shows up every day. He cares about you and wants to make you happy and safe. This is just a contribution of chromosomes."

Miles studies the picture with an expression I recognize. For a long time, I craved my father like a cold glass of water on a hot day. Until I learned he was nothing more than a mirage.

"You can always talk to me about the hard stuff, Miles. There's nothing you could tell me that would push me away."

"I know, Mom."

"Someday, you'll want to have secrets. And that's fine. But promise me that if you're hurting, you'll talk to me. I might not be able to fix it, but we're a team. We carry our problems together."

Miles doesn't answer but instead holds up the photo. "Can I keep this?"

"Sure." It's just a color printout on plain copy paper, and I'm ashamed I never thought to print out a better one, anticipating that my child might someday want it.

He starts to stand, but then crashes into me, wrapping his arms around my neck, and I savor the weight of him.

"I love you, Mom."

"I love you more," I whisper.

"Not possible," he says, sliding off the bed and disappearing into his room.

Y CHROMOSOME

Since the beginning of time, male heirs have been prized above daughters. In some cultures daughters were even discarded or sold. Up until the twentieth century, males inherited everything—status, titles, land, and family history. If you look through a microscope, you can find that history living inside the Y chromosome.

When I was in third grade, I overheard my friend's mother confide that she hoped her new baby would finally be the boy her husband had been waiting for. As if my friend and her younger sisters were placeholders that didn't count. I wondered if things would have been different had I been a boy. If my father might have stuck around if there'd been a son worth staying for.

There's no denying the Y chromosome is special. It's the smallest of the twenty-three chromosomes that a father passes on to his son. But while other chromosomes recombine with those from the mother, the Y chromosome is passed on in its entirety. It wasn't until the late-twentieth century that we learned the Y chromosome wasn't the same in all men. We can now look at a group of men and trace the paternal line based on tiny variations on their Y. These differences provide a road map through time, allowing us to chase paternity back to one common ancestor.

The oxytocin inhibitor lives on the Y chromosome, making it an inherited trait. This means men are genetically predisposed to engagement or apathy. And with this discovery comes great hope—saving millions of children from the misery Rose and I endured. I want to eliminate the effect of the oxytocin inhibitor gene, and with it, the story of loss that so many people pass on to the next generation.

No part of my father's Y chromosome exists in me or Rose. Miles carries his donor's Y, and Mikey and Josh carry Henry's. Whatever flaws might be found on my father's Y will end with him.

Chapter Twelve

L iam lives on a small walk street, a pedestrian-only enclave. Tall trees flank the property, giving a sense of privacy and security. I forget sometimes how much money Liam makes designing video games that generate millions of dollars in sales. To me, he's just Liam. But he lives in an amazing cottage with a sunny window seat and a tiny retro kitchen renovated with yellow and black tiles and a vintage Aga stove he never uses.

After dropping Miles off with Rose, I let myself in with my key and Liam calls out from his office, "Five more minutes and I'm all yours."

I kick off my shoes and lie down on the couch. It's been several weeks since I've been here. My eyes catch on a book left out on top of the bookshelf. *Structures of Life: Organic and Biological Chemistry 2nd Edition*. I smile at the image of Liam, home alone and studying one of his old chemistry textbooks as a way to connect with my child.

Liam emerges from his office and sits on the end of the couch, lifting my feet into his lap. He starts massaging my left foot and a tiny groan escapes me.

"What do you want to do tonight?" he asks. "Dinner on Main Street? A movie?"

"Just this." I wiggle my right foot, and his fingers knead the arch, a week of standing in the lab and at the front of a lecture hall melting away. Nights at Liam's are my chance to escape, to step into an alternate reality where I have no responsibilities. I don't have to force anyone to take a bath, brush teeth, or get to bed on time.

"How's Miles liking karate?"

I half expected an *I told you so* when I first told him I'd signed Miles up. But of course, being Liam, he just smiled and said, "Good." So far, Miles has loved the discipline and the power of it. He's even talked to a few of the kids in his class, which makes me hope that he'll have more than just Nick on his list of friends.

"He tells me he uses his mental ninja to ward off Ethan."

Liam snorts. "I'll have to try that one the next time my boss tries to staff me on dual projects."

He slides my feet off his lap and turns so he's facing me. "So listen," he says. "I met your dad the other day when I was over at Rose and Henry's."

I stiffen. "Rose never told me she was spending time with him, that he was going over there."

"He asked about you."

"Really? Strange, he's not one for updates."

He rests his elbows on his knees and looks at me. "I just . . . I don't know. He seemed really sad. Like, hungry for any little thing I could tell him about you."

"I spent most of my childhood feeling that way. I'm glad he knows what it's like."

"Paige," Liam says. "Maybe you could give him a break."

I sit up and hug my arms across my chest. "If you're imagining facilitating some big reconciliation, stop right now. It's not going to happen. Not all of us grew up with a scoutmaster for a father."

Liam's eyes bore into mine. "Have you considered how it might help Miles to have a relationship with his grandfather? I've tried to step up, but it isn't me he wants."

I can't believe what I'm hearing. "Are you kidding me? After everything he put me through, you're suggesting I offer up my child so my father can break his heart too?"

Liam clasps his hands in front of him and looks at me. "How could he hurt Miles?"

"By letting Miles get close to him and then packing a bag in the middle of the night and disappearing."

"Miles isn't you, Paige. I get that you're hurt. You have every right to be. What your dad did to you and Rose was terrible. But Miles has a devoted parent who loves him. He's got an incredible extended family that embraces him. You've done a tremendous job surrounding him with love. Even if your father decides to leave again, Miles will be okay. You made sure of that."

I wander over to the bookshelves and pull the switch on the small lamp that sits on top, trying to distance myself from what he's saying. I turn back to Liam. "You're arguing both sides. Miles is craving a father figure. You're suggesting I let my father play that role, and then in the next breath telling me that Miles will be fine if he leaves again. Maybe you're right. Maybe Miles would be okay. But I can't set my child up for something like that. Please don't ask me to." I'm trembling, angry and hurt that despite what I've told Liam about my father, he still doesn't get it.

Liam crosses the room in two steps and folds me into a hug. He presses his lips to the top of my head and says, "Okay. I'm sorry."

We stand that way until Liam's phone rings from the other room. "I don't need to get that," he says.

I pull away, wiping my eyes with my sleeve. "No, it's okay. Go."

Liam leaves, and I step into the kitchen and splash cold water on my face, drying it with a paper towel. What Liam said makes sense. Miles has a lot of people he can count on. But a relationship with Miles would require a relationship with me. And I'm not willing to give that.

Liam emerges from his office and stands in the doorway to the kitchen. "Let's get some dinner. Anything you want."

"Sushi," I say.

He cringes. "I was going to say anything you want *except* sushi."

"Sorry, too late." I grab my coat, and we walk out the front door together, Liam's arm holding me close to his side, right where I love to be.

———

We bring dessert home to eat in front of the TV. I unload two plastic containers of chocolate-chocolate cake onto the counter, feeling like a reset button has been pressed.

Liam pulls two plates from the cupboard behind us. "Normally, I'd eat this straight out of the box and use the plastic fork they throw into the bag," he says. "But since you're here, I'll use real plates and silverware."

"Classy," I say, following him into the living room, where we settle onto the couch.

I'm just about to take my first bite of cake when my phone rings, and I see it's Rose's number. "Hello, Rose," I say.

But it's Miles. "Hey, Mom? Aunt Rose wanted me to call you because she doesn't believe you let me watch *Ninja Beasts*."

I sigh. "Put her on the phone."

"Do you know what that show is like?" Rose's voice is critical. "Have you even watched an episode?"

I close my eyes. "If you don't want him to watch the show at your house, just tell him he can't watch it at your house."

"That's beside the point," Rose argues. "That show is trash. You shouldn't let him watch it at your house either."

"Rose," I say, mustering all of my patience. "Can we talk about this tomorrow? When I pick up Miles?"

"Sorry! Right. Talk tomorrow. Say hi to Liam for me."

I hang up and say, "Rose says hi."

Liam flips through shows on Netflix. "What do you want to watch?" he asks.

"How did we get here? Netflix on a Saturday night?" I laugh. "We're so . . . domestic."

Liam sets the remote on the table and pulls me closer, so that every inch of my body touches his, and smiles into my eyes. "Something wrong with domestic?" he whispers.

"Nothing at all," I say, relaxing into his embrace.

He kisses the tip of my nose and then my lips and my neck. Tiny nerve endings explode, and I tip my head back, giving him better access. My breath quickens, and I press into him.

Liam takes my hand and leads me into his bedroom, and I leave my phone on the coffee table, unwilling to think about anything except him.

—

Later that night, we lay on the couch, the ending credits of *House of Cards* on TV and the remains of our dessert on the coffee table. Liam leans over and kisses my neck.

"I love your place," I say. "It's so quiet. Peaceful."

He smiles. "That's funny. Because I love *your* place. It's a home. With people living real lives in it."

"You never told me that before."

Liam shrugs. "This place is nice. But it feels like a hotel. Somewhere I can sleep between days at work or time with you. It's more of a waiting room than a home."

I start to gather our plates, but Liam's expression stops me. "What's wrong?"

"I was just thinking of the day I moved in here five years ago. I had just landed the job with New City Games, and my dad flew out to help me. We sat right out there, on the front step, with pizza and a six-pack. And he told me to enjoy my time here, but that the end goal wasn't to have a career with a lot of money; it was to build a life and a family."

I put the dishes back down, giving Liam my full attention. "I love your dad."

Liam gives me a small smile and says, "He's a smart man." He looks down at the hardwood floor, nudging the edge of the blue-and-green rug that covers part of it with his toe. When he looks up again, his eyes are worried, the crease between them more pronounced. "He said, *Be patient. Be a good man, and good things will come.*"

I move toward him, slipping my arms around his waist. "You are a good man. And this is good."

Gently, he pushes me back so that he's looking at me. "But I'm still in this limbo."

I try to read his face. "What are you trying to say?"

"I feel like my real life is with you. And Miles. And when I'm not with you, I'm just . . . waiting."

My eyes scan the living room. Clusters of photographs—Liam and his parents, Liam and me, and even one I managed to snap of

Liam and Miles—dot the surfaces, and I imagine him here alone every night. Dumping his take-out containers in the recycling bin. Wiping down an already clean counter. Putting his single dish and fork into the dishwasher, where they would probably sit for weeks before it's full enough to run a load. I remember what it's like to live alone, being free to stay up late or sleep in, to eat whenever I want, to work late at the lab, or to go for a predawn run. I feel constrained by a life that is still so solitary in so many ways, yet so filled with the love of another.

Liam pulls me close to him again. "I want more than this, Paige. More than a weekly dinner at Rose's and occasional over- nights where I can kiss you good night and fall asleep next to you. I want to be there for all of it."

What Liam wants isn't unreasonable. But it's the opposite of what Miles wants, and once again I'm caught between the two of them.

The Netflix menu is still displayed on his large-screen TV, and he picks up the remote and turns it off. I'm on edge, know- ing where this conversation is going. We look at each other, nei- ther of us speaking.

Finally, I say, "I want what you want, Liam. Don't ever doubt that."

He leans forward. "Good. Then let's make a plan to get there."

"It's not that simple."

"It *is* simple. It can be as simple as we want it to be. I love you. You love me. I want a life with you. With Miles. I'll take as long as you need me to take, but I want to know where we're going."

"It's never that simple with a child. You know that." A small thread on the couch cushion catches my attention, and I pull on it gently, twisting it between my fingers.

"I'm not suggesting I move in next week," he says. "But I'd

like to start going in that direction. Maybe we take a trip, just the three of us. Or maybe I start spending one night a month there, to get Miles used to the idea."

I'm shaking my head, my thoughts knotted, trying to untangle the complications of what he's suggesting. Already, I'm imagining what it would be like to see Miles wake up and find Liam asleep in my bed. "You make it sound like it'll be simple for him to learn how to adapt. But it's his home too. His life, and I have to put his needs first."

"I'm not some guy you just met, Paige. We've been together over a year. Miles has known me almost his entire life. It doesn't get much safer than that."

I look out the window, streaks of color fading into a dark sky. "It's not a matter of safety. I just don't think the timing is right."

Liam looks away from me. "Either you want me in your life, or you don't. You wouldn't let me come to the picnic, you reject my advice about the bullying—"

"I didn't," I interrupt. "I signed him up for karate."

"After the fact. Your first response is always no. You insist on keeping me an outsider, only letting me in when it suits you. When it feels safe. All I'm asking is for you to commit to a plan to move forward. Like I said, nothing has to happen now. We can go as slow as you want. Just *let me in*."

I swipe the hair off my forehead. "I let you in. I've given you more than I've ever given to anyone else. You know my family. You know my son. How can you say I don't let you into my life?"

Liam shakes his head, incredulous. "You have so many walls built up around you, you can't even see them."

"I don't know what you want from me," I say. "I'm giving you everything I've got."

"You're not," Liam says. "You're giving me everything you *want* to give. There's a big difference."

Just then my phone buzzes. A text from Miles from Rose's number.

I forgot my karate clothes. Can you bring them when you pick me up?

Liam watches me read the text, and my fingers itch to reply. But I don't. If I don't pay attention and think about what I'm saying, I might lose something precious.

I flash back to a memory. I don't know how old I am, but I'm crying. My father sweeps past me, suitcase in hand, and Rose grabs at his leg as he's walking out the door. My mother picks her up and wipes away her tears, oblivious to her own. And I realize now, I don't want to ever live through that again. My reluctance is about protecting Miles, but it's also about protecting myself. Although Liam knows all parts of my heart, he doesn't know all parts of my life. My tendency to yell at bedtime. The times Miles gets so frustrated with a game or a project that he clenches his fists and kicks things across the room. As much as I love Liam, he's still an outsider I'm afraid to let all the way in.

I set myself on this course years ago, before I knew what I wanted or what the cost would be. "I don't want to fight with you tonight," I tell him. "Can we table this for another time?"

"When, Paige? While we're at dinner at Rose's? Or when I'm hanging out at your place, being ignored by Miles? This is the only private time we get."

"Which is why I don't want to waste it."

"That's the difference between you and me," he says. "I don't think this conversation is a waste." He grabs the remote and pulls up another episode of *House of Cards*, his face a mask I can't read.

"I'm sorry," I say, though the words are barely a whisper. I want to pull him toward me, brush the hair off his forehead, and reassure him that my life belongs with him, that someday we can have what he wants. But I can't. I stare at the screen, the three feet between us feeling like a mile.

GENETIC DISORDERS

A genetic disorder is defined as a medical condition caused by a DNA abnormality, which can be inherited in several different ways:

Autosomal Dominant: One mutated copy of the gene is enough for a person to be affected by the condition. *Ex: Huntington's, Marfan syndrome*

Autosomal Recessive: Both copies of the gene in each cell must have the mutation in order for it to manifest. Meaning, the parents each must have at least one copy of the mutated gene that they pass forward to offspring. *Ex: cystic fibrosis, sickle cell disease*

X-Linked Dominant: Caused by mutations on the X chromosome. In females (who have two X chromosomes), the condition may, or may not, present. But in males (who only have one X chromosome), a mutation on the only copy of the gene will cause the disorder. *Ex: fragile X syndrome*

X-Linked Recessive: Also caused by mutations on the X chromosome. In males (with only one copy), the condition will manifest. In females, a mutation would have to occur in both copies of the X chromosome to cause the disorder. *Ex: hemophilia, Fabry disease*

Y-Linked: A mutated gene on the Y chromosome will cause the disorder. Because only males have a Y chromosome, the mutation can only be passed from father to son. *Ex: Y chromosome infertility, oxytocin inhibitor gene*

Mitochondrial: This applies to genes in the mitochondrial DNA (mtDNA). Only females can pass these mutations on; however, they will pass to both male and female offspring. These mutations can appear in every generation; however, fathers cannot pass these disorders on to their children. *Ex: Leber hereditary optic neuropathy*

Chapter Thirteen

Dinner with Jackie and Aaron couldn't have come at a better time. They live in a one-story white house with a picket fence, roses in front, and a stone path leading to the door—straight out of a fairy tale. We stand on the porch, next to chairs and benches with brightly colored cushions, where I imagine they sit to watch Nick ride his bike or scooter along the sidewalk. Maybe they enjoy a glass of wine or a cup of coffee while they put their feet up and talk.

Miles bounces next to me, eager to get inside, and Liam stands behind me, holding a tray of lemon squares. He bends down and brushes a quick kiss against my lips. I lean into him, appreciating his solidness, hopeful this evening will smooth out the rough edges leftover from our fight last weekend.

When Jackie opens the door, a cozy smell of roasted garlic and thyme envelopes us. "Hello!" she cries, giving me a quick hug. She takes the plate from Liam and says, "You must be Liam. It's so nice to meet you." To Miles she says, "Nick's in his room. Straight back that way, to the left." She points Miles in the right direction and leads us through the house, filled with deep, squishy chairs, bookshelves, and family photographs scattered across surfaces. From the back of the house, the sound of a blender cuts through the air.

"Aaron's mixing drinks." She leads us into an expansive kitchen and family room space that opens onto a trellised patio.

Aaron stands at the counter with his back to us, expertly tilting the blender to fully mix what looks like margaritas.

"Honey, they're here," Jackie shouts, and Aaron silences the blender, turning to greet us.

"Welcome!" He reaches out to shake Liam's hand and then pours margaritas into four waiting glasses and passes them around. "I hope blended is okay with you. Sadly, we're out of salt."

"This works for me," Liam says.

I turn and survey the room. The kitchen opens up into a lived-in family room, complete with a piano, sectional, and flat-screen TV. A wall made entirely of sliding glass leads onto the patio with a table set with colorful plates and mismatched glasses. The whole effect is funky and charming, just like Jackie.

"Jackie tells me you design video games," Aaron says to Liam. "Have I heard of anything you've worked on?"

Liam leans against the counter and launches into a long list of games I've only heard of because he's mentioned them.

"You worked on *Golom 2000*? Holy shit."

"I was just one of many on the team," Liam says, though I can tell he's pleased with the acknowledgment.

"Is level thirteen really impossible to beat?"

"And we're out . . ." Jackie says, pulling me by the elbow through the door and onto the patio. We sit in chairs with purple and orange cushions, and I sink back, setting my margarita on the table.

"This place is amazing," I say. "Did Aaron design it?"

Jackie takes a drink and nods. "Over the course of four long years," she says. "It was a nightmare. He's really good at his job, but he obsesses over details. Midway through, I would have happily moved into a yurt if I'd had the option. I just wanted it to end."

I laugh. "A ringing endorsement."

"His clients love him. But I will never put myself through that again."

Aaron and Liam emerge from the kitchen, each carrying a platter of assorted cheese and crackers.

Aaron grabs a cracker and turns to Liam. "If I were to load up *Golom 2000* after dinner, could you beat level thirteen?"

Liam laughs. "I might know a few tricks."

They return to the kitchen, and Jackie's eyes follow them.

"Does he ever sit down?" I ask.

"Nope. He loves entertaining—the preparation, the planning. I love the eating and the talking. When we got married, I wanted to have our engagement party downtown, at this restaurant with an incredible rooftop deck, three-hundred-sixty-degree views. But Aaron wanted to host it himself, do all the cooking. His mother taught him to cook—it's their *thing*." Jackie smiles. "I can't really complain though. I'm in charge of weeknight meals, but Aaron takes over on the weekend."

A shout of laughter filters out through the open windows. A shadow passes across her face, the relaxed edges bunching up, as if she's trying not to cry.

"Are you okay?" I ask.

"I'm glad you guys could come tonight. Aaron needs the distraction."

"What's wrong?"

Jackie scoots her chair closer to mine and lowers her voice. "He doesn't want anyone to know, but I've actually been hoping to get you alone so I can get your thoughts as a geneticist.

A couple of days ago, his dad was diagnosed with Huntington's disease."

"I'm so sorry." My words fall empty between us. Huntington's is a degenerative disease, attacking the central nervous system. There is no cure. Only a prolonged—and painful—decline.

Jackie shakes her head. "It's hit him really hard." She bites her lip and looks down at the drink in her hand. "I'm worried. About Aaron, but also about Nick. The reading I've done so far isn't good."

I sip my drink, careful to choose my words so they're accurate but still encouraging. "The Huntington's indicator is based on CAG repeats—a tiny sequence of DNA—on a specific gene. Any more than thirty-five repeats guarantees the development of the disease at some point in the future. More than twenty-seven means he won't develop the disease but could still pass the gene onto offspring. Ideally you're looking for less than twenty-seven. Aaron has a fifty percent chance of inheriting the gene, but the fact that he's already in his midforties is a really good sign. The earlier you develop it, the more severe the onset. And his father wasn't symptomatic until now, so even if Aaron does carry the gene, it might be decades until symptoms appear. Have you talked about predictive testing?"

Jackie shoves her drink aside. "We've talked about nothing else since we found out. I want him to do it. I don't want it hanging over our heads, worrying every time he drops something or trips, thinking, *Is this it?*"

"But he doesn't," I say.

"If it were just him, I'd accept that he doesn't want to know if some horrific fate is out there waiting for him. But we have Nick." She looks again toward the kitchen, where Aaron and Liam work side by side at the counter. "I need to know that

Aaron doesn't have the gene so I can stop worrying about Nick."

"Even if Aaron has it, that doesn't mean Nick will. And you wouldn't be able to test Nick until he's eighteen anyway."

"That's such a bullshit rule," Jackie says, swirling her melting margarita around in the glass.

"I get it," I say. "But it's meant to protect Nick and his rights as an individual."

Jackie sets her glass down hard, spilling a little on the table. "But he's mine. My child. What about my rights as his mother?"

I reach out and put my hand over hers. "I know."

Just then, my phone rings from inside my purse—my mother. I reach down and press ignore. "Sorry about that."

Something in my expression must catch Jackie's attention. "Everything okay?"

"Nothing worth mentioning."

Jackie reaches for a cracker. "Please don't think I hold the monopoly on drama," she says. "In fact, I'd rather talk about yours, if you don't mind."

It feels a little selfish, unloading my problems onto her, so shortly after learning what real problems sound like, but I also know the relief of losing yourself in a situation that holds no pain for you. "It's my mom," I explain. "She's trying to get me to spend time with my dad."

"You're not close?"

I laugh. "No."

I tell her about Dad and how my mother falls all over herself every time he returns. Then I tell her about the lunch he didn't show up for. "I don't know why she's pushing so hard this time. He's never going to change, but I'm the only one who can see it." From the kitchen, Liam laughs, and Aaron soon joins him. A melancholy contentment rises inside of me—gratitude for these new friends, but sadness because none of us gets a free pass from tragedy or pain.

"Maybe something's different this time," Jackie suggests.

"Believe me, nothing's different."

Jackie turns so she's facing me, tucking her knee under her. "My dad died in 1989."

I'm about to say something, but she holds her hand up.

"He was an asshole. Critical. Angry. Emotionally abusive. My mother was like a pill bug, rolling into a ball every time he'd start in on her. Nothing was ever good enough for him. He dropped dead of a heart attack while I was in college. He grunted goodbye in September, and that was the last thing he ever said to me."

She pauses. I wait for her to tell me the rest, how she wishes she had the time to forge some kind of truce with him.

But she doesn't. "If I'd been braver, I would have cut him out of my life a lot earlier. I wasn't strong enough to stand up to him. My mother wasn't either. But since he's been gone, she's reinvented herself. She's the head children's librarian at the Rockaway public library. She volunteers at my old elementary school, working with struggling readers. She would never have had the nerve to do any of that when my dad was alive. She'd still be scrambling, making sure dinner was on the table at precisely six o'clock, or that he had the right brand of peanut butter in the cupboard. Good for you for setting boundaries and sticking to them. Some men don't deserve to be husbands or fathers." She laughs, but it sounds hollow. "But you already know a lot about that."

I lean back, my thoughts a jumble. This is the first time anyone has said I was doing the right thing. "My mother and Rose say I'm cold and unforgiving. Liam thinks I'm making a mistake."

Jackie's eyes soften. "You're neither cold nor unforgiving, at least as far as I can tell. You're just protecting yourself. There's nothing wrong with that. I think *you* should be the one to choose how much you're willing to let him in. No one else."

My phone buzzes with a voice mail. My thumb hovers over the play button before jumping over and hitting delete.

Boundaries.

I drop my phone back into my purse as Aaron and Liam begin carrying out platters of food. Aaron calls for the boys to come to dinner, and they barrel through the door after him, loud and excited about the robot they're building.

"Mom, please tell me we're not going to eat and run. Nick and I have at least another two hours of work," Miles says.

I laugh. "Well, we probably won't stay for two hours, but you can have some time after you eat."

Miles sags. "Well, it's better than nothing," he says, plopping into a chair next to Nick. I marvel at the miracle that they found each other.

Liam slides into the seat next to me, and I can tell he's thinking the same. His gaze travels between the boys, and I reach under the table and squeeze his hand.

"So, Miles," Aaron says, once we've started eating. "Did you ever make that chalk?"

Miles turns in his seat to face Aaron. "No, my mom was out of baking soda."

"I'm sure I could find some for you before you go," Aaron says.

"Thanks!" Miles beams at Aaron.

"Liam was a chemistry major for a little while," I tell Aaron.

"Only for a semester," Liam says. "Then I switched to computer science." He turns to Miles and Nick. "Back then we used computers that took up almost the whole room."

"Cool," Nick says, taking a bite of his roll.

Miles looks at Liam as if he's a stranger who just came in off the street and sat down at our dinner table.

"It's amazing how much technology has changed, just in our lifetime," Jackie says, glancing between Liam and Miles. "Liam, tell us about some of the games you're working on right now." To Nick she says, "Liam designs video games."

"Which ones?" Nick's eyes spark with interest, and I detect a slight thaw from my son. I shoot Jackie a grateful look, and she winks at me.

After the boys have finished eating, they excuse themselves to go back to their robot, leaving the four of us sitting around the table picking at the remnants of my lemon squares and drinking coffee.

"That was delicious," I say.

"Thanks," Aaron says, leaning back, stretching his legs out beneath the table. "I love to cook."

Liam puts his arm around me and says, "Paige and I are taking a cooking class in March. *A Night of Asian Fusion*," he says in his game-show-host voice again.

Jackie smiles. "Aaron's mother used to sign the two of them up for cooking classes when he was a teenager. While everyone else was going out to movies or parties, Aaron was learning how to blanch tomatoes and make hollandaise."

Aaron grins. "Are you complaining?"

"Definitely not," she says. "Aaron comes up with these incredible combinations. It's like he has a sixth sense. We joke that somewhere on his family tree is a famous French chef."

"You should take one of those DNA tests that can tell you

where your ancestors are from," Liam says. "A guy I work with did it. All his life, his dad went on and on about their Irish roots. But it turns out he's mostly German and Russian."

Like a record scratch, the mention of a genetic test silences the table. Liam looks at the three of us, confused.

"Jackie tells me you designed this house," I say, trying to pivot gracefully and failing. I reach under the table and squeeze Liam's knee.

Aaron twists his glass in his fingers. "I trained as an engineer. My dad wanted me to build bridges and skyscrapers. I tried it for a little while and found it to be too corporate and impersonal. I sort of slid into environmental engineering sideways."

"Aaron went to MIT," Jackie says.

"I love designing houses that are functional and eco-friendly. Each project is different. It allows me to build, but to also focus on the people and the space, not the money."

"That sounds like everyone's dream job," I say. "To be in it for the art, the pleasure of creating something important."

"I've been very lucky," he says, giving Jackie a sad smile.

An argument erupts inside the house, and Nick's voice calls, "Dad!"

"That's me," he says, rising from the table and tossing his napkin next to his plate. "Be right back."

Jackie watches him go and then turns to me. "Nick tells me things have gotten better for Miles at school," she says, "and that Miles has told him some things about his father. Did you decide to show him the donor profile?"

Liam's eyes travel between me and Jackie, measuring our words and trying to figure out when this might have happened and why I never told him. And the fact that I didn't sits like a stone in my stomach.

"I did, and it seems to have helped a little bit," I say, trying to keep my tone light. To convey to Liam that I haven't locked him out yet again.

"I'm so glad," she says.

I feel a shift in Liam's demeanor, a leaning away, even though he hasn't moved in his seat. Aaron returns from inside the house. "Crisis averted." He sits again and turns to Liam. "Jackie tells me you surf?"

Liam's eyes lock on to Aaron. "Every chance I get. You?"

"Occasionally. I picked it up when I moved here. I used to live in the San Francisco area, where most of the water sports happened on the bay—stand-up paddling, windsurfing, sailing. Only the very brave surf in the bay area."

My breathing loosens, the tension dissipating a little bit.

I check my watch, surprised it's already 9:30. "It's late," I say. "We should get going."

Jackie smiles. "Thanks for coming," she says. Her eyes hold mine, and I know she's thanking me for more than that.

We head into the house. "Miles!" I call. Jackie and Aaron follow us to the front door, where Miles soon joins us.

Aaron snaps his fingers and says, "Hold up a minute," and disappears back into the kitchen. He returns with a Ziploc bag. "Baking soda," he says, tossing it to Miles.

"Thanks," Miles says.

Aaron reaches out and squeezes his shoulder. "No problem. Let me know how it turns out."

Miles's eyes shine. "I will. Thanks."

Jackie gives me a hug and points to my purse. "Drop the rope."

I'm confused at first, until I realize she's talking about my dad. "Hang in there," I whisper.

The ride home is silent, and I know Liam's angry with me. When we pull up in front of our house, I hand Miles my keys. "I'll be inside in a minute."

I watch him scamper across the lawn and into the house.

"I should have told you," I say, hoping to preempt the fight I know we're about to have. "I'm sorry."

"This is never going to change, is it?" Liam's voice is quiet. Exhausted. "You keep me in my box, trotting me out for date night and family dinner. If I want anything more, I have to leave work early or sneak in after Miles goes to bed. Everything is on your terms. You can't even be bothered to tell me about something as significant as showing Miles his donor profile." Liam stares out the windshield, his face a stony mask.

"I wasn't trying to hide it from you."

"I know. That's the problem. It never occurred to you that I might want to know something like that. You claim to be so frustrated that Miles won't accept me, but he treats me exactly like you do. He's never going to let me in because you've taught him *he doesn't have to*."

His words slam into me, as if I've been punched. "That's not fair."

He turns to look at me. "Why didn't you tell me you were going to show him his donor profile? Why did I have to hear about it from Jackie?"

I look down at my hands. "I don't know. It just didn't come up."

"It didn't come up because you compartmentalize your life. Me on one side, everyone else on the other. And it's getting lonely over here."

"You're being ridiculous."

His voice is low. "No, Paige. I'm tired."

I press my fingers over my eyes and snap. "I'm tired too. I'm tired of being badgered. By you, by Rose, by my mother. Why can't anyone accept no for an answer? No, I'm not ready to move in with you. No, I don't want a relationship with my father, and I sure as hell don't want Miles to have one. I have a PhD from Johns Hopkins, for fuck's sake. I'm capable of making decisions for myself and my child."

"No one's questioning your ability to make decisions," he says. He starts to say something else, but stops himself, leaning his head back on his seat instead, exhaling hard. "I can't keep having this argument, or smiling through whatever scraps you want to throw my way. We had a nice time tonight. I like Jackie and Aaron. But it's always this way. I get a taste of what it could be like to be a family. But then we're right back here—me pushing you to let me into your life and you strong-arming me out of it." He looks at me. "So I'm going to give you what you want: space. You can do whatever you want with it. I'm going to use it to sort through whether I want to keep putting myself through this."

I can feel the emotions stirring. Betrayal, disappointment, resentment, fear. A potent cocktail I know all too well. "I guess I'll let you get to it then." I shove open the car door and slam it behind me, striding across the lawn toward the house without looking back. I don't hear him pull away from the curb, but when I look out the dining room window, he's gone.

HUNTINGTON'S DISEASE

The Huntington's gene is found on chromosome four. It's an autosomal dominant gene, meaning only one parent needs the gene in order for it to be passed on to offspring. These are the statistics:

- Huntington's disease affects approximately thirty thousand people in the United States.

- Approximately 150,000 individuals live with a 50 percent risk of inheriting the disease.

- 1 to 3 percent of cases are sporadic, meaning an individual develops the disease with no family history.

- The disease ranges anywhere from ten to thirty years in duration.

- Adult onset usually begins in middle age, though it can happen later.

- Early onset begins in childhood or adolescence. The duration for early onset is usually shorter, only ten to fifteen years.

- Predictive testing* can determine whether an individual has inherited the gene. One hundred percent of individuals with the Huntington's disease gene will develop the disease at some point in their lives.

---

* *Genetic testing for Huntington's disease is prohibited for children under the age of eighteen, as the child may not fully comprehend the implications of testing. However, a child under the age of eighteen who presents with early-onset symptoms may be tested to confirm a diagnosis of early-onset Huntington's disease.*

Chapter Fourteen

I lie on my back and stare up through the leaves of a tree to the blue sky above it, a light wind caressing my arms. Damp earth seeps through the blanket I've spread on the grass, but I don't care. I only want to float in this space of silence and not think of anything.

Rose collapses on the blanket next to me and tosses an empty water bottle into her bag. Across the field, Mikey runs laps with his soccer team, while Miles and Josh play on a climbing structure nearby.

"Please don't start in on me today. I don't have a lot to spare right now, Rose."

She sighs. "Then you're going to hate me even more because I have to tell you something."

I roll onto my side and sit up.

"Dad's got cancer."

"Right." I sweep my hair off my forehead. "Remember when he thought he had Parkinson's? Turned out he was just drinking too much coffee. Did Dr. Google diagnose him again?"

"It's pancreatic cancer," she says. "He's got six months, tops. That's why he came home."

The ground seems to shift beneath me, my confidence wavering. "And of course, Mom's going to drop everything and take care of him. Forget about the years he left her to do every-thing alone."

"He needs us now." Rose hugs her arms across her chest and looks toward the field where Mikey plays.

"He ditched us for most of our lives, Rose. Where was he when *we* needed *him*? Why should I care now, just because he's sick? He made his choice when he walked out."

Rose flinches, and I regret my words. Despite everything Dad's done, she still loves him. And I love her. "I'm sorry."

Pancreatic cancer is a horrible disease. It's swift and brutal. I try to remind myself that it's a fitting end for someone who could leave us so quickly and cruelly, but uncertainty begins to take root. My father has always been a loose end for me, a tether to the anger and resentment I've carried since childhood.

If what Rose says is true, my loose end is about to be cut away. I try to imagine what it will feel like, to live in a world where my father doesn't exist. "How's Mom?"

"She's devastated," Rose says. "She's waited forever for him to come back. And now that he has . . ."

I stare across the grass, toward the playground. Kids jump from the climbing wall, dance across a suspended bridge, swing from the bars, travel down the slide on their stomachs.

So many times I've imagined what it would feel like to find out my father died. A car accident, a heart attack—it never oc-curred to me he might come home to die, that watching him waste away would be his final gift to us.

"This changes everything," she says. "I know you. You pre-tend to have this heart of steel, but not even you could turn your back on this."

"It doesn't change anything," I say. "In fact, it makes it even more clear."

"How can you sit there and deny him the opportunity to know you and Miles?"

Since Liam and I broke up, I've been numb. Under normal circumstances, I would have jumped into this argument with both feet. But I feel as if I've just returned from war—weary, battle-worn, battered.

Rose continues. "When you had Miles, you talked about the importance of extended family. How you wanted all of us to have a role in raising him." She points to herself. "I've done my part. I love that child like he's one of my own, and I can't stand the thought of his missing out on knowing the only grandfather he's ever going to have." Her lashes grow wet with tears. "Dad doesn't have a lot of time left. Someday you're going to wake up and realize you had a choice in this, and you chose wrong."

I let her words hang in the air, the sound of a tennis ball hitting a racket from somewhere behind us. "You deal with Dad by giving him chances. Again and again. But that's not me." I pick some grass and let it fall through my fingers. "I don't trust people to do what they say they're going to do. Dad taught me that."

"And look how well that's turned out for you."

She's trying to bait me. I turn to her and pull my knees against my chest. "I think it's served me well. I never wanted Miles to know the pain you and I felt. Liam was the only man I ever let close to him, but he walked away too. I protect myself so that when these things happen, they don't destroy me. Now Dad's going to die and . . ." I trail off, unsure how that sentence ends.

"And?" Rose prompts.

I shrug. "I lost him a long time ago."

I look across the field and see Mikey ambling toward us, sweaty from practice. My phone buzzes: a text from Liam. I freeze, stuck between anger and yearning. But when I open it, the message is brief. *I dropped off some of your stuff at your house. My key is on the kitchen table, along with your spare car key.*

I hold my phone up so Rose can read it. "You say I'm closed off, that I don't let people in. This is why." I stand, brushing the grass from my jeans. "We'll see you at Josh's party on Saturday." As Mikey passes me, I pull him into a loose hug.

He slips out of my grip and says, "See you later, Aunt Paige."

Rose's eyes meet mine, and for once, she has nothing to say.

MUTATION

A mutation is a permanent change in the DNA sequence. Some mutations are inherited, while others are acquired during our lifetime, direct results of our environment and our experiences. Events—both mundane and traumatic—can cause a mutation.

Cancer is a specific kind of mutation that occurs in concert with another gene malfunction. Meaning, we all have some cancer cells in our bodies, but they never grow or develop because other genes suppress them. In order for a cancer mutation to take hold, a silent genetic breakdown has to have already occurred. I think about how long ago this breakdown began for my father. Did it start when he left us the first time, a single cell mutating as he packed his bags and slipped away in the middle of the night? I would imagine abandoning your family must leave some kind of biological mark.

My mother used to always tell Rose and me, "You reap what you sow." But it was my father she should have said that to. He was careless about everything—physically and emotionally. He moved through life believing he could outrun the consequences of his choices. He may be able to convince Rose to forgive him, or my mother to remain devoted, but this just proves biology is smarter than we are. Be it several days or several decades, biology doesn't forget. Everything catches up to us eventually.

Chapter Fifteen

I'm dishing out slices of cake in the kitchen when Rose careens through the open back door and grabs a few plates, carrying them out into the crowd of kids. "Sit down at the table, and I'll serve you," she calls over requests for corner pieces or the frosted number ten in the center of the cake.

Liam decided not to come. "He thought it would be best," Rose said when we arrived.

I nodded and unhooked his key from my key ring. "Can you give him this next time you see him?" My voice was cold as I slid the key onto the hall table and made my way toward the backyard, trying not to think about how I'd just relinquished my final link to Liam.

Now I hear the front door open and close and my mother's voice calling, "Hello? Anyone home?"

"In here," I say. It's unlike my mom to show up to a grandchild's birthday party so late, but she's been off her game lately because of Dad. When I turn, I stop short. Behind my mother, carrying a long rectangular gift that can only be another LEGO set, stands my father. I study his face, looking for signs of the cancer that's eating away at him. His skin looks papery thin, and his coloring is chalky. His hair, which used to be dark and wavy like mine, has thinned and is now the color of dingy white laundry.

"Hello, Peanut," he says.

Peanut. The name he used interchangeably for Rose and me when we were kids. When I was younger, I treasured the times he'd use it for me. I'd feel like I'd done something right, that I had somehow been chosen. When Rose got the name, I'd ignore her for hours, jealous she had to come along and steal him from me. It wasn't until I was older that I started to wonder if he called us Peanut because he couldn't remember which of us liked school and which preferred to collect hair ribbons.

"Hi, Dad," I say, turning back toward the cake, dragging the knife through it.

"Aren't you going to give your father a hug?" my mom asks. "You haven't seen him in a while."

I freeze.

"Don't worry about it, Beth," my dad says before I can answer. He walks into the yard, where Rose takes the gift and hugs him. My mother huffs past, leaving me to finish the cake on my own.

———

After the last of the cake has been served, I wipe down the counters, avoiding the backyard and the prospect of falling into small talk with Dad or getting a scolding from Mom.

Rose comes into the kitchen.

"You can't hide in here forever," she says.

"I'm not hiding; I'm cleaning. You should thank me."

She rolls her eyes. "Mom said you refused to say hello to Dad."

"I said hello. Mom just found it insufficient, expecting me to throw myself into his arms and forgive him for all the horrible things he put us through, simply because he's got cancer."

"Don't be a bitch."

I toss the sponge into the sink. "I think we should go." Miles has had his cake; we can leave with minimal arguing.

"Stop," she says. "I'm sorry. Come outside." She pulls my arm, and I let her lead me into the backyard, where a swarm of kids are running off their sugar high. My parents stand next to the back fence, my mother's arms wrapped around Miles, who's in conversation with my dad.

In three strides I'm in front of them. "What's going on?"

Miles looks at me, alarmed by my tone of voice, and I smile at him, though I'm anything but calm. "Why don't you go and play," I tell him. "We're leaving in a few minutes."

Miles runs off, and my mother says, "Really, Paige. That was unnecessary."

I round on her. "I've made my wishes clear."

Before we can get into it, my dad holds up his hand. "Beth," he says. "I've got this. Go help Rose."

She gives me a warning look before walking away.

"Why'd you come back, Dad?"

"I'm dying. I want to be near my family."

I think about all he's missed, the times he could have shown up—to birthdays, Rose's wedding, the births of his grandchildren. Of all the times he could have stood up for us or wiped away our tears. And now he's returned to collect the few pennies he's invested, not nearly enough to carry him to the end of his life.

"I know I've made mistakes in the past," he says. "I want to know you and Rose better. I want to know my grandchildren."

I watch Miles chase a soccer ball across the yard, Josh right behind him.

"He looks like you at that age," my father says.

"Please don't," I say.

He nods. "I know I don't deserve anything. Not after the years I strung you girls along."

I pause to look at him, wondering if I heard him right. It's easy to say the right things when there isn't enough time to do anything different. "So why come back?"

He keeps his eyes on Miles and says, "When you know you're going to die, things simplify. All of a sudden, I knew where I needed to be. I knew what I needed to do. I want to use these months to make things right with your mother, you, and Rose."

He faces me again, and I look into his eyes, the exact same shade of blue as mine, though they're watery, tinged yellow with age. Or sickness. "The problem is that while you've cleared your conscience, we're still stuck with the memories. The years you didn't show up. The years you promised to stay and then left again while we slept. What the hell are we supposed to do with *those* memories, Dad?"

Parents are starting to arrive to pick up their kids. Goodbyes are being said, and I want to make my exit. "I'm sorry you're dying. It's a vicious disease, and I wouldn't wish it on my worst enemy. Even you." I turn away and call, "Let's go, Miles!"

Miles runs toward me, and when he reaches us, my father says to him, "It was nice to meet you."

Miles smiles. "You too."

I look back and forth between the two of them—the man who fractured my heart and the boy who put it back together again.

Behind us, the kitchen door opens, and I know my mother is watching our departure. But I don't turn around. I guide Miles out of the party, fighting the urge to run. I know it's futile. The only way to keep my father away from Miles would require me to isolate him from the rest of my family.

And I could never do that to him.

THE SCORPION AND THE FROG

A Fable

Once there was a scorpion who needed to cross a river. He asked the frog for help. "Please," the scorpion said. "Can you carry me on your back across the river?"

The frog said, "No. You're a scorpion and you'll sting me."

"I won't," the scorpion promised. "I will be forever grateful."

"No," said the frog. "I don't believe you."

After much argument and assurances that the scorpion would control himself, be on his best behavior, and would be indebted to the frog for the rest of his life, the frog agreed.

Halfway across the river, the scorpion stung the frog. As they were both drowning, the frog said, "Why did you do this? Now we're both going to die."

And the scorpion replied, "I'm a scorpion. I don't know any other way to be."

Chapter Sixteen

"We've got a problem with Scott's oxytocin levels," Bruno says, dropping a pile of reports on my desk as he enters our office.

"What kind of a problem?" I ask, sifting through them.

Bruno sits at his desk and puts his feet up. "Look for yourself."

I flip the pages until I get to the lab report. I scan the numbers, and when I reach the line measuring oxytocin levels, I see a red *+0.02%*. I quickly read through the rest of the report, comparing his last blood draw with earlier ones. Everything else is the same. The only variance is his oxytocin levels.

"This is a lab error," I say.

"You'd better hope it is," he says. "Or we're fucked."

I read the report again. Oxytocin production is a biological response to the birth of your own offspring. You can either produce it or you can't. You can't grow it like a muscle.

"I guess it's no longer an IRB violation to send Jenna back. Get her scheduled," I tell him.

"Already done," he says.

—

The sun is just starting to set as I make my way down the Third Street Promenade. Nan emailed last week to inform me that since I hadn't signed up for anything, she was assigning me to the class fund-raising committee, which was holding its first meeting at Italia, an upscale restaurant far beyond my budget. *Everyone needs to do their share,* her email chirped, making me want to slam my computer into the wall.

I spot Jackie hurrying from the opposite direction, long skirt swishing around her ankles and silver bangles decorating her wrists.

She grabs my arm when she reaches me, leaning in. "I accidentally parked next to Nan in the lot, so I had to hide in the back of my minivan until she was gone."

I laugh, imagining Jackie curled up behind the driver's seat, among old Cheerios and dried-out pens.

We make our way through the dining room and find Nan and her committee tucked into a corner, with notebooks and pens sitting next to their bread plates and glasses of wine. "Hello, ladies!" Nan calls, waving us back.

Jackie and I huddle together, sliding into the two empty seats near the end of the table. Nan sits at the head, of course, but I'm at the foot, staring down the table at her as if we are hosting a party together.

Jackie pulls aside a passing waiter. "Can we get two martinis, please?" She gives me a questioning look, and I smile and nod.

"Okay." Nan claps her hands. "Thanks so much for coming. This is going to be the best fund-raising event the school has ever had. We're hoping to raise enough money to buy iPads for every student." She makes a show of sliding her notebook to the side and says, "But let's save the business for dessert and make this a moms' night out." The ladies lining each side of the table smile and give a reserved golf clap.

"Jesus help me," Jackie mutters under her breath. "We have to sit here all the way to dessert?"

Just then, the waiter arrives with our drinks, and we dive for them.

"The only way through is drunk," Jackie whispers.

Across the table, Nan starts complaining about how her Pilates instructor's honeymoon will disrupt the class schedule, and the other moms murmur their sympathy and sip their wine.

"Have you heard anything about the job?" I ask Jackie.

She grimaces. "I didn't get it."

"I'm sorry."

She shrugs. "It was a long shot. I've been out of the workforce for almost ten years. I'm a dinosaur. They can hire someone right out of college who won't have any family obligations, no school pickups or parent conferences." At the other end of the table, Nan has moved on to describing her father's villa in France. Jackie huffs. "Nan's father leaves her a villa. Mine left me a collection of Budweiser beer koozies," she says, rolling her eyes. "Speaking of," she says, "how are things with your dad?"

"Actually," I say, setting my drink down, "he's sick. That's why he came back. Cancer." I busy myself with my napkin, smoothing it across my lap.

To my relief, Jackie doesn't spout any of the usual sympathy or platitudes. She nods slowly, and takes another sip of her martini. "Does that change anything for you?"

"Not really," I say, "other than the fact that now everyone is mad at me."

A waiter appears, depositing a basket of bread in the center of the table and Caesar salads in front of each of us. I pick up my fork and ask, "How are you?"

She sighs. "The same. It's nice to be out of the house—even for this." She leans closer and lowers her voice. "I need a break. It's like every time I'm in the same room with Aaron, the conversation veers into an argument. The only time we're not fighting is when Nick's around, because we haven't told him about his grandfather's diagnosis yet."

"Aaron still doesn't want to get tested?"

"No. We're supposed to meet with a genetic counselor to go over our options. I'm hoping that might change his mind."

I take a piece of bread and rip it in half. "Well, knowing whether he carries the gene or not won't change anything for him—today, tomorrow, or even next year. I'd want to know too, but at least there's time."

"I know," she says. "That doesn't make it any easier though."

—

"Paige," Nan calls out, pulling my attention back to the table. "Since you're the only one who wasn't with us last year, why don't you tell us a little bit about yourself."

I set down my fork. "Well, I'm Miles's mom, and I'm a geneticist at Annesley."

The other ladies smile, but Nan's got more questions. "That sounds interesting." She picks up her wineglass and takes a drink. "Is Miles your only child, or do you have more?"

"No, he's my only one."

Her lips form a sympathetic pout. "That's too bad."

"Not really," I say. "It works for us."

"And your husband?"

I smile sweetly. "I decided not to bother with a husband. I used an anonymous sperm donor instead."

Next to me, Jackie snorts as Nan's mouth falls open. I take another sip of my martini, thankful Jackie ordered something strong.

"Can I please get another one of these?" Jackie asks, holding out her martini glass to a passing waiter.

"Well, that's . . . unconventional," Nan finally says.

I look around the table, all eyes on me. "It's not that unusual. It's what highly educated, professional women do these days."

"Or, we latch on to the first rich man willing to put up with us. Right, Nan?" Jackie lifts her empty martini glass in a toast.

Nan's face turns a pasty white before flushing deep red. She raises herself up slightly and says, "Boys need a father. So much of what's wrong in the world is because our boys don't have a steady hand at home to guide them."

Jackie shoves her chair back and stands. "Fuck off, Nan."

"We should go," I say. "I'm not sure this is the best committee for either of us."

I toss a few twenties on the table and lead Jackie through the crowded restaurant, but before we leave, Jackie shouts, "I'll pray for you Nan!"

We fall through the doors and into the cool night air and collapse into each other, laughing. "Do you want me to take you home?" I ask. "I don't think you should drive."

Jackie ignores me and steps closer. "Don't let them scare you off. You're no different than the rest of us." She gestures toward the restaurant. "We all wanted a kid, so we found a man. Some of us got lucky and found good ones. Others just found rich ones." She takes a deep breath and looks into the crowd. "You've got a great kid. It doesn't matter how you got him."

Her words soften me. Somehow, Jackie knows exactly what I need to hear.

She continues, "It's good for Nan to get her boat rocked every now and then. Maybe she'll steer clear of you for the rest of the year." Her eyes catch on a group of people who have just exited a bar across the promenade. "Hey," she says. "Since our dinner got canceled, let's not waste your babysitter."

"Then who's going to drive?" I ask.

She waves my words away, unconcerned. "Aaron will come and get us. Nick's sleeping at my in-laws' tonight."

I follow her across the street, and we enter a dark room teeming with the scent of exotic spices, salsa music, and waitstaff maneuvering trays of mixed drinks through the crowd.

"I'm not cool enough to be here," I say, looking down at my gray slacks and navy blue sweater.

"Nonsense," Jackie says, snagging a table in the corner.

We order a pitcher of sangria from the waitress, and when it arrives, Jackie pours our drinks and asks, "What's Liam doing tonight?"

I take a big gulp and briefly worry about mixing wine and gin. But in this moment, all I want to do is get drunk with Jackie. "I don't know. We broke up." Saying it aloud makes it impossible to ignore the accumulation of everything I took for granted. The cups of coffee Liam would leave in my car when he surfed County Line. The way he'd unload my dishwasher because he knew I hated doing it. All of the tiny pieces of our life together assembling into a giant hole I want to fill with alcohol.

Jackie looks shocked. "What? Why? And why didn't you tell me sooner?"

"I didn't want to get into it in front of Nan," I say, noticing the way the sangria warms my stomach, the way it turns my sharp edges soft. I should drink to excess more often, I decide.

"Is it because of Miles?" she asks.

"No. He says I don't let him in enough, that I don't include him in my life."

Jackie's expression is the perfect blend of angry and skeptical, and I hang on to it. "What does he expect you to do? Your child has to come first."

"Exactly," I say. "Let's talk about something else."

Jackie ticks off forbidden topics. "No Liam or Aaron. No kids. No school stuff. No work. No Huntington's." She looks alarmed. "What's left?"

I laugh and feel myself relax. It's a relief to be around someone who doesn't want to pick apart my life, lining up my flaws and bad decisions to be examined. "I don't know."

Jackie pours more sangria into our glasses and glances at a table of young women next to us. "What kind of life would you live, if you were their age and could choose anything?" She takes a sip of her drink. "I'd want to live in New York, right in the heart of Manhattan. Maybe in a high-rise apartment with views, and have an important job downtown."

"What kind of job?"

"I don't know. One where I had an office and an assistant to take my lunch order. And a coffee cart that came by once an hour. I'd wear power suits and killer heels. How about you?"

Science is all I've ever wanted to do. But I try to stretch away from the ruts in my life to something completely different. "Maybe something abroad," I say. "Like a travel journalist. I'd write about foreign locations, stay in hotels for free, fly from one place to another, and immerse myself in the culture. The foods. The smells . . ." I trail off, imagining it, until I realize I've chosen another career that would leave me isolated and alone. Maybe that's just who I am. There's nothing wrong with being self-reliant and independent. It wasn't until I tried to be something different that things started going wrong for me.

"That sounds amazing," Jackie says.

The women next to us laugh and clap as one of them does a shot. From behind me, a man says, "I can get one of those for you, if you like." His voice is warm and intimate in my ear, and for a split second I think it's Liam, somehow intuiting I'd be here, come to ask me to forgive him, and a rush of adrenaline floods me.

But when I turn, it's the face of a stranger, leering at me through glassy eyes that are shot through with red. "No, thanks," I say.

He turns his attention toward Jackie. "How about you? You look like you know how to have fun."

Jackie smiles at him suggestively. "I love to have fun. But I'm finishing a course of antibiotics and my doctor says I can't *have fun* until the sores heal."

The guy recoils, as if he's been slapped, and backs away. "Maybe next time?" Jackie calls after him, but he's already gone, off to find his next victim.

"You're terrible." I laugh. But the exchange has left me feeling empty, the realization that I'm a single woman in a bar, fending off drunk assholes. Suddenly, I feel woozy and all I want is to go home. "Can you call Aaron and have him come and get us?" I ask her. "I should go home and relieve Gemini."

Jackie shoots off a text and says, "Gemini? That's your babysitter's name?"

I'm reminded of what Liam said when I first told him Gemini's name. *She puts the "pair" in au pair. You're lucky because she usually only looks after twins*. I feel a sense of loss, like a missed train, departed from the station.

"Two waters," Jackie says to a waitress passing by. She puts her hand over mine. "You miss him."

I shrug. "Yeah." It's the first time I've said it out loud, and it doesn't make me feel better. "But I don't see how it could have worked. He wanted more than I could give him."

"Life is long. Lots of things can still happen."

—

Twenty minutes later, Aaron's standing over our table, grinning. "Well, look at you two. My wife, drunk on a Tuesday night. Who would have thought?" He slides into the chair next to Jackie. "You girls ready to go home?"

"I need to use the bathroom," Jackie says. "I hope there isn't a line."

Aaron watches her walk away and then turns to me. "Jackie really needed this tonight. She's had a hard time with my dad's diagnosis and what it means for our family. She says you've been a real help though, talking to her about the statistics and what they mean. Thanks."

"No problem."

His eyes dart between me and the back of the bar. "Since I have you here," he says, leaning forward, "I was wondering if I could ask your advice on something."

His face is stretched and desperate, and I feel sorry for him. "Of course."

He glances again toward the restrooms and then out the front window toward the street. "I hate putting you in this position," he finally says, "except I don't know who else to ask."

Cold adrenaline sharpens my focus, knowing he's about to ask me how to tell Jackie he's tested positive. I'm already formulating a way to assure him she can handle it.

He takes a long, shaky breath. "About twelve years ago, I was a sperm donor. Jackie doesn't know—it was before we met."

I feel as if my chair might slip out from under me, and I wonder if I've heard him right. Am I drunker than I thought? "I'm sorry," I say. "I couldn't hear you. What did you say?"

But he says it again. "A long time ago, I was a sperm donor."

I nod, as if this were something innocuous about himself that he's shared with me—like the fact that he used to play basketball or he was once a camp counselor—and I take a sip of my water to buy myself some time as I scramble to process what he's just said.

"Since you work in genetics," he continues, "I was hoping you could tell me what my ethical obligations are. About the Huntington's."

I study his face, looking for signs he knows how I conceived Miles, but there aren't any. He wants my opinion as a geneticist, not as someone who used a donor.

"I'm not an attorney," I tell him, measuring my words carefully. "And it will probably vary by clinic." I fight to keep my voice steady and clear. "Which one did you use?" I grip my water glass, willing him to say names of clinics I know of but didn't use. Hillcrest Reproduction. Cryogenics of North America. Crenshaw Cryogenics.

"American Cryogenic Bank," he says.

I feel the air rush out of me, but I pull myself together before he notices. ACB has donors from all over the country. Tens of thousands of men, all across the United States. It would be almost statistically impossible for Aaron to be ours. *Almost.* The word floats through my mind, like a whisper, causing me to nearly choke. I close my eyes, seeing Miles and Nick, their heads tilted toward each other as they talk about chemistry.

I shake my head to clear it. I need to stay calm. This can't be what I think it is. "You absolutely have an obligation to inform the clinic," I say. "They'll need to notify the families who used your sperm."

Aaron looks at his hands, splayed on top of the table. I study the contours of his face, the way his cheekbones blend into his jaw, the set of his eyes, the arc of his nose, and pick up my water glass, draining it, the chill of ice racing to my temples.

Over his shoulder, I see Jackie making her way toward us, and I sit up straighter in my chair. Aaron follows my gaze and says, "Please don't mention this to Jackie. I'll tell her. Just give me some time." When she arrives at our table, he stands and says, "I'd better get you two home. We can bring you back tomorrow to get your car," he tells me.

I wobble, gripping my chair for support. "That's okay," I say. "Rose can bring me."

"It's no trouble," Jackie says, wrapping her arm around Aaron's waist and letting him lead her toward the door. I follow behind them, my mind a mess of questions I can't even begin to sort into any kind of sense.

OUR HISTORY AND MISSION

The Donor Sibling Registry (DSR) was founded in 2000 to assist individuals conceived as a result of sperm, egg, or embryo donation that are seeking to make mutually desired contact with others with whom they share genetic ties. Without any outside support, the DSR has single-handedly pioneered a national discussion about the donor conception industry and families, with its many media appearances and interviews. DSR advocates for the right to honesty and transparency for donor kids, and for social acceptance, legal rights and valuing the diversity of all families.

The DSR's core value is honesty, with the conviction that people have the fundamental right to information about their biological origins and identities.

The donor conception industry is largely a for-profit enterprise, and after the "product" has been purchased, most doctors, clinics, egg donation agencies, and cryobanks do not engage in discussions and activities which acknowledge the humanity and rights of the donor-conceived. It is our mission to bring these concepts to the public arena for discussion, as has been done in many European countries, as well as New Zealand and parts of Australia.

Since 2000, we have provided support and connection to families which have been developed via donor conception, advocated for the rights of the donor-conceived, and educated the general public through national media interviews and appearances about the issues, challenges and rights of the donor-conceived community.

Parents are sometimes not prepared for their children's curiosity and desire to know more about their genetic background. In order to move out of the secrecy and shame that has for so long shrouded donor conception, the DSR will continue to educate parents and the general public on the importance of honoring and supporting their children's natural drive to know more about their identity.

The DSR also ensures that the donor-conceived have a safe place to search for their biological identities and to make these connections with their half-siblings and where possible, their donors as well. **When matching on the DSR, make sure to ask a few pieces of information from the donor profile that have not been posted, and that only the donor, or someone with the donor's profile, would know.**

Chapter Seventeen

"Oh my god." Rose stops midstride to face me head-on. We're only halfway around our first lap of the Annesley track, and the crisp October air bites through my light sweatshirt, raising goose bumps. Sycamore and pine trees rise behind the old brick-and-stone stadium, which surrounds us on three sides. The fourth opens to a majestic view of the Pacific Ocean.

I called Rose first thing this morning and begged her to meet me because despite our disagreement over Dad and the tension that has settled between us, Rose is still my person, the one I turn to when I don't know what to do.

Her hands press into her temples as if to physically keep her head from exploding. "Tell me exactly what he said."

I start walking again, keeping my eyes on the track in front of me. I tell her about Aaron's dad's diagnosis, his past as a sperm donor, and how he asked me for advice last night at the bar.

Rose lurches to a stop again. She grabs my arm, holding me in place. "Do you think he's Miles's donor?"

A runner approaches from behind, passing us on the left. I try to match my breathing to hers—in and out, one step at a time. I start walking again, pulling Rose along with me. "No. I think it's nothing more than a very disturbing coincidence," I say, trying very hard to believe it myself.

But Rose's thoughts barrel ahead. "But if he is Miles's donor, could Miles have the Huntington's gene too?"

I look away, toward the ocean. "Theoretically, yes. But, Rose, the chances of that are infinitesimal."

Rose nods. "There's no way," she agrees. "If he donated *before* he met Jackie, then he can't be your donor. Miles and Nick are the same age."

I close my eyes. I need Rose to help me chase away the possibility, not force me to argue the opposite. "Frozen sperm doesn't expire. Some clinics discard it after twenty years, but theoretically it lasts forever. He said he donated about twelve years ago. It fits the timeline."

Rose is stunned into silence. We're barely walking at this point. "Oh my god." The realization of what this might mean for Miles—the uncertainty, the fear—settles onto her face. The panic that kept me up all night pokes through her voice. "What did you say when he told you?"

"Nothing. Because there's nothing to say."

"But what if you're wrong? What if it is him? And what about Jackie? What will you say to her?"

I look across the stadium at the empty bleachers rising toward the treetops.

"I don't know," I admit.

Rose is incredulous. "This could be Miles's father. His *brother*."

I need to gain control of this conversation. "There's no reason to think that, Rose. Thousands of people use ACB every year." The wind whips my hair around my face, and I struggle to tuck it behind my ears. "If you were to travel to New York and meet someone on the subway who has a friend in Los Angeles named Henry, would that mean this person knows *your* Henry?"

"Possibly," she says in a low voice. And I know she's right.

I think about Miles and Nick together, subtle similarities I didn't register as significant until now. The identical arch of their backs as they observed the grasshopper at the school picnic. The way they finish each other's sentences. Even the way they walk is the same—a lopey, zigzag gait that I should have recognized. I chastise myself. Close friends often finish each other's sentences or adopt each other's mannerisms. Similarities prove nothing.

Rose's voice pulls me back. "How could the clinic have let Aaron donate? Don't they screen for genetic diseases?"

"They can't screen for everything. Huntington's isn't one of the tests."

Rose looks incredulous. "How could he put so many families at risk?"

"I don't think he knew. If one of Aaron's grandparents had it, it's likely no one talked about it. In those days, they would have been sent away to an institution, forgotten. Or maybe they passed away before the onset of symptoms."

We round the end of the track, walking directly into the wind. In a low voice, Rose says, "I don't know, Paige. I have a bad feeling about this."

I don't look at her, instead focusing on the back of the runner in front of us, rounding the corner with her smooth stride and loose limbs. I want to run after her and keep on running, away from this place I've landed. "Bad feelings aren't proof," I say.

Rose gestures toward the bleachers, and we sit down in the first row. The cold metal of the bench seeps through my pants, chilling me even with the shining sun. "Isn't there something you can do?" she presses.

"If he notifies the clinic of his father's diagnosis, we can get proof that way," I tell her.

"So you're going to sit back and wait?"

"Do you have a better suggestion?" I look down at my knees, and notice a tiny hole in my running tights. "It's very unlikely," I repeat.

Rose looks toward the ocean and back again. "I hope you're right."

"When have I ever been wrong?"

Rose gives a shaky laugh. "Lots of times. I still have that scar on my knee from when you convinced me I could fly."

"I'm not wrong about this," I tell her. "We're worrying over nothing." I don't think Rose believes me any more than I do.

———

Back at work, the steadiness I rely upon settles over me, like a heavy cloak blotting out the rest of the world. Jenna, Bruno, and I sit in my office, having just returned from the lab, where I reran Scott's last sample myself. The results are the same.

I turn to Jenna. "What do we know about oxytocin?"

She smiles, familiar with this routine. I don't believe all knowledge rests with the PhD. Younger minds and eyes are sometimes much more flexible. "It's a hormone that's released by the pituitary gland. It's responsible for pair bonding."

"And what do we know about the inhibitor?" I ask her.

"It impedes the release of oxytocin from the brain," she says. "Therefore, the subject has trouble with bonding and attachment."

I look at Bruno. "What do you think?"

"I think the sample is corrupted," he says. Jenna starts to argue. "No offense," Bruno says to her. "It happens."

"How do you explain my getting the exact same results then?" I ask. "No variance."

Bruno shrugs. "I can't."

A thread of a hypothesis is growing inside of me. "Bio 101, Jenna. Talk to me about gene expression."

"We all have genes waiting for the right conditions to express themselves. Cancer genes. Obesity."

I nod. "What if something in Scott's life has caused the inhibitor gene to turn off?"

Bruno says, "DNA methylation?"

I think of the lecture I gave my freshman biology class in September on mutation and methylation and shake my head. I turn to Jenna. "We need another sample. Can you schedule something with Scott this week?"

—

After Jenna leaves, I make my way back to the lab, to distance myself even further from the worry that chases after me. When the door clicks shut, I pause, taking in the scene. The room is long, with white walls and high windows. Scattered across the space are several workstations with grad students and lab assistants bent over them. I check the log by the door and see that several samples are waiting to be processed and pull up a stool to an empty workstation, snapping on gloves. Most lead researchers spend the majority of their time in an office, reading reports and soothing administrators, but I've made sure that will never happen to me. I don't ever want to lose the feel of the lab, for my hands to forget the precise steps involved in extracting DNA. When I look through a microscope and see an entire world—

a unique set of instructions for a human being—it's a magic that still takes my breath away. It's a meditation that corrals my racing thoughts into a box where I can keep them separate, until I'm ready to think about them again.

"Hey there, Dr. Robson," someone calls from across the room. But I'm already focused on the task at hand, hypnotized by the low hum of equipment, my body finally relaxing enough so that I can forget everything else.

MTDNA

There are lots of things about my mother I hope I've inherited. Her strength and determination are just two of them. She never faltered when we were growing up, never wavered in her belief that she could do everything. I only now realize how much she kept hidden from us—the loneliness, the self-doubt, the isolation of being a single mother when single mothers were rare.

Genetically, we are inextricably linked to our mothers through mitochondrial DNA. It's a unique form of DNA that isn't found in the chromosomes. In fact, it isn't part of the genome at all. It lives in the cell between the nucleus and the cell membrane. Like the Y chromosome, mtDNA does not combine with genes inherited from your other parent but is passed on, whole, to you. It will live inside of you—the story of your mother, and her mother, and all the mothers who came before. A boxed set of every mother in your line, back to the beginning of time, stamped onto every single one of your cells, replicating throughout your entire life. Complete and unchanging.

When Miles was a baby, I used to think he could sense the exact minute I woke up, because the moment I opened my eyes, he'd start to cry. Or I'd know he was going to fall a fraction of a second before he did. Even to this day, he'll sometimes start talking about the very thing I was just thinking about. Humans have a long history of stories about a mother's intuition. Could it be connected to the exact replicas of the mtDNA living inside the cells of our children?

The scientist in me refutes this, but the mother in me knows it's true.

Chapter Eighteen

When my mother arrives at my door, carrying Miles's Halloween costume, I know I can't avoid her any longer.

"Cool! Thanks, Grandma!" Miles grabs the costume. "Did you remember the ninja star?" He rifles through the bag, tossing everything onto the floor.

"Miles," I say. "Grandma worked hard on that costume. Don't throw it on the floor." To my mother, I say, "Ninja star?"

She laughs. "Relax. It's just cardboard, covered with tinfoil."

Miles pulls it out of the bag and holds it up. "I think this will work," he says. "Come into my room so I can show you the book I was telling you about last night. You aren't going to believe the photos they have of Jupiter in it."

My mom laughs and kisses him on top of his head. "In a minute. I need to talk to your mom first."

Miles scoops everything up and says, "Okay, but don't take too long," before disappearing back into his room.

"What did you want to talk about?" I lead her into the living room, where the late-afternoon sun slants through the windows, making a bright spot on the wall behind the couch. I slide the curtain closed, and the room dims, both of us taking our battle positions on either end of the couch.

"Stop being a shit."

Well, I guess we're skipping the niceties. "You came here to tell me that?"

"No." She smooths her blue nylon pants over her knees, avoiding my eyes. "Actually, I came here to tell you that even though I disagree, I will honor your desire to keep your distance."

I'm shocked. My mother never gives up a position once she's established it. "Why now?"

"Because your father doesn't have a lot of time, and I don't want to spend it arguing with you. Accept him, don't accept him, we all need to move on."

"And how does Dad feel about this?"

She looks down, picking an invisible piece of lint off her pants. "He was the one to suggest it."

"Of course he was." Always running away when things get tough. "What about Miles? Is Dad going to keep his distance from him too?"

"I'm happy to come here to spend time with Miles. But you can't insulate him from the world. He's going to come into some contact with your father occasionally."

She senses my hesitation and says, "What do you think will happen, Paige?"

"I'm scared he'll get hurt."

My mother scoots closer to me on the couch. "You're not scared for Miles. You're scared for yourself." She looks toward the window, squinting at the bright light seeping through the curtains. "I know what you think of me. I see the silent judgment in your eyes every time your father comes back and I let him." She looks at me, challenging me to deny it. "I gave up the possibility of having a normal family by loving your dad. I never questioned whether he'd return; I just trusted he would. That's what kept me going when things got tough. But I don't regret it.

He's the love of my life." She looks down at her pants again. "I am sorry about what it did to you girls though."

"The only thing we ever knew for sure was that we could never count on him."

"I thought I was doing the right thing, making sure you had a relationship with your father, as unconventional as it seemed." She folds her hands on her lap. "Your dad and I had a long talk last night. It's not fair to force him on you, and if you feel more comfortable staying away, he will honor that. And I will too."

I can tell this doesn't sit easy with her.

"Why do you care so much about whether I have a relationship with him?"

She looks at me, incredulous. "He's a part of who you are," she says. "Whether you like it or not."

I start to argue, but she holds up her hand.

"Let me finish. Forgiveness doesn't mean forgetting, or even having a relationship with him. It means understanding what happened, looking beyond your version of the past and seeing things from someone else's perspective."

"I have," I say. But she looks at me like she used to when she caught me in a lie, as if she can see inside my brain. My version of the past is the lens through which I view my world. To remove it would mean looking at everything I've done—Miles, my study, my father, and Liam—differently. And I'm afraid of what I might see.

She takes my hand and squeezes it. My mother's hand has been a constant in my life, smoothing my hair, drying my tears, yanking me into the dentist's office or across a street. But as I stare at our intertwined fingers, I notice how swollen and bent hers are and remember that she too is getting old.

"I feel lost, Mom. Like I can't do the right thing for anyone. I'm always disappointing someone—you and Rose, Liam, Miles."

She sighs and pulls me closer. I let myself lean into her, the floral scent of her lotion enveloping me, reminding me of the many times she sat with me like this when I was younger. "You're letting fear make your decisions," she says. "Fear of letting Liam all the way into your life and fear of upsetting Miles if you do. Fear that your father hasn't changed and fear that he has, because then you'd have to do something about it." She tucks a piece of my hair behind my ear, and I try not to notice the slight tremor in her hand.

"So what should I do?" I ask, hoping for one of the solutions she used to give me. *Try again. Ignore what they say. Tell them you're sorry.*

She kisses the top of my head like she did to Miles, like she's done to me thousands of times. "I can't tell you that. Life is scary. But that doesn't mean you shouldn't live it."

DNA METHYLATION

DNA methylation is a process that occurs in every single cell of your body, more than a billion times per second. Methylation is critical to cell health and controlling gene expression. But like anything that happens so frequently, errors can occur. Scientists are learning that faulty DNA methylation can also be triggered by outside factors, such as trauma. Or grief.

Chapter Nineteen

"Have we heard anything from Jorgensen about the bridge grant?"

Bruno gives me a funny look. "Nothing yet," he says. "But you've asked me that twice already this morning. What's the matter with you?"

I look down at my desk, sorting a pile of pens and pencils. "I've got some stuff going on," I admit. "It's . . ." I trail off, shrugging into silence.

"Want to talk about it?" he asks.

I want to tell him all of it. But I don't have the energy to face his brand of honesty right now. "Not really."

Bruno nods just as his computer pings, and he swivels to read the email. Something must catch his attention, because he sits forward suddenly and begins furiously tapping his keyboard.

"What is it?" I ask.

"We got the second set of labs back for Scott Sullivan," he says, his eyes glued to the screen. "His oxy levels are still elevated. In fact, they're slightly higher than last time."

I quickly log on to the secure database and pull up Scott's file too.

We're quiet, each of us drawing our own silent hypotheses.

"Now what?" he finally asks.

"I don't know."

"At this rate, he might not even qualify for phase two."

Bruno and I look at each other across the desk, our years together silently communicating what neither of us want to say out loud.

"You're still thinking methylation, aren't you?" he asks.

I gather my laptop and some papers off my desk and stand. "I think it's too soon to think anything. I need to get some air, a change of scenery. I'll be down the hill at Dillon's if you need me."

—

I arrive at the coffee shop, with its wide-open views of Point Dume and the Pacific. I need to sit down with the Sullivan file, away from the lab, where my perception can sometimes be skewed. I pull up the file again and scan the labs, starting with the blood draw from that first day in the hospital five years ago. His levels remained static until the draw a few weeks after Mara's death. That's when they began to creep up. Methylation can cause a slow genetic change, usually occurring across months, years, or even generations. If we're getting gradual methylation of Scott's inhibitor gene, that could explain the small increase in his oxytocin levels.

Late October sun angles across my table and pulls my eyes across the highway to the beach beyond. It's deserted, save for a few surfers on the tail end of their morning surf session. My eyes automatically search the cars in the beach lot, looking for Liam's, but I know that even if he surfed this spot today, he'd be long gone by now.

I return to the file, pull up Jenna's interview notes, and go back to June, the last visit with Mara. I read through everything, then look again out the window and think about her final day and what she left unfinished, believing she had more time. What kind of mess would I leave behind? What would I have wished I'd said? And to whom?

On impulse, I log on to my email and pull up Miles's class roster. I scroll down until I find Aaron's contact information and copy his address into a new message. My cursor blinks, waiting for words that won't come.

Dear Aaron, I think we need to talk.

No.

I have a crazy question for you that will sound ridiculous.

Also not good. I can't think of a scenario in which this conversation ends well. I either embarrass myself with my outrageous imaginings, or I drop a bomb onto the lives of people I care about. As long as the words stay inside my head, no one can get hurt. I delete the email and look across the restaurant, where I see an older man sitting a few tables away, shoulders hunched over his cup of tea, an untouched Danish sitting on a plate next to him. His features seem vaguely familiar until I realize I'm looking at my father.

More unfinished business.

As if sensing my stare, he looks up, and our eyes lock. He hesitates, offers a half smile, then resumes his stirring.

A combination of resentment and regret creep up inside of me. It's easy to keep my distance when I can fool myself into believing he doesn't exist. But watching him eat alone in the same restaurant as his daughter breaks something inside of me.

"Dad."

He looks up, his tea halfway between the table and his mouth.

I gesture toward the empty seat across from me, surprised to find myself hoping he'll accept.

His eyes fill with a mix of gratitude and apprehension, and I smile to show him I mean no harm.

He carries his tea and Danish across the restaurant and slides in across from me. "Good morning," he says.

"What are you doing here?" I ask. Dillon's is out of the way and caters more to the Malibu crowd.

He shrugs. "They have the best selection of Danishes on the west side." He stirs his tea and takes a sip. "How have you been?" he asks.

His words feel formal, like something he'd say to an acquaintance. Which I guess I am.

"I'm well," I finally say. "How are you feeling?"

"Pretty good, considering." He sips his tea, his familiar blue eyes studying me over the rim of his cup.

"What medications are you on? What kind of treatment plan?" I latch on to these details so we don't have to discuss anything personal.

He sets his cup down and gestures toward my laptop, ignoring my questions. "Work? Your mother says you're running an important project through the college."

"I'm studying the effect a certain hormone has on new fathers," I tell him. "We've discovered a genetic inhibitor in some men that keeps their body from releasing it."

"That sounds interesting. Why are you here and not in the lab?"

I rest my arms on the table, then pull them onto my lap, the echo of my father's stern voice saying, *Elbows, please*, playing in my mind. "I'm trying to make sense of some data. But something screwy is going on with one of our subjects, and the test results aren't making sense."

"What do you think it is?"

"At first, a lab error. But his results keep coming back the same."

He takes a sip of his tea. "And?"

I shake my head, unwilling to put into words what I'm beginning to suspect. That grief has caused a biological response in Scott, which has affected him enough to alter his brain chemistry and his cells. "We're not sure yet, but we're working on it."

He raises his eyebrows. "You must have some theories?"

I cross my arms. "Nothing I'm ready to talk about yet."

He nods, as if he expected to be shut down, and wipes his mouth with his napkin. "I must get back to your mother. It was a real treat to visit with you. I hope we can do it again?"

My head jerks up, his abrupt farewell catching me by surprise.

He gathers his things, oblivious.

I don't know why this shocks me. He's always been this way, leaving before anyone else is ready to let him go.

I consider his request. Do what again? Have another thirty-second conversation? *Let's do this again sometime*, or *I'll call you*. The phrases are meaningless. Nothing more than empty words that really just signal goodbye.

My father hesitates, as if wanting to say something more, but then decides against it. "Regardless, thank you for inviting me to join you today."

After he's gone, I shove my laptop away, surprised that instead of feeling angry at his sudden departure, I feel guilty that maybe I could have tried harder to hold him here. I think of my mother's advice from the other day and wonder if this is the life I'm too scared to live—and whether it's worth it.

ANNESLEY COLLEGE LABORATORY RULES AND PROCEDURES (EXCERPT)

Updated 2016

Los Angeles, California
2009

GENERAL SAFETY AND LAB USE

Unauthorized work in the laboratory is *forbidden*.

Unauthorized personnel (including undergraduate students) are not permitted in the laboratory *under any circumstances*. Authorization may be granted by Dr. Robson on a case-by-case basis.

No one under eighteen is permitted in the lab at *any time*.

Chapter Twenty

"Trick or treat!" Miles's voice floats over Josh's and Hannah's, and the woman who answers the door oohs and aahs over their costumes while Rose and I stand on the sidewalk. I'm dressed up as Jessie, from *Toy Story 2*. Liam and I came up with our costumes together—I'd be Jessie, and he'd be Woody—because Miles had been obsessed with the movie. I've got a Western shirt on, with blue jeans and cowboy boots, and I've fixed my hair in a long braid down my back. Liam's costume was equally simple—jeans, boots, a vest, and cowboy hat. This afternoon, I snuck away to the mall, where I bought a new pair of pants that hugged my hips and made me look like a movie star in a tabloid magazine rather than a tired-out geneticist who spends too much time in the lab. I'm not naive enough to think that simply by wearing a costume, I can remind Liam of everything we used to be. But somehow I've bought into the magical thinking that if we can stand next to each other, me as Jessie and him as Woody, that for a few minutes I might feel like I've gotten something back again.

Miles races down the path, holding up his candy. "Twix!" he shouts. "The giant size!"

"You should let me check that for safety," Rose says, adjusting her Cleopatra wig. She looks more like Cher than the Egyptian queen.

"Put it in your bag, Miles. Don't let her near it."

Rose shoots me a look and whispers, "You know you're going to eat that the minute he falls asleep tonight."

"Which is exactly why I don't want you near it." I pull out a mini Snickers from my pocket that I stole out of Miles's bag while he retied his shoes, and I pop it into my mouth before he can see.

The kids race past us and on to the next house. The night is perfect—there's a slight chill to the air, but not so cold that kids need coats over their costumes. The street is crowded with groups—large bands of teenagers out for an evening of mischief and parents with small children dressed as pirates and princesses. Miles's ninja costume has been a hit at every house we go to, and I make a mental note to tell Mom. "What's Mikey doing tonight?" I ask.

Rose shrugs. "He says they're trick-or-treating, but I think they're probably just taking advantage of being able to roam the neighborhood after dark." She looks at me sideways. "You look good. Kind of hot. Like a hot cowgirl."

"Thanks. Liam and I planned to be Jessie and Woody a month ago. It seemed silly to go through the trouble of getting a new costume."

"I'm sure it had nothing to do with the fact that Liam is back at the house with Henry, handing out candy." To the kids she calls, "Hannah, wait for us at the corner!"

"It's a costume, Rose. Not a love letter." I pick up my pace, hoping Rose can't see the truth in my eyes.

—

After three hours and a huge bonanza of candy, Rose and I call it a night. The kids beg for one more street, reminding us that it's Friday and they can sleep in tomorrow, but I'm exhausted. "Time to head back to the house so you can empty your bags and start trading."

"Everyone knows that's just an excuse for you to steal our candy, Aunt Paige," Josh says to me.

I touch my finger to the tip of his nose. "I don't steal. I sample."

When we get to Rose's, we follow the kids up the walk and through the front door. As I move through the quiet house, I wonder if Liam has already left, and I feel a pang of disappointment. But then I hear his voice in the kitchen, laughing at something Henry's said.

Nerves flutter through me. This is the first time I've seen him since we broke up, and I suddenly don't know what to do with my hands. *It's just Liam*, I remind myself.

As I walk through the dining room and into the kitchen, I pull up short. Liam leans against the counter, drinking a beer, but he's not wearing the Woody costume. Instead, he's repurposed it into a Han Solo costume. When he sees me, the smile falls off his face.

"Hi," I say.

"Hey."

Rose and Henry look awkward, and Rose says, "Maybe we should go check on the kids."

I feel a surge of anger at how eager he is to shed even the smallest connection to me. And I feel foolish that I thought it could be any other way. "No, it's fine," I tell them, not wanting to be alone with Liam. To Liam I say, "You changed your costume."

He looks down, as if he doesn't remember what he's wearing, and then back up at me. "Yeah. This just seemed simpler."

I nod. "Simpler. Right." What could be simpler than a costume he already has?

"Don't be that way, Paige."

"What way?" I stare at him and his eyes lock on to mine, each of us dug into our own anger, unwilling to give any ground to the other. Finally, I turn to Rose and Henry and say, "We should go. It's late."

I walk into the living room, where the kids have spread their candy on the floor and are sorting through it, trading Almond Joys for Milky Ways. Rose follows me. "You don't need to leave," she says.

"We do. Miles is going to a beach party tomorrow and should probably get to bed."

"In November? Whose party?"

"It's a Founder's Day celebration at the Turner House." The Turner House is one of several private beach clubs in Santa Monica. Most of their events happen during the summer, but they're famous for their Founder's Day party every November.

"Who do you know who belongs to the Turner House?" Rose asks. But then she says, "Oh. Right. Never mind."

"You don't have to say it like that."

She pulls me aside and whispers, "Yes, I do. Do you really think it's a good idea for him to go?"

I watch Miles pile his candy back into his bag and say, "I think we're both getting worked up over nothing, worrying about something that isn't logical or possible. Besides, once he heard about it from Nick, I didn't have a choice. It'll be fine."

"Are you going too?"

"No, I have too much work to do."

"You can't just ignore this and hope it will go away," she says.

"There is no *this*." I step away from her and turn toward the living room, where Hannah and Josh are still sorting candy. "Happy Halloween, you guys."

"Good night, Aunt Paige," they say, not looking up from their task. Rose watches me, annoyance and worry etched across her face, as I walk out of the room.

—

The next morning my eyes are gritty from lack of sleep, and no amount of coffee can erase the fuzziness in my head. Rose texted me this morning. *Sorry last night was such a disaster. You guys will find a new normal.* But what I'm realizing too late is that it's our old normal I want. Except the old normal wasn't good enough for Liam.

When I pull up to Jackie and Aaron's, Jackie is loading beach bags into her car, and Aaron and Nick huddle on the grass. A prickle of unease, like a warning, passes over me as I survey the scene, but I shake it off.

"Miles!" Nick calls. "Come over here! My dad is going to show us how to win the rocket contest."

Miles bolts from the car, not even bothering to shut the door. Jackie leads me over to the porch.

"What's that?" I ask.

She smiles. "Every Founder's Day, the club has all these different activities for the kids. Relay races, crafts, eating competitions, and the rocket contest."

The boys kneel next to Aaron, who holds a two-liter of soda and a package of Mentos. "We have to get our bottle to explode the highest," he tells them. "Watch." He uncaps the soda, and the boys draw nearer.

"Aaron's been waiting to do this competition for years," Jackie says. "You can't enter without a kid, and up until now, Nick's been too scared."

I watch Aaron hand out the supplies to the boys, giving them quiet directions the entire time. He lets the boys do the work, asking questions, giving suggestions, but ultimately letting them figure it out. This is the first time I've seen the three of them together since my conversation with Aaron, and I search for differences—hungry for anything that might prove he isn't our donor. But when his head tips toward Miles's, it's impossible to miss the identical shape of their eyes or the symmetrical way their hair curls over their ears. I glance at Jackie, certain she sees it too, but she just smiles, a tinge of sadness in her eyes.

"Any word from Liam?" she asks.

I give her the basics of what happened last night, and Jackie winces. "Ouch."

Miles whispers something in Nick's ear, and they both burst into laughter. I look at Jackie, and a fissure opens inside me, leaking uneasiness and dread.

When they're ready to toss the bottle, Aaron turns to us and says, "Watch this!"

He hands it to Nick, who tosses the bottle onto the sidewalk, where it bounces and then shoots up into the air, a fury of fizz. The boys scream and laugh, dancing out of the way as a cascade of soda rains down on them. The bottle lands and explodes, a river of leftover soda running down the driveway and into the gutter. Aaron's laughter floats over everything.

Jackie turns to the boys. "Okay, over to the hose before you get in the car."

Aaron picks up the bottle, which has split in half, jagged plastic edges poking through the label. He jerks his hand back as a tiny stream of bright red blood seeps from his finger. "Caught an edge," he says. "Be right back." He jogs up the stairs and through the open front door.

From behind us, I hear Miles say to Nick, "That was so cool. What do you get if you win?"

But I don't hear Nick's answer because Jackie says, "Why don't you join us?"

I shake my head. "I wish I could. But I've got a ton of work to do. It's not often I can get eight uninterrupted hours in the lab on a weekend. My pile of paperwork is almost as tall as Miles." I smile, but it feels forced. "How's Aaron doing?" I nod my head toward the house.

She gives a tiny shrug. "The same. We're at an impasse."

Aaron joins the boys at the side of the house, and I hear them giggling, unable to tell the difference between Nick and Miles, the sound of their laughter blending together into something almost musical.

"Look what I found!" I hear Aaron yell, and the boys shriek. Aaron comes around front, each boy tucked under an arm, like footballs. Miles laughs, reflexive and deep, the same laugh as when I tickle him. A shiver runs through me, and I cross my arms over my chest.

Of course the boys are similar. They're best friends. They adopt each other's speech patterns and expressions. It's what humans do. But I'm beginning to lose my grip on that rationale. Desperate to reset my racing thoughts, I say, "Can I use your restroom?"

"Of course," Jackie says.

I walk through the quiet house, toward the powder room that sits off the family room and kitchen. After locking the door, I sit down on the closed toilet, resting my head in my hands. I close my eyes and take a few deep breaths, trying to ease the tight knot of fear pinching my chest. When I open them again, they land on a wadded-up paper towel soaked with blood in the trash can next to me, an empty Band-Aid wrapper on top of it. Almost like it's waiting for me. Time seems to slow down for a few seconds, as if to mark this moment in my mind, the one that links *before* to *after*.

And then it moves again, reminding me I have a limited window in which to act. I rummage around in my purse and find a crumpled Ziploc that holds a couple of Q-tips, which I toss into the garbage. My shaking hands turn the bag inside out and lift the bloody paper towel from the trash can, careful not to touch it. I seal the bag and stash it back in my purse, my heart pounding. The consequences of what I'm planning to do are nothing more than faint smudges on the edge of my periphery.

By the end of today, I can put to rest the fear that's been chasing me since Aaron's revelation, and I can go back to supporting my friend as she worries about her husband and son. *But if it's a match . . .* I squash that thought before I can finish it and run cool water over my hands. From beyond the closed door I hear Jackie tell the boys to get in the car and Aaron rummaging around in the kitchen, asking Jackie where their membership card is. I stare at myself in the mirror. There's no turning back.

——

The lab is deserted when I arrive, which is typical for a sunny Saturday morning. I swipe my card key and flip on the lights, letting the cool antiseptic smell calm my nerves. *Just another subject, just another sample,* I tell myself, snapping on gloves and removing the bloody paper towel from the bag. I break open a set of sterilized scissors from its bag and set to work snipping the towel into tiny pieces I can dissolve and test. My pulse slows, my breathing evens, and I let procedure take over. I swab the plastic spoon Miles used to eat yogurt in the car this morning, and soon both samples are vibrating in a bead beater, suspending the DNA in liquid. Then comes the centrifuge, and all that's left is pure DNA.

When I've got enough from each sample, I set up plates for comparison. I move through the motions, keeping my mind on the surface. I think about next steps, about how many plates I'll need, not wanting to dive down into outcomes. I glance back at the paper towel pieces—plenty left to test for the Huntington's gene if I want to. *If I have to.* I pull up short, momentarily frozen by the weight of what I'm doing, my integrity as a scientist pushing up against my protective instinct as a mother. This is illegal. If anyone were to discover what I've done—even off the clock—it could compromise our study much more significantly than any Scott Sullivan visit authorizations I made. I would lose my job. I'd be unhirable.

And yet, I can't seem to care about anything other than answers. I push on. Of course, the mother in me has won.

———

I glance at the clock on the wall, relieved to see that two hours have finally passed. I pipette the DNA into a gel for comparison and set up a dozen slides, before positioning the first one under a microscope. *Please don't be a match. Please don't be a match. Please don't be a match.* I imagine the DNA lined up next to each other with no matching lanes, the zigzag of genetic strangers, and I can almost feel the weight of fear lifting. I breathe out slowly, centering myself, and count to ten before leaning forward to the microscope.

The match jumps out at me immediately. Right at the top, two bands lined up together so exact there can be no other interpretation.

"Oh my god," I whisper.

With shaking hands, I secure the next slide, praying for a mismatch. But with each passing slide, the answer pulses through me. *Paternity. Paternity. Paternity.*

I roll backward on my stool, dizzy.

Aaron is Miles's donor.

I pull off my gloves and press my fingers against my temples. Images of Miles running around and laughing with Nick and smiling up at Aaron—every cell inside of him responding to this man in a way I've never seen before—play in my mind.

What now?

The answer looms large in front of me: get a definitive answer about Huntington's. Most labs that test for the gene have premade tests, but I know I could design one in less than an hour and get the results in two. I've already violated Aaron's privacy once today without consent. What's one more test?

A thump down the hall jolts my attention toward the door. Bruno's distinctive whistling launches me off the stool and into action. I swipe everything—the slides, pipettes, vials, the plastic spoon, and the remains of the bloody paper towel—into the biohazard container at the end of the lab. I flick off the machines, shove the stool back to the workstation, and leap toward Jenna's desk in the corner, where I flip open a binder with Scott Sullivan's name on the spine, just as the door beeps and Bruno enters, pocketing his key card.

"What are you doing here?" he asks, pulling up short. He's wearing a tie-dyed T-shirt with Bob Marley's face on it.

"Miles is at a party, and I thought I'd get caught up on paperwork." I focus on pushing air in and out of my lungs and tuck my hair behind my ear with a trembling hand. I glance toward the biohazard bin, my chance to test for Huntington's now lost. I'm relieved, my sanity returning one breath at a time.

Bruno glances at the logs behind me. "Looking at Scott's log, I see."

I shrug. "Just chasing after ghosts."

Bruno perches on the edge of Jenna's desk. "I know. I did the same thing last week. There isn't anything out of the ordinary, except that he's the only subject whose spouse has died."

I try to appear thoughtful, as if I've spent all morning thinking about Scott. Bruno starts to say something, but I cut him off by closing the file and saying, "I'd better head out. I need to pick up Miles. See you Monday."

Bruno looks startled by my abrupt departure, but I'm already out the door, a frozen mask of fear etched across my face.

———

When I reach Pacific Coast Highway, I turn right instead of left, toward Jackie's. I need to drive out some of the adrenaline of nearly being caught before I'm able to face Jackie and Aaron. I pick up my phone and dial Rose.

"It's a match," I say as soon as she picks up.

"What? Where are you?" I put her on speaker, and her voice fills the car. "What's a match?"

"Miles and Aaron. I ran a DNA test this afternoon." I slam on the brakes at a red light, barely registering the traffic around me.

"Back up. How did you run a test?"

I explain as quickly as I can, glossing over the questionable ethics, but Rose knows better. "Is that legal?"

"No." I let the word hang there, challenging her to argue with me about it now.

"Shit," she says. "So now what?"

I pull into a deserted beach parking lot and sit, watching a seagull forage in a trash can. My eyes travel down the coast, toward Santa Monica and the Turner House, where Miles unknowingly plays with his father and half brother. "What am I going to do?" I ask.

"Nothing," Rose says. "You're going to do nothing. You're going to pick up Miles, say *Thank you for taking him*, and you're going to drive away. And then you're going to put some distance between you and them."

"I can't do that to Miles," I say. "It'll kill him."

"They're brothers," Rose says, her voice low and urgent. "Eventually someone's going to see it and put it together. And then what will you do?"

"I didn't have time to test for Huntington's," I tell her, as if she hadn't spoken. "I need to convince Aaron to get tested. Now, more than ever."

"Why not just test Miles?"

I shudder. "Bruno almost caught me," I tell her. "I can't risk it again."

"Not even for this?"

"I'd lose my job, Rose. No university would ever hire me. I couldn't even teach."

She's quiet for a moment. "I know you want Miles to have his friend, but you need to look at the bigger picture. What happens if Jackie finds out? What do you think that will do to her?"

"You've seen the boys together," I tell her. "This is what he's been craving. And somehow—miraculously—I found it. There's no way I'm going to take that away from him now, despite the risk." I feel heartless for saying it, but it's the truth. Miles is different because of Nick and Aaron. He deserves to have what I never did.

"The longer you allow this to continue, the more likely it is they'll find out, and you'll lose them anyway."

"I won't do it," I say. The seagull is pecking at an empty McDonald's bag, ferreting out stale french fries one at a time.

"Paige," Rose says, her voice gentle. "Too many people will get hurt. Including Miles.

I pinch my eyes closed. When I open them again, the seagull is gone, and all that's left is a bunch of trash strewn across the ground.

———

When I arrive at Jackie's, she's back on the front porch. I make my way toward her slowly, counting my steps, trying to appear calm.

"How was it?" I ask, sitting on the chair next to her and tucking my hands under my thighs, hoping they won't betray my nerves.

"Wonderful. Perfect weather, great food. Aaron kept the kids busy the entire time, so I was actually able to sit and read a book. I wish you could have come."

I offer a wobbly smile. In another universe, under different circumstances, that would have been nice.

Just then, Miles rounds the corner of the house. "Mom! We won! Our bottle flew the highest, and we won first prize!"

I try to muster enthusiasm. "Wow! How exciting. What did you win?" My words taste bland; my mouth feels full of sawdust.

"Free ice cream!"

He zooms past me into the house, and Nick follows. Aaron sits on the step, brushing sand off his feet with an old beach towel. "It was amazing," he says, and to Jackie, "I'll put every-thing away and pull out a pizza for dinner."

"Thanks, babe," Jackie says, and he tosses the towel aside and heads for the car.

We sit in silence, the sound of the boys' voices lingering in the air around us. The truth swells inside of me, pushing against my skin until it's so tight I feel I might split apart. I sneak a glance at Jackie, her bare feet propped up on a low table, obliviously flipping through her phone, and it hits me. I will never again sit next to her with the ease I once felt. It won't matter whether Jackie knows or not. I will see it, every time I look at her, every time she calls, every time we chat in the yard. And it will grow. The longer I say nothing, the larger this secret will loom. But if I do what Rose suggests, I won't even have this. The thought of losing Jackie is agonizing.

From inside the house, Nick calls, "Mom, can you help me find the *Mario Kart* disk?"

"It should be on the shelf with all the other video games," she yells through the doorway.

"It's not there!"

"Excuse me," she says. She slips through the front door just as Aaron rounds the corner and joins me on the porch. He sits on the step, resting his arms across his knees, his large hands dangling between them.

"How are things?" I ask, hoping maybe he's finally found clarity.

"They've been better," he says. "But I'm surviving."

I glance behind me, to make sure Jackie isn't near. "Jackie says you still don't want to get tested."

"It's not that simple."

Impatience blooms inside of me. "Those families have a right to know," I say, keeping my voice quiet. "If you refuse to get answers for yourself, you at least owe them the information they need to make their own decisions."

"I appreciate your advice, but it's a lot more complicated than you can imagine."

His complete dismissal of my child and countless other children—including Nick—causes me to abandon any sympathy I had left for the position he's in.

"Your selfishness will have devastating results."

"No offense, Paige, but mind your own business. This doesn't affect you."

"It does," I say, my voice dangerously low. "It affects Miles too."

Confusion flits across his face, and he opens his mouth to speak. But I interrupt him.

"If you had the decency to notify ACB, in a few days a letter would land in my mailbox, telling me that the donor I used to conceive my son has discovered he's a potential carrier for Huntington's."

Aaron's eyes widen with every word I utter and dart between me and the door where Jackie could appear at any moment.

"Jackie never told you I used a donor?" I ask.

"You have to be mistaken." His face pales, but his eyes darken. He looks toward the open door and then back at me.

"I wish I was. I only realized it might be possible when you said you used ACB. I didn't want to believe it, but now I think I have to."

"So you don't know anything. Not for sure."

The image of the matching DNA bands burns behind my eyes, linking me to this man forever. "Take a closer look at Miles and Nick together, and you'll see it too," I say. "I have the donor profile and baby picture if you don't believe me."

"That's hardly proof," he says. He leans his head back against the porch rail and pinches his eyes closed, as if he could squeeze the truth away by simply not looking at it. "How do I know you're not some crazy stalker?"

I lean closer, fighting to keep my voice quiet. "Why would I *want* you to be our donor?" I hiss. "What do I stand to get out of it? Believe me. I wish it were anyone but you."

I glance at the door again. We don't have a lot of time before Jackie returns and interrupts us. "Regardless of whether you believe me, these are real people, Aaron. Real families who have a right to know if their children are at risk. I understand why you don't want to know for yourself. But you have an obligation to the children you helped conceive. Growing up, getting married, having kids of their own. How could you let that happen without disclosing what you know?" I stand and walk toward the front door, just as Jackie returns.

"I found it under his bed," she says, rolling her eyes. "Along with an empty bowl I'm pretty sure had ice cream in it once."

I smile, but it feels stiff and forced. "Miles, we need to go!" I call. To Jackie I say, "Thanks for taking him today. Sounds like he had a great time."

"See you at Nan's next weekend?" she asks.

I groan. Nan's hosting a silent auction fund-raiser and dinner. Everyone is *strongly encouraged to attend.*

The look on my face makes Jackie laugh. She pulls me into a hug as Miles comes down the hall. "Buck up. Safety in numbers." I sink into her for a moment, savoring the weight of another mother with worries as big as my own, wondering how much longer I'll have her in my life.

Over her shoulder, I watch Aaron's eyes track Miles all the way to the car.

YOUR APPOINTMENT WITH A GENETIC COUNSELOR: WHAT TO EXPECT

Genetic counselors often work in hospital settings, in coordination with medical doctors, and consult with patients about a variety of issues such as:

- Prenatal diseases/conditions

- Genetic mutations such as the BRCA gene

- A relative who has been diagnosed with a genetic condition or disease

Meetings with genetic counselors are always in-person, where a patient can:

- Discuss test results (including possible further testing)

- Review treatment options

- Learn how to discuss test results with family members

- Learn about disease prevention/management

Chapter Twenty-One

I stand in the doorway to Miles's room on Wednesday evening. "Get your shoes on," I say. "And a coat. We're going on an adventure."

Miles looks up from the book he's reading, confused. "At eight o'clock at night?"

"Car's leaving in five minutes," I say, and push off the doorframe, in search of my car keys. I feel like the entire world has shifted sideways, and my thoughts are dominated by worry—about Miles, about Aaron, and about the secret I so carelessly dropped the other day. I need a distraction. Not work, where I'm consumed with worry over Sophie and whether Scott will qualify for phase two. I need Miles. I need to lose myself in my son.

"Where are you taking me?" he asks from the back seat. The evening traffic has died down, and the streets are empty as we drive out of the city and toward Malibu. "Are we going to Annesley?" he asks.

"Sort of." I don't tell him any more. It's the perfect night—cold air and a clear sky. The farther away from town we get, the darker it becomes. My car winds up the road, past the main entrance to Annesley, and I see Miles's eyes track it. "Just a little farther," I tell him.

We turn onto a service road above campus—more of a fire

trail than a road. It's tucked between two hilltops, and the lights of Santa Monica are blocked. It's dark, so when I pull over and park, I leave the interior car light on so I can see and pull a large box out of the trunk.

"I borrowed this from Mark Swinger in the astronomy department," I tell him. "It's an automated telescope. We can program coordinates into it and look at anything we want."

"No way," Miles says, bouncing on his feet.

When I have it set up, I say, "So what do you want to look at first?"

"Mars," he says without hesitation.

I look at the list Mark gave me and punch some numbers into the small black box. The telescope begins to move. When it stops, I take a quick peek, and Mars glows through the lens, a giant rust-colored ball. Incredible. I step aside and let Miles look.

"Wow," he breathes. His small shoulders are hunched over the telescope, absolutely still. Crickets chirp in the dark hills that surround us, but other than that, the night is silent. I feel as if we've stepped out of time, just the two of us, and I wish we could stay here, cocooned between these hills, where the drama of Aaron or the pain of my father, Scott, and Liam are a distant smudge on the horizon.

Miles glances at me and smiles. "This is so cool." He returns to the viewfinder. "Did you know that on Mars, you can jump three times higher than you can on Earth? That's because there's less gravity there."

These are the moments I dreamed of when I decided to have a child—just the two of us, discovering something together. I take a deep breath, and the cold night air fills me, sharp and refreshing. My mind tries to problem-solve—what will I do next, how can I make this right with Jackie and Aaron—and I take another breath and hold it, suspending everything for just a few seconds. As I let it out, I imagine I'm blowing my fear out too. The pain that's been a constant companion since Liam and I broke up, pain I didn't want to acknowledge until now. There's no one here to pretend for. Just me and Miles. The way I'd always intended it to be.

"Let's look at something simple," Miles says, pulling me back. "The moon."

I plug in the coordinates and gesture for Miles to take a look. But he shakes his head. "You go first."

I peer through the lens and laugh. "It's like I could reach out and touch it," I say. "I can practically see rocks on the ground, the contours of the crater." I take in the details, marveling at how something so familiar can look so different. That through a device invented four hundred years ago, everything we take for granted could be cast as something magical and new.

This is the comfort I feel when working in the lab—the idea that there is so much more beyond our field of vision. Whether I'm looking at the tiny particles of our cells or the enormity of the solar system, I'm reminded again that we are all nothing more than stardust. Every atom in our body started out there, an explosion of elements at the beginning of time, traveling through the millennia and leading to this moment with me and Miles alone on a hill above the city. I think of my favorite Carl Sagan quote, and I whisper it aloud, like a prayer. "'The cosmos is within us. We are made of star-stuff. We are a way for the universe to know itself.'"

—

Nan's neighborhood is filled with large homes set far back from the street, and from down the block, the faint lilt of a string quartet rises and falls into the cool evening air. I tuck my purse tighter under my arm and wobble over the sidewalk in heels that pinch my feet, wondering why I'm not at home on my couch instead.

When I found out Rose and Henry weren't going to be here, I almost didn't come. I spent the last week alternating between anxiety and anger, waiting for Aaron to drop the bomb on Jackie and our subsequent collective fallout. But so far, everything's remained the same: chatting with Jackie at morning drop-off about homework or the food in the cafeteria, fielding texts about a playdate in a couple of weeks, answering the phone to ease her worries about Nick and Aaron—which only adds to my tension, because her worries are now mine.

In the backyard the party is in full swing. The large, flat lawn is lit by fairy lights and overlooks the canyon below, offering unobstructed views of Malibu and the Pacific Ocean in the distance. Houses atop this hill sell for tens of millions, and as I look around, I feel outclassed and outmoneyed.

Musicians play in the corner, and waitstaff wander among the attendees, bearing trays of hors d'oeuvres. Guests hover around silent auction tables, signing their names to whatever is being sold to raise money for our school technology fund. I float, unacknowledged, between groups of parents who sip from crystal goblets that reflect the final glimmers of a sunset darkening the sky from brilliant pink to a deep purple.

A waiter approaches with a tray of stuffed mushrooms. I take one and a cocktail napkin, nibbling as I wander across the lawn. What I really need is a drink. But the bar is a long and lonely walk across the grass, so I decide it can wait. I finish the mushroom and crumple the napkin in my fist, watching the sun sink below the horizon, when someone grabs my elbow from behind.

"Thank God you're here," Jackie whispers in my ear, and I

smile, despite myself. "I've been listening to Baylor's mom tell me all about her liposuction. She didn't come right out and say I needed a referral, but she practically programmed her doctor's number into my phone."

Jackie's dress is a shimmering dark blue and hugs her curves in all the right places, making my black sheath dress look like a potato sack. "You look gorgeous." I survey the crowd. "Where's Aaron?"

"Over there," she gestures toward the pool, lit up with underwater lights that cast undulating shadows across the terraced pool house. He stands with a group of men on the pool deck, hands shoved into his pockets, leaning back on his heels. As if sensing our stare, he turns away from the conversation and looks at us. Jackie squeezes her hand into a fist twice, then flashes a sideways peace sign. Aaron nods and peels away from the group.

"What was that, your gang sign?"

Jackie laughs. "No, we made it up years ago, when we had to go to tons of work parties for Aaron. It means *Get me a drink*. He'll bring one for you too because I told him to bring two. We also have one for *Let's get out of here* and *You've got food in your teeth*."

My stomach somersaults as I'm reminded again that I'm an interloper who has inserted herself and her child into Jackie's family. And that because I was angry at Aaron, I've created a situation where it's only a matter of time before Miles and I lose all three of them.

She looks at me. "Are you okay?"

"I'm fine," I say.

Aaron approaches, balancing three drinks between his hands. "Paige." His eyes slide over mine, avoiding direct contact. The smell of his soap—sandalwood—and a trace of Jackie's perfume envelop me. I smile tightly and take the glass from him.

"Have you bid on anything yet?" Jackie asks him, nodding toward the auction tables.

Aaron looks surprised, as if he's forgotten why we're here. "Not yet. Anything interesting?"

Jackie shrugs. "The usual. Floor seats to a Lakers game. A weekend in Catalina. A trip to Paris." She looks at him. "Should we try for the Lakers tickets? Your dad would love that."

Aaron's eyes shift away, toward the canyon, and he says, "He's not really up for big outings these days."

Jackie turns to me to explain. "He's been having some trouble getting around." To Aaron she says, "We could use a wheelchair so he wouldn't have to walk far or worry about all the stairs."

"Drop it, Jackie." His words are blunt and heavy.

I turn away, trying to quell the panic that this might someday be Miles. When I turn back to them, Aaron's eyes meet mine, the secret we share straining the air between us.

Finding my voice, I say, "Excuse me," and walk away before either of them can respond. The sun has set, and I stand at the edge of the property as Nan steps in front of a microphone and welcomes the crowd. I look behind me, at Jackie and Aaron, still locked in a heated discussion.

"Thanks so much for coming out tonight to support Elmwood Elementary. We have lots of exciting auction items, so get your bids in before ten! And a special thank-you to those who so generously donated to such a worthy cause, including my handsome husband, Dr. Stephen Parker, who contributed several free consults." She pauses while the crowd claps.

I turn to face the ocean. The moon is bright enough to illuminate the surface of it, and from this distance it looks as smooth as polished stone. I peer over the edge of the property and find a gentle, landscaped hill extending down into the canyon. I walk along the edge of the fence, until I find an opening tucked into the far corner. Stepping through it, I follow a twisting path that winds around tall shrubs and plants, sporadically illuminated with lights until I come to a small, flat plateau with a bench overlooking the twinkling lights of the Malibu coast and the endless expanse of ocean. The sounds of the party float above me, remote and distant, while the wind carries the smell of salt and the sound of the waves crashing on the shore far below. I feel secluded and safe, and I settle in to drink my wine.

Footsteps sound on the gravel path behind me, and I spin around, aware of my isolation, to see the familiar shape of Aaron turning the corner, a fresh glass of whiskey hanging low in his hand.

"Mind if I join you?" He steps forward and sits on the bench next to me without waiting for a response, the space heavy with everything that needs to be said.

I'm the first one to break the silence. "Why'd you do it?"

He doesn't ask what I mean. He just closes his eyes and takes a deep breath, exhaling heavily and saturating the air with the smell of whiskey. "It was so long ago," he says. "When I was younger—before Jackie—I had a problem with gambling. My dad bailed me out the first few times I got into trouble, but that only made it worse." He gives a rough laugh. "A friend of mine had been a donor and said it was easy money once you got through the red tape. I don't think either of us really thought through the implications of what we were doing."

He turns toward me. "I was only a donor for a year before I finally realized I didn't want that for myself—to spend my life scraping money together and living in a casino. Then I met Jackie, and I didn't know how to tell her. I fooled myself into believing it didn't matter, that it would never come out. I tricked myself into thinking, with all the choices, no one would ever pick mine. It would sit there, unused. And if they did, it wouldn't matter because I was anonymous. But now . . ." He trails off. "Here we are."

Lights dot the hill adjacent to us, sparks of warmth in an otherwise cold and lonely landscape. "She would have understood," I tell him.

He leans forward, resting his forearms on his knees. "Probably," he says. "The fear got to be larger than the fact."

I know a little something about that. "I need you to understand something," I say. "Before he met you, Miles was lost. Alone, no matter what I tried. But then he met Nick, and by extension you. Miles feels so at ease when he's with you and your family, like he's known you forever." I turn so I'm looking at him. "And now he isn't wandering around the track every day by himself. You did that. You and Nick. I can't tell you what that means to me." This is my last chance to get Aaron to see the importance of letting Miles have this. I touch his arm gently. "I don't want this to be happening either—but it is. You don't want to hurt Jackie, and I will do anything to protect Miles."

Aaron stares out at the ocean. Nan's voice floats down to us, announcing one more hour until the bidding closes. We both look up the hill, and I wonder if Jackie's noticed both of us are missing.

"Do you really think Miles is mine?"

"Don't you?"

In a quiet voice, he says, "Tell me about him."

Tears prick my eyes, and for a moment we are just two parents, sitting in the dark, talking about our child. "He could read before he turned four," I whisper. "It made it impossible for me to take him to a restaurant, because he'd read the menu and insist on eating dessert for his meal."

Aaron laughs, sending a charged thrill through me that something our child did pleases him so much. I think of all the moments in Miles's life Aaron can never have and how Miles would never know how delighted Aaron would be by them.

"He's always loved math and science. One time, in kindergarten, I caught him in the kitchen trying to conduct an experiment on the stove. He had a pot with an inch of vinegar at the bottom, and a box of baking soda on the counter. *I wanted to see if heat would make the reaction stronger.*"

Aaron shakes his head, grinning. "My mother could tell you stories like that," he says. "I once set the garage on fire."

"Don't tell Miles," I say, and then stop short, because Miles will probably never know any of this.

"He's a great kid," Aaron says, his voice softening to almost a whisper. "That day at the beach with him . . . He just brings such a joy to everything he does."

I let Aaron's words sink into me, absorbing them like a sponge.

"I know the other day, I made it sound like I didn't believe you," he says. I start to speak, but he holds his hand up and continues, "But I can see the similarities, now that I'm looking for them. Not just between me and him, but also between the boys." He sighs. "I never thought I'd have more than Nick," he continues, looking down at the ground. His face looks haggard, as if he's aged twenty years in the span of a week. "Sure, I knew there might be other kids out there, but they weren't *mine.* Miles—" He closes his eyes for a moment and then opens them, his anguish palpable. "It's like being gifted a piece of me. But I don't know how to fit him into my life. Hiding something invisible from my wife was one thing. But now Miles is here, in front of me, reminding me this can never stay a secret . . . I have to tell her."

My chest tightens, though I expected this. Of course he can't keep this from Jackie. It would be unreasonable for me to think he would. "I'll do whatever makes you the most comfortable," I tell him. "If you want definitive proof, we can run a paternity test. I know a reputable lab that will put a rush on it." I won't risk another test on my own.

He nods. "I think that would be wise. Jackie's going to push back pretty hard on this. It would help to have absolute proof."

I touch his arm. "And just so you know, when you run a paternity test, that's all they look for. They won't see anything you don't want them to see."

"Thanks. I'm not ready to go there yet. But I've thought a lot about what you've said, and I'll notify the clinic of the risk." He finishes his drink and turns the empty glass around in his hands. "The thing I've been struggling to get Jackie to understand is that we're already either doomed or saved. Knowing for sure won't change anything. I just don't know if I have it in me to know my future like that."

I understand what he's saying, and it's possible when Miles turns eighteen, he'll come to the same conclusion.

"If I could undo anything—for Nick or Miles, or any of the other kids—I would. In an instant." He leans back, closing his eyes. "I'll call you first thing Monday, and we can set up a test for later in the week."

We sit there, shoulder to shoulder, nothing left to say. The ocean appears motionless below us, but I know the currents beneath the surface are so strong they'll pull you under and carry you far out to sea.

FEDERAL GOVERNMENT GUIDELINES

Adherence to the principles of **good clinical practices** (GCPs), including adequate **human subject protection** (HSP) is recognized as a critical requirement to the conduct of research involving human subjects. Many countries have adopted GCP principles as laws and/or regulations.

WHAT IS GOOD CLINICAL PRACTICE (GCP)?

GCP is defined as **the standard for the design, conduct, performance, monitoring, auditing, recording, analysis, and reporting** of clinical trials or studies involving human subjects. It protects the rights, safety, and well-being of the subjects, and ensures that the quality of the data is accurate and reliable.

Chapter Twenty-Two

Monday finds me in my office, buried in a budget report. Running the numbers twelve different ways, cross-checking line items until all I can see are the digits on the page.

Bruno startles me out of my trance when he sits in the chair across from me. "Are you trying out for a guest-lecture spot in the math department?" he asks, logging into his computer.

I look up, bleary-eyed. "What time is it?"

"Eleven."

"It's that late?" I grab my phone to see if maybe he's wrong. But he's not. And I have no missed calls.

"I've never seen you pay that much attention to a budget report," Bruno says. "Things must be pretty bad."

I make a noncommittal sound and flip through the pages outlining the NIH grant that will close out phase one, trying not to think about Aaron, or why he hasn't called me yet.

"I've got a draft of the phase two trial letter. Can you look at it?" he asks. Jorgensen finally approved our bridge grant last week, and Bruno got right to work pushing forward to phase two.

He waits for me to answer. When I don't, he continues, "Scott still qualifies, but just barely."

"Sure," I say, not really listening to him. I return to the report, happy to dive back in, the mindless columns the only thing that soothes my nerves.

An hour later, my phone rings, and I nearly jump out of my skin. But it's only Rose. "Hey," I say.

"We're meeting with Dad's palliative care team next week, and I wanted to offer you an opportunity to join us."

When I don't say anything, she sighs. "Hospice is recommending it for all family members," she says.

Before I can stop myself, I say, "Is it already time for hospice?"

"It's just an introductory meeting," she explains. "That way we can ask any questions we might have, Dad can make end-of-life decisions, and we'll all be on the same page before anything happens."

A curious mixture of guilt and sadness washes over me. I want to be able to set aside my anger and hurt and show up for something like this—at the very least to support my mom and sister—but I feel locked into my stance as an outsider looking in.

"Anyway," Rose continues, her tone abrupt. "I thought you'd want to know."

"Thanks," I say, ashamed I can't even ask her to keep me posted. But the words stack up inside of me, unable to move into the open.

Rose hangs up without saying goodbye, and I tip my head back against the window and stare up at a steel-gray sky, tracking a flock of crows as they fly toward the hills, trying not to worry about why I haven't heard from Aaron, or what it might mean.

Around one o'clock, my phone rings again. But it's not Aaron. It's Jackie. I hesitate, wondering whether Aaron decided to blow off the test and just tell her. I let it ring three times before I find the courage to answer it.

"Hi," I say, turning toward the window for privacy.

At first I can't understand her. Her words sound garbled, as if she's underwater. Then I realize she's crying.

"Jackie," I say. "Are you okay?" She knows. And now she's calling to unleash her anger on me.

"Sorry," she chokes out. "It's just . . ." She trails off again into sobs, and I hold my phone tight, bracing myself for the onslaught. She takes a deep breath and tries again. "There's been an accident. I need you to pick up Nick after school and take him home with you."

"What do you mean? What happened?" My voice must be louder than I intend because Bruno looks up in concern and mouths *Miles?* I shake my head and try to focus on Jackie.

"It's Aaron," she says, her voice thick with tears. "There was an accident at work. He was on-site and—" She breaks down again, and I wait for her to continue. "He was up on the roof of a warehouse, looking to see where they could put solar panels. And—" A fresh wave of crying fills my ear.

"What happened?" I can barely bring myself to ask the question.

"He fell through," she manages to say.

"Oh my god." I cover my eyes with my hands, thinking of Aaron, broken and bloody on the floor of some old warehouse. It's impossible. I was just talking to him on the side of a hill less than forty-eight hours ago.

"His partner just called me. He's coming to take me to the hospital. I don't know how long we'll be, so I need you to pick up Nick after school."

"Of course," I say. "Whatever you need."

She takes a deep, shuddering breath. "Thanks."

The line goes silent between us. Finally I say, "Call me as soon as you know anything."

"I will. Knowing Nick's covered is a huge help. Please don't say anything to him."

"I'll make something up." I'm already scrambling for a lie an eight-year-old would believe for why his mother and father are unable to pick him up. Or cook him dinner. Or put him to bed.

"Thanks. I don't know what I'd do without you, Paige."

We hang up, and I stare down at the students moving through the quad below. I feel Bruno come up behind me and put a hand on my shoulder.

"What happened?" he asks.

I swivel around to face him. "Aaron had an accident at work today." I can't bring myself to say more, and I marvel at how Jackie could get any words out at all. Tears prick my eyes, and I swipe them away. "I have to tell you something," I say, filling him in quickly, on how I discovered Aaron was my donor, and how he was going to tell Jackie. Until this happened. I tell him all of it, only omitting the DNA test I ran in the lab.

"Oh my god, Paige. Why didn't you tell me sooner?"

I push away from my desk. "I need to get Nick and Miles." The thought of staying here, surrounding myself with lab reports and anecdotal data gathered by lab assistants, is stifling.

"No problem," he says. "Take as much time as you need. I'll take care of things here."

"Thanks." I grab my coat and keys, slinging my purse over

my shoulder. "Don't forget to—" I start to say, but the words escape me. All I can think about is Aaron and the way he laughed at the stories I told him about Miles.

Bruno guides me toward the door. "Go."

———

Later that night, I sit at Rose's dining room table, the remnants of a meal surrounding us, while Nick, Miles, and Josh play outside in the deepening twilight. I'd picked the boys up at three, feeding them a line about a last-minute appointment Jackie and Aaron had to attend. Delivering the lie while driving helped conceal the truth. I took them to Rose's, the tension from our earlier phone call vanishing as soon as I'd told her what happened, knowing she would prop me up as she's done thousands of times before.

But now it's nearing eight o'clock, and I don't know what to do next.

"What if you don't hear from her?" Rose asks.

"I'll text her and let her know I'm taking Nick back to my place."

I've already sent her one, giving her Rose's address and telling her we'd wait for her there, but she didn't respond. I haven't heard from her since her first phone call, and I'm terrified of what that means. She'd have called or texted by now if there was good news, and her silence weighs heavily on me.

We sit, nursing glasses of wine, the clock in the hall ticking the minutes away. Finally, I whisper, "What if he doesn't make it?"

Rose takes a deep breath and reaches across the table to squeeze my hand. "Try not to let your mind go there."

I bury my head in my arms on the table. When I look up,

Rose is staring out the window at the boys—the brothers—chasing each other around the yard.

I push my chair back. "I guess I'll get them home and into bed."

"You can stay here if you don't want to be alone."

"Thanks," I say. "But I think it'll be easier if we go home. Nick can sleep on the trundle in Miles's room."

"Okay." Rose rises, following me toward the backyard. "Call me when you hear something. Anything."

"I will."

As we make our way down the hall, the doorbell rings. We stare at each other, frozen. Henry comes out of the living room, where he's been reading, his glasses slipping down his nose, a finger holding the place in his book. "Do you want me to get that?" he asks.

I nod, unable to speak. No one else would be ringing Rose's doorbell this late at night.

He steps toward the door and peeks through the side glass. "It's Jackie," he says, and swings the door open.

She stands there, eyes red-rimmed and trembling.

As if drawn by a magnet, I walk toward her, wrapping her in my arms. She begins to sob on my shoulder, her body heaving and trembling, and I start to cry. She doesn't have to say anything. I just know.

"He's gone," she chokes, then dissolves into heavy sobs as I hold her, tears streaming down my cheeks. The house, Rose, Henry, everything fades away. It's just the two of us, holding on to each other.

She pulls away, wiping her eyes.

Rose comes up from behind and leads us into the living room, where the boys won't see us. "Mikey!" she calls up the stairs.

"Yeah?"

"Get the boys out of the backyard, set them up with a movie, and stay in there with them."

"But I'm doing my homework," he says.

"Just do it!" she snaps. Mikey appears at the top of the stairs and takes in the scene, his expression shifting from resentment to worry, rushing down to do as he's told.

Rose slides the paneled doors closed behind us and walks Jackie over to the couch. I sit next to her, taking her hand.

Jackie closes her eyes and takes several deep breaths. "Do you have something to drink?" she asks.

Henry jumps up, returning with a bottle of whiskey and four glasses. He pours Jackie an inch, and she drains her glass.

We sit, eyes on Jackie, waiting for her to begin talking whenever she's ready. Henry hands me a glass, and I hold it with shaking fingers, afraid to miss anything she might say.

She takes a deep, shuddering breath and begins. "The doctors said his internal injuries were too severe. There was nothing they could do." Another sob breaks through. "He died around three." I take her glass from her and envelop her in another hug, swallowing hard. At three, I was in the car with the boys, oblivious.

"I'm so sorry," I whisper.

She nods and pulls away again. She presses her hands against her eyes, trying to stem the flow of tears. "I called his parents as soon as I heard, and they met me at the hospital. His mother's a mess."

"What about you?" I ask. "What can we do for you? I can keep Nick tonight if you want to just . . ." I trail off, unsure what she might want or need.

She shakes her head. "I want to go home. I want Nick at

home with me—oh God, what am I going to tell him?" She crumbles again, sobbing into my shoulder.

I hang on to her, letting my own tears fall down my cheeks and into her great mass of hair. Across the room, Rose and Henry grip each other's hands so tightly I can see the bones through their skin, and I try to wrap my mind around how we could have lost Aaron so soon after finding him.

"I'm here for whatever you need. You know that, right?" I push her away so I can look into her eyes.

She nods, fumbles in her purse for a tissue, and blows her nose. "I'll tell Nick tonight. Keep him out of school tomorrow. Maybe for a while. There's a lot to do." The words catch in her throat.

"Let me help you. I can make calls. Sit with you. Whatever you need."

"Thanks." She closes her eyes for a moment, her lids looking bruised. When she opens them again, she says, "I'm afraid to stop moving. If I do, it will all catch up to me and . . ." She pinches her lips together, fighting back more tears.

"If you need me to take Nick, just say so."

She nods again and stands, wiping her eyes with her sleeve. "Okay."

We follow her down the hall to the family room. The boys are splayed across the couch watching TV. Jackie walks up to Nick and kneels in front of him. "Time to go, honey."

Nick takes one look at her face, tearstained and raw from crying, and gets up without argument. "What's wrong?" he asks. "Where's Dad?"

"Let's just get home and we can talk."

"Okay," he says hesitantly. He casts a doubtful look over his shoulder as he follows her out of the room.

Later that night, I lie in bed, staring at the faint shadows that flicker and weave across my wall and finally let my thoughts land on how this changes everything. My secret is safe, my friendship with Jackie intact, and I'm washed with equal parts shame and relief.

I close my eyes but sleep doesn't come. Instead, I see Aaron's face, his expression ragged as he explained the weight of his fear, and my eyes fly open as I wonder whether Jackie had enough presence of mind to ask for a genetic test on Aaron. I doubt it. And now we'll never know.

GENETIC ATTRACTION

Genetic attraction is a trope that shows up every now and then in pop culture—two people drawn to each other for unexplained reasons, only to discover they're related. Proponents describe it as a phenomenon that happens when the emotional bond between a parent and child or between siblings is disrupted, that when they meet, there's an actual biological response in their cells.

Genetic attraction is documented in many animals, most notably mice, whose amplified sense of smell allows them to identify their blood relatives simply by scent. However, there's almost no scientific evidence to support its existence in humans.

We do know our brains are hardwired to help our relatives, to take risks for them that we wouldn't take otherwise. *Blood is thicker than water.* Miles and Nick each got half of their DNA from Aaron. They are first-degree blood relatives, biologically programmed to protect each other. The chemistry between them is obvious, but I'm the only one who understands how deep it goes, that it's not just based on shared interests but a shared biology.

So while most scientists think genetic attraction is a fuzzy science that has no real merit other than anecdotally—I find myself wondering if, for humans, genetic attraction manifests differently. We can't smell our relatives, but maybe—somehow—we can sense them.

Chapter Twenty-Three

Rose and I stand by a window overlooking Jackie's backyard, while several older women ferry platters of food from the kitchen to the crowd who've come to pay their respects to Aaron. One stands out, with a flowing skirt and wild, curly hair that's almost completely gray. She must be Jackie's mother. She scurries around, not making eye contact with anyone. I imagine her in an earlier life, bullied by Jackie's dad, trying not to ruffle anyone or draw attention to herself.

I scan the backyard for Miles and Nick, who disappeared outside somewhere. My eyes catch on a familiar figure, the broad surfer's shoulders covered in a nice suit. "You didn't tell me Liam would be here," I say.

"I didn't know," she says.

Liam sits on a bench in a corner with Miles and Nick, his eyes covered by sunglasses, saying something to the boys. Miles laughs, and a tiny smile cracks across Nick's face. I wish I could hear what he'd said. I haven't seen Miles laugh since I told him about Aaron, and it makes me feel better to see him smiling again.

Liam reaches an arm across the back of the bench, past Miles, and puts a hand on Nick's shoulder. And then something extraordinary happens. Miles leans into Liam—just curls himself under Liam's arm, and the three of them sit like that for at least five minutes. I can't tear my eyes away from them.

I feel Rose watching me. I turn and offer a weak smile. "It's nice to see them talking."

She nods, and when I turn back to the window again, Liam's gone, and now it's just Miles and Nick alone on the bench. I scan the yard for him, but he's disappeared. Rose nudges my shoulder and tilts her head toward the hallway as Liam walks into the living room. He stops in front of Aaron's parents, Leonard and Beverly, to say something. Then he looks over at Rose and me, still by the window, and raises his hand in a silent farewell before walking out the front door.

I feel the jolt of his departure, like a rumbling beneath my feet. I fight the urge to follow him, reminding myself that he chose this. Rose still watches me. "What?" I ask.

She shakes her head. "Nothing."

In a corner, Aaron's parents sit surrounded by friends. Beverly looks as if she's going to crumble at any moment, while Leonard sits, stone-faced, next to her.

"Those poor people," Rose says. "As if they haven't endured enough with his diagnosis." After a moment, she says, "Do you think Aaron's mom knows something?"

There had been a moment at the church, when the family had exited a small side door into the sanctuary, right next to where we were sitting. Jackie looked glad to see us, touching her hand to her chest as if to say *Thank you*, but Beverly had been rooted to the spot, staring at Miles. Leonard had to practically drag her up to the front. As she walked toward her son's casket, she turned her head several times, looking at us over her shoulder, placing us in the crowd.

"I don't know," I say now. "There's definitely a resemblance between Miles and Aaron, but it seems unlikely she'd connect the dots so easily. Aaron said he donated because he needed money and didn't want to ask his parents, so I doubt it. Miles probably just reminds her of Aaron, in the same way a stranger on the street can make you think of someone you know." I say this because I need it to be true, not because I believe it. "I think it just spooked her."

But it's keeping me from approaching them to offer condolences. I turn away, not wanting to catch Beverly's attention now.

I'm about to suggest we leave when Jackie emerges from the back of the house. She's pulled her hair back in a silver clip, and her face looks polished and clean, as if she's just washed it. She sees us and comes over, hugging first me, then Rose.

"Thanks for coming," she says.

Rose rubs her arm and says, "How are you doing?"

"Actually, I'm doing okay. It's a relief to have the service over."

I flash back to the casket, cold and dark at the center of the altar, and I understand.

"What can we do to help?" I ask.

Jackie looks around the room, at the groups of people. "Nothing, really. I don't even know most of these people. They're friends of Aaron's from growing up or college. Or Beverly and Leonard's friends." She gives a strangled laugh. "In all the years we were together, I guess I never really made my own friends. I was just happy to be with Aaron. But now—" She presses her lips together. "I'm glad *you're* here."

I reach into my purse and pull out a cylinder, wrapped with a gold string, and hand it to Jackie. "This is for you."

She looks confused. "A certificate?"

"There's a national registry of stars. You can pay to have one of them named after a loved one. So . . . I had one named after Aaron."

Next to me, Rose breathes, "Oh, Paige. That's lovely."

Jackie unfurls the certificate, and I explain it to her. "I got one in the Orion constellation. The hunter. It's not one of the bigger stars, obviously. But you can definitely find it with a telescope. Maybe, when things settle down, we can go. You, me, and the boys. It'll be visible every year, November through February."

Jackie scans the certificate and the map, tears pooling in her eyes. "I don't know what to say," she whispers. "This is incredible. Thank you."

I reach out and pull her into a tight hug, wishing I could do more. Wishing I didn't have so much to hide. "You're welcome," I say.

Jackie pulls away and glances over to the corner where Aaron's parents sit. "I'd better go check in with them. They aren't doing very well."

"Of course," Rose says.

She rolls up the certificate and reties it, slipping it onto the mantel behind a vase. Then she approaches Beverly and Leonard, their faces tilting up toward her, as if they hope she'll tell them something that will change this awful reality in which they've found themselves. Beverly reaches up to take Jackie's hand, and Jackie squats down in front of her, gripping both of her hands, and says something that causes Beverly to break into silent tears and Leonard to look even more stoic. My eyes travel to his hands, which are restless in his lap.

"Let's go out back," I suggest to Rose.

Outside feels more like a party. Kids run around in their church clothes, laughing, and I find Miles and Nick in the center of a small knot of boys. I wander over to an empty table and sit. Rose slides in next to me.

"What an incredible gesture," she says. "How did you think of it?"

I shrug. "One of the guys in the astronomy department told me about it."

"How are *you* doing?" she asks.

"Okay, I guess. It's not really my tragedy, you know?"

"I suppose. Except you've lost something significant. So has Miles. It's okay to let yourself feel that."

Tears well up and threaten to fall, so I tip my sunglasses down over my eyes. "Thanks."

We're silent for a few minutes before she says, "What about the clinic? Aaron never told them, and now he can't."

The responsibility sits inside of me, low and heavy. "I know. I've been thinking about that nonstop. But if I notify the clinic, they'd have to confirm with Aaron. Which means they'd eventually contact Jackie."

Both of us turn to look back at the house, where, inside, Jackie is trying to comfort Aaron's parents despite her own grief.

"It would destroy her," I whisper.

"But ethically—" Rose starts.

"He donated twelve years ago. That means any child conceived with his sperm wouldn't be of age for several more years. I don't have to do anything immediately."

Rose nods. "So now what?" she asks. "You're just going to continue holding on to the secret and hope that no one will discover the truth?"

"I'm not going to abandon Jackie now. It's my secret, and I sure as hell won't ever say anything." I look across the yard to Miles and Nick, sitting shoulder to shoulder at a picnic table.

I know what I'm doing is wrong. It's deceitful, and it tears me apart because I love Jackie and I'm terrified the truth will come out, somehow. But Miles trumps all. And he always will. "I can't take Nick away from him."

"And if Jackie finds out?"

I'm growing exasperated. "How could she possibly find out?"

"Even though Aaron's not around to tell them doesn't mean there isn't documentation somewhere."

"There's no documentation identifying *us*."

I look at Miles and Nick again, sitting there, in nearly identical poses, not talking or moving, simply staring off into the crowd. My stomach clenches. Light and dark hair, fair and olive skin. Different, yet unmistakably similar.

"Right," Rose says, following my gaze. "I'm sure you're right."

TAKOTSUBO CARDIOMYOPATHY

No one's ever died of a broken heart. Except why do we have so many phrases that describe the physicality of grief? *Heartsick.* *Heartbroken. Heartache.* The heart bears the brunt of our grief, and it takes a toll. Takotsubo cardiomyopathy is a condition that mimics a heart attack. Its cause? Severe emotional or physical stress. Turns out, you can die of a broken heart after all.

Chapter Twenty-Four

M iles and I arrive at Rose's for Thanksgiving a half hour late. When she opens the door, I hand her the pecan pie I made and follow her back to the kitchen. My parents sit next to each other on the couch, and Miles races past them. "Hey, Grandma. Hey, Grandpa," he calls, before joining Josh in the backyard with a soccer ball.

"Happy Thanksgiving," I say from the doorway.

"Same to you," my father says, and my mother beams.

I slip into the kitchen before either of them can start a deeper conversation. I made the gesture, now I'm going to put some distance between us.

I hadn't wanted to come, but Rose talked me into it. "It just seems like a facade," I told her when she suggested it. "All of us, sitting around the table pretending we're a Norman Rockwell Thanksgiving portrait."

"Where else are you going to go?" she asked. "Denny's?"

"Maybe we'll go to Bruno's," I said, although I knew Miles would kill me. He loved Bruno but thought Bruno's eclectic group of friends were weird.

"Just come. Maybe you could bring Jackie and Nick."

"I already invited them, but she said no. They're not going

to celebrate this year, just try to get through the weekend with pizza and movies."

"God," Rose said. "I can't even imagine it."

I couldn't stop imagining it—how brutal it must be for them, living among the artifacts of Aaron's life, as if he might return any minute. To have to constantly remind yourself he never will.

"I won't make it a big production," Rose said. "I promise."

"Fine," I agreed.

Now I stand in her kitchen, watching Rose baste the turkey. "Not too much longer," she says, checking the thermometer.

I pour myself some wine and gesture toward the small kitchen table, where a game of Risk is set up. "World domination?" I ask.

Rose smiles, closes the oven door, and begins mashing potatoes. "The kids are playing that with Dad."

My head snaps around. "Dad's playing games? That's new."

Rose tests the consistency of the mashed potatoes and resumes mashing. "I know. But he loves it. It's sweet."

I study the board and count up players and colors. Five. "Are you or Henry playing too?"

"No, just the kids and Dad."

"Who's the fifth?"

Rose freezes, and suddenly, I know. "Miles," I say, turning on her. "When is this happening?"

She brushes a piece of hair off her forehead with the back of her hand and resumes mashing. "Tuesdays, while you're teaching your night class."

"Rose—" I start.

But she interrupts me. "Look. I'm sorry. It started a couple of weeks ago. Miles seems to love it. It's not hurting anyone."

I set my wineglass on the counter. "It's hurting me," I say.

She comes out from behind the stove and pulls me toward a chair. "Would it make you feel any better to know that Miles is much more engaged with Mikey, Hannah, and Josh than he is with Dad? I promise you, he loves the game, but he doesn't give two shits who's sitting in that fifth chair."

I picture the way Miles is around strangers—except Aaron—and know what Rose says is probably true. Miles has a way of tuning adults out. It's what he's done to Liam for years. Mom said this would happen, and Rose is right. His cousins, Rose, and Henry are more than enough buffer.

—

Dinner itself is uneventful, as I position myself as far away from my father as I can. It isn't until after dessert and the kids have left the table that my father turns to me and says, "So, Paige, have you figured out that work issue yet?"

My mother's eyes shift between us, sparkling and hopeful.

"No," I say to him. I turn to my mother and explain. "I ran into Dad at Dillon's a few weeks ago when I was trying to get caught up on some work." I hope my tone will communicate that this isn't the reconciliation she's been hoping for.

But my mother latches on to this tenuous link. "Peter, Paige is working on the most interesting study." She turns to me, her face flushed, finally discovering the opening she'd been waiting for. "Paige, tell your dad about it. It's fascinating!"

Something inside me shifts. First, it's Tuesdays with Dad playing Risk. Now my mother wants me to catch Dad up on my study, as if he's just been out of town for a couple of weeks. All of the grief and tension I've been suppressing begins to unravel.

"We're studying why some men abandon their children," I

say, looking directly at him. "They carry a gene that physically impedes their ability to bond. I've found a way to fix you, Dad, if you're interested. I could give you some of the synthetic hormone, and maybe for the first time, you'll be able to resist the urge to disappear on us."

Rose's fork freezes midway to her mouth, and my mother looks horrified. *"Paige,"* she scolds.

With a flush of shame, I realize I've gone too far—no hormone can keep my father from leaving us this last time.

I pinch the bridge of my nose, warding off a headache that's growing behind my eyes. "That was uncalled for. I'm sorry," I say to all of them. "It's been a tough few weeks."

My father holds up his hand to wave away my words, and I can't help but notice the slight tremor of his fingers, making me feel even worse. "Don't worry about it," he says. "It's understandable." He turns to me. "I know, better than you might think, what I've put you through."

"Don't try to pretend my not wanting anything to do with you is the same as what you did to me and Rose."

He folds his napkin carefully, the entire table watching him. "I'm not talking about that," he says. "Your study makes a lot of sense to me. My father was a cold and neglectful man. If what you say is true, I'm glad whatever my father passed on to me wasn't passed on to you."

My mother reaches out and places her hand over his.

Rose stands, almost in tears. "Would anyone like more coffee?" she asks, holding up the pot and looking around the table, desperate to move the conversation forward.

I shake my head. "It's getting late. I think Miles and I should go."

Four pairs of eyes watch me push back from the table and

stand, but no one speaks or tries to stop me. "Thanks for dinner, Rose. It was delicious." I set my napkin on the table and walk toward the bottom of the stairs, where I call for Miles and tell him to say goodbye to everyone while I wait by the door.

He heads into the dining room, and it isn't until I hear him say, "Goodbye, Grandpa," that what's left of my resolve shatters, leaving me wiping away tears, alone in the dark foyer, wondering what kind of person I've become, and whether I'm so different from my father after all.

— ⬩ —

The following week I sit down with Jenna and Bruno. "I want to look at Scott's inhibitor gene," I tell them.

Scientists have only been able to study the before and after of a gene methylation in humans. No one has ever observed one while it's happening.

"The one from his most recent sample?" Jenna asks.

"All of them." I wait for Bruno to object, which he does.

"We can't allocate lab resources for something like that," he says. "It's not in the IRB. If we get audited, we couldn't explain it."

"We're rerunning samples we've already gathered, which does fall under the IRB," I argue. "Look it up."

Bruno pulls up the document we wrote five years ago and scans it. I wait for him to get to the consent section. When he does, his eyes lock on to mine, a flicker of excitement growing.

I offer a tiny smile and shrug. "I drafted it so that we could retest any of the subsamples at any time. It doesn't limit what we're testing for." I turn to Jenna. "I want you to coordinate it. Do you have time?"

She nods. "I can spread out my caseload, no problem."

"Has he signed up for phase two?" I ask Bruno.

"Yep. He says the study was important to Mara and she would have wanted him to see it through."

If there's a way for the inhibitor gene to turn itself off, I want to find it. Not just for the scientific discovery, but for myself. For the little girl who always hoped someday her father might change into someone better. I think about my father, playing Risk with the kids, and wonder what's changed. The fact that he's dying? Or something more?

I turn to Jenna and begin to outline how I want her to isolate and compare Scott's inhibitor gene, the air between us crackling with possibility.

Nativists believe in the idea that genetics determines everything, not just your hair and eye color, but also your personality and abilities. Nurturists believe that what you were exposed to as a child—both physically and emotionally—shape who you ultimately become. But the truth is, both sides are correct. Our genes influence our behavior, and our behavior influences our genes. And our life experiences are what activates or silences all of it.

Scientists have recently discovered a gene that might be responsible for perfect pitch, the ability to identify any note, or to produce a specific note on demand. But just because you have the gene doesn't mean you automatically have the ability. That skill has to be developed through exposure and instruction. Genes must sometimes wait for experience to turn on.

Can someone without the gene learn perfect pitch? Perhaps. We can modify behavior and train our bodies and minds to behave a certain way, and changes can occur on a cellular level too. This is how our genes were designed—to take their cues from experiences and the environment around them.

A long time ago, I chose to silence my pain instead of dealing with it. I'm paying the price now. My instincts are asleep, no matter how many times Rose yells at me, telling me what to do or reminding me what's at stake, I can't seem to hear her clearly. Her advice is a tangle of notes, unfollowable.

If nurturists were to study me, they'd say this is a learned behavior, that my childhood taught me to be disengaged and distant as a means of protecting myself. But if a nativist were to crack me open, maybe she'd see a genetic variance caused by the repeated heartbreak of a little girl who believed she would never be enough, so eventually, she stopped listening.

Chapter Twenty-Five

I'm snooping in Rose's closet, looking for a sweater of mine that she borrowed a year ago that I'd like back. She claims it's hers, so I have to snatch it without her knowing. I ease the door open while she's busy in the bathroom, planning to grab it and shove it in my bag before she catches me, when I see a gorgeous red dress hanging on the back of the door, tags still on.

I hold it in front of me and look in the mirror. "What's the new dress for?" I call.

Rose comes out of the bathroom and pulls up short when she sees which one I'm holding. "Oh, it's for a party next weekend." She turns away and begins organizing the jewelry on her dresser, a sure sign she's hiding something.

"Rose?" I ask.

She turns around. "It's for Liam's holiday party."

I sit down hard on the bed, the dress in a pile on my lap. Of course, Liam's annual holiday party. I feel as if my life is spinning away from me, leaving me stranded somewhere I don't want to be.

Rose takes the dress and hangs it back up. "Don't wrinkle it."

I turn on her. "No, we wouldn't want you to show up in a wrinkled dress for Liam's big party."

"Paige, what would you have me do? Not go?"

I close my eyes for a moment and then open them again. "It's like I've been lifted right out of his life," I say. "Everything stays the same—same holiday party, same guests, same everything. The only thing missing is me."

She sits down on the bed next to me. Late-afternoon sunlight hits the corners of the room, and I can see dust in the air, floating on invisible air currents. A pair of Henry's muddy running shoes are kicked off in the corner next to an overflowing laundry basket.

"Paige, you lifted yourself out."

"Why do you keep blaming me? You act as if I did this all on my own."

"You are hanging on—so tight—to this idea of safety. *If I can just stay over here, inside this square, nothing can hurt me.* But look around you! You can't protect yourself from getting hurt. Aaron still died. You still lost Liam. Dad's going to die too, and it's going to hurt like hell, whether you want to admit it or not. Life cannot be lived inside the penalty box."

"Oh, you're making hockey metaphors now?" I joke. But what Rose said makes sense. I'm lonely. I miss Liam's calls. His jokes. The way he'd wrap me in his arms and squeeze just the right amount until I relaxed into him. I flop back onto the bed. "This isn't how I want it to be."

Rose lies down next to me and I wiggle closer to her, the two of us staring at the ceiling. "Remember when we were little and you'd crawl into my bed at night because you were scared I'd disappear before morning?" I ask.

She links her pinkie with mine, the way we used to. "You taught me how to be brave. And I can't, for the life of me, figure out how or when you forgot."

—

We've got the preliminary results from the tests Jenna's running on Scott's old samples, and I'm running through them, again and again, trying to track what's going on. She's gone back to the very first sample we took in the hospital after Sophie was born, which shows a fully intact inhibitor gene on his Y chromosome. She's making her way through subsequent samples, and she's matching them up with the anecdotal data to make sure there isn't a different inciting event, prior to Mara's death, that escaped our notice the first time.

Bruno comes into the office near the end of the day and tosses a stack of lab reports on my desk. "While you and Jenna work on your science fair project, we've got four grad students rotating through the lab on a twenty-four-hour schedule to cover you guys. Jake Murphy skipped all his classes yesterday."

"Get the names of his professors. I'll make a couple of calls."

He sits at his desk and stares at me. "You seem . . . motivated to figure this out."

I flip a folder closed and open a new one. "I'm always motivated to figure something out. You know that."

He shakes his head. "This is different."

I look up at him and shrug. "Maybe it is. I can't help but think of what this means for all the kids out there whose fathers are like mine." Before he can lecture me on Sophie Sullivan again, I say, "This isn't some attempt to save anyone. It's more for myself, to be honest. The idea that a father can change like this means much more to me than it might to you."

Bruno grabs a folder from my desk and opens it. "What are we looking for?" he asks.

—

As I'm leaving my office, Jackie calls. "Hi," I say, "I've been thinking about you." A cold winter wind bites through me. I wrap my arms around myself, hugging my purse to my chest.

"Beverly is driving me crazy. She keeps calling, harassing me about Christmas or just crying into the phone. I feel for her, I really do, but I can't take it. I can't be that person for her, you know?"

"Maybe you should be honest. Tell her you need some space."

Jackie snorts. "She doesn't know the meaning of *space*. The morning after our wedding, she called us from the lobby of the hotel, wondering if we were interested in meeting for breakfast."

I laugh. "What'd you do?"

"We went downstairs and had breakfast with her." She sighs. "I've told her I can't handle doing a regular Christmas. Not this year. I feel bad for Nick, but I think we both need a change of scenery. Neither of us can deal with getting a tree or decorating without Aaron." Her voice catches.

"Maybe you guys could go somewhere totally different. The Caribbean, maybe. Or India."

"Actually, that's why I called. I was thinking you and Miles might like to come up to the cabin with us. We could have a different kind of Christmas. Skiing, hot chocolate, sledding. Unless you have plans? I don't want to tear you away from your family."

"We don't," I tell her. Rose has been talking about a big family Christmas with our dad. And even though I know she's right, that there are a thousand ways for me to get hurt in this world, I can't bring myself to attend. "That sounds great."

"Good." She sounds relieved. "I was thinking we could leave next week, right after the boys get out for vacation."

"Perfect," I say. But the way Beverly looked at Miles at the funeral still haunts me, and I try not to think of what I might be running into.

SECRETS

Scientists have found a strong correlation between keeping a traumatic secret and the onset of anxiety, depression, and other biological symptoms. A study done in the 1970s linked traumatic secrets to hypertension, influenza, and even cancer. Neuroscientists have found that keeping a secret can impact brain function as well. Through EEGs and blood tests, they've shown that writing a secret down and then destroying it, or revealing a secret to another person, led to tangible health benefits such as improved sleep and T cell counts.

However, studies have also shown that for individuals who have learned of a traumatic secret, the biological damage can have a long-lasting, negative impact.

Chapter Twenty-Six

I feel like a girl on the run. Jackie has the volume cranked up to Bon Jovi's "Livin' on a Prayer," and we sing along—loudly and badly—while Miles and Nick look appropriately horrified in the back seat.

Taking a trip with Jackie wasn't exactly what Rose meant when she said I needed to step outside of the penalty box. But I'd rather be up here, singing bad eighties anthems with Jackie than home alone, thinking about the party I wasn't invited to.

The song ends, and I reach across the console and turn the volume down just in time to hear Nick say, "I don't understand. How is the game multiplayer if you're not connected to the Internet?"

"The interface is different," Miles says.

I turn to face the boys. "What are you talking about?"

Miles looks at me, his face void of any expression. "The new game Liam is working on."

"How did you find out about it?"

Miles glances at Nick, as if to say, *You see what I have to put up with?* before turning to me and saying, "He told me."

"When? Where?" Trees whiz by my window, and my head spins.

Miles shrugs. "I don't know. Tuesday? I was at Aunt Rose's."

So now it's not just Tuesdays with Dad; it's Tuesdays with Dad *and* Liam. For all Rose's assurances that I haven't been erased, it sure seems like I have. At least on Tuesdays, when everyone knows I teach a late class. I should drop it, but I can't resist. I look over my shoulder again and say, "What was Liam doing at Rose's on Tuesday?"

Miles's answer is frustrating in its brevity. "Talking to me about his new video game."

Jackie glances at me with sympathetic eyes and says, "You okay?"

"Sure," I say, my mood ruined. I train my eyes forward. "Are we almost there?"

———

Finally, she puts on her turn signal, and we glide off the highway and onto a small road that backs up to one of the ski resorts. Jackie pulls up in front of a large A-frame, with windows reflecting the bright snow back at us.

The boys leap from the car, and Miles, inexperienced with snow, sinks in a drift up to his knees. "Mom!" he calls, half laughing, half crying.

"You're okay," I tell him, lifting him under his armpits and pulling him out. We wobble and slide our way to the front door and step into a cavernous room with a floor-to-ceiling fireplace made entirely out of river rock. Worn leather chairs and couches flank the fireplace, and a backgammon table stands next to a corner window that overlooks the back of the resort. My eyes travel upward to a mezzanine that looks down into the living room. Nick is already upstairs, looking over the railing.

"Miles, come up and check out our room!"

Miles sprints upstairs, disappearing from sight. "Take off those pants and shoes!" I call after him.

Jackie stacks logs and twists newspaper in the fireplace, and soon she's got a fire going. She stands, wiping her hands on her pants. "It's five o'clock somewhere. Want a cocktail?"

"Gin and tonic?" I ask.

"Absolutely," she says, and I follow her into the kitchen, where she pulls a half-empty bottle of gin and an unopened bottle of tonic water from a cupboard.

As she mixes the cocktails, she says, "I feel like I've stepped out of one life and into another. I can pretend we're celebrating the holiday and Aaron is home working." She gives a shaky smile. "That's not unhealthy, right?"

"It sounds like an excellent coping strategy to me," I say.

I take a sip of my drink, letting the bitter lime and fizzy tonic slide down my throat and settle my stomach before following her back to the living room.

"We never did holidays here, so I don't feel like I have to hide from the memories the way I would have at home." She looks out the enormous window, swirling the ice in the glass, before looking back again. "And Nick needs this. He's been having a really hard time. I think he forgets every once in a while." She looks so sad, tears pooling in her eyes. "He'll seem normal, and then his expression will just crumble. I can literally see it slamming into him. And I can't fix it." She rubs her eyes, as if to blot out the image.

"How did Beverly take the news of the trip?"

"Not well. Luckily, Leonard intervened on our behalf."

"And how is he doing?"

"Okay, I guess. The same."

This would be a logical segue to ask about the testing. *Were*

you able to have Aaron tested in the hospital? Oh, I've been wonder-
ing, did you or Aaron's parents think to request a test for him that day?
But no matter how I approach the question, it feels intrusive and
self-serving. I swirl the ice in my glass. I can only assume if she
did, she'll eventually tell me about the results. Aaron's words
on the hill come back to me. *We're already either doomed or saved.*
Knowing for sure won't change anything.

I gulp the last of my drink, which is mostly water now that
the ice cubes have melted, and stand.

"Can I get you another one?" I ask, holding up my glass.

"I'm good, but help yourself," Jackie says, leaning back in her
chair and propping her feet on the low table between us. "What's
mine is yours."

Her words stop me for a moment, and I can feel Rose's sharp
gaze judging me from three hundred miles away. I hurry into
the kitchen, chased by my guilt, and pour a new drink—going
a little heavier on the gin than the tonic. I've run away from my
problems with Liam and my dad, but I've stepped into a different
set, with much more significant consequences.

―

"I have to tell you, I'm not a very good skier," Jackie says as the
two of us sit in the chairlift, gliding to the top of the mountain.
We've just left the boys at ski school and are taking the first run
of the day.

"You're kidding, right?" Snow and trees reflect off her goggles so it's impossible to see her expression.

"I kind of suck," she admits, turning to me with an awkward
smile.

I'd assumed she was an expert and could lead me down the

hill. But now we're floating toward the top of a mountain, and I've got no idea how we're going to get down.

Her goggles reflect the shock and terror on my face, causing a bubble of laughter to well up inside of me. "Shit," I say.

She giggles, a slow build toward a full belly laugh, and the next thing I know we're collapsed into each other, laughing so hard tears are streaming from our eyes, and my goggles fog up so much that I have to prop them on top of my head so I can see.

"Oh no!" She points at the operator shed looming in front of us and the steep ramp intended to carry us down and away from the lift.

I clutch my poles tighter, my muscles tensing. "Keep your tips up," I say, repeating something a friend once told me.

"My tits?" she says, turning toward me at the last minute. Shocked, I look at her as my skis touch the snow. The chair pushes me forward, but I stand too late. Jackie's skis veer toward mine, and soon we're rolling in a ball down the ramp, forcing other skiers to jump out of the way. Something pokes me hard in the side, but I'm too busy disentangling myself from Jackie to pay attention to what it was. As I look up, through cockeyed goggles and a skewed hat, I see Jackie splayed facedown, skis crossed behind her, covered in snow and cackling hysterically.

She catches sight of me across the way as skiers glide between us off the lift, skis perfectly parallel. Someone angles to a sharp stop, throwing a shower of snow into my face, leaving me sputtering.

Jackie laughs even harder. The absurdity of the situation is contagious.

"Ladies, get off the ground before you get hurt," the lift operator calls to us from the shed. "I have to stop the lift if I leave the shed. Do I need to stop the lift?"

This sends us both into a new gale of laughter. "We're okay!" I try to push myself up onto my knees but my crossed skis keep me from kneeling, so I reach behind and release my boots from their bindings. Jackie has rolled onto her back and is sprawled out, spread-eagle, looking up at the sky. "Paige, get over here!"

I drag my skis and poles behind me, nearly colliding with a couple disembarking from the lift.

"Sorry," I shout behind me, settling myself next to Jackie. Coldness creeps through the insulation of my coat and ski pants. We lie there, staring up at the sky, the green tips of the pine trees a dark contrast against the endless blue sky.

She breathes, long and slow. "This place always restores me."

"Ladies! *Get up off the ground!*"

"In a minute," she whispers to me. I turn to face her and notice a tear sliding down her cheek. "I feel closer to him here."

I take her mittened hand and squeeze it.

The lodge is a cavernous room with the feel of a men's club, with dark wood, a roaring fireplace taking up an entire wall, and a bar lining the other side. Leather chairs are scattered across the room, intimate and cozy despite being able to accommodate at least a hundred people. Floor-to-ceiling windows frame the mountain, crawling with skiers.

We sit in large armchairs, warming up with Irish coffees.

"Enough of me and my problems," Jackie says. "What's going on with you?" She leans back in her chair, propping her stocking feet up on a low table between us.

"Well . . . you're not the only one hiding up here from her family," I say. "Turns out, my entire family is gathering on

Tuesdays—with Liam—for dinner and game night." I explain about the games of Risk and about Liam's holiday party.

"Wow, that must feel like a huge betrayal," she says.

I think about it. "I don't feel betrayed so much as I feel left out. Like there's a giant phone tree going on behind my back. *She's gone! Come over!*"

Jackie smiles gently. "I don't need to tell you that's not true, do I?"

"I know, but it feels that way."

"You miss Liam," she says. Not a question, a statement. I don't even bother denying it. "Is there anything you can do to fix it?"

I shake my head. "I don't think so." I think about everything that's come to pass since we broke up—the discovery of Aaron as Miles's donor and my decision to conceal it from Jackie—and I shudder at the idea of telling him. I don't want him to see how lost I am, how much I've messed everything up. I'm hanging by a string, just trying to make it, minute to minute—with my dad, with Jackie, Aaron, and Miles. There's no way he'd want to jump into this mess with me. There's too much ground to make up. I look out the window, the glare of the sun bouncing off the snow and making my eyes water. In a quiet voice I say, "He wants all access to my life, and I just don't operate that way. There are things I don't think he'd understand or agree with." That's as close as I'll come to telling Jackie the truth.

She studies me, thoughtful. "Everyone has things they keep private. I did with Aaron." Jackie takes a drink from her mug and continues, "I'm sure he did with me."

"What do you mean?"

"No relationship is completely open. If it won't impact things going forward, then leave it alone. But you also have to trust their love. You have to believe that no matter what, no matter how hard, they won't walk away."

Except Liam did walk away.

Jackie continues, "I don't think there's anything I wouldn't have forgiven Aaron for," she says, her eyes growing wet. "When you love someone, forgiveness is easy."

"What if what he did was unforgivable?" I ask, my voice just above a whisper.

"Even then," she says. "It might have been hard, but I loved him."

I look down into my mug. It's easier to forgive someone when you know they're never coming back, when you know there's nothing else they can do to hurt you. I think of my father. When he's gone, he'll be done disappointing me. Will I be able to forgive him then?

When I look back up at her, she smiles. "You don't *have* to do anything about Liam," she says. "But just know that if you want to, you can."

I think about what Rose said, about how she can't figure out when I forgot how to be brave. I wish I knew.

We fall into an easy silence, looking into the fire, lost in our own thoughts. I don't know what I hate more—the weight of the secret that sits inside of me or not believing in Liam enough to tell him.

SIBLING RELATIONSHIPS AND THEIR IMPACT ON SOCIAL-EMOTIONAL HEALTH

Allison Monroe, Columbia University Press

The sibling relationship is one of the most important and long-lasting relationships a person can develop. This bond affects a child's social-emotional development and has far-reaching consequences well into adulthood. Positive sibling relationships contribute to higher cognitive ability, emotional stability, and greater independence.

FROM THE DONOR SIBLING REGISTRY WEBSITE: SUCCESS STORIES

5 Kids on Vacation—Oh My!

My partner and I conceived our son via donor eight years ago. We have recently connected with four of his genetic siblings and took a trip to Great Wolf Lodge to meet them. The kids (two boys, three girls) connected immediately. I can't describe how incredible it was—as if they were just picking up a conversation they'd started years ago. Two of them could be twins; they look so much alike! I admit, we had reservations at first—what if the kids didn't get along? What if our son got hurt or was rejected in some way? But our fears were put to rest immediately. This was truly a gift—for all the kids, and for those of us who love them. I can honestly say I feel as if our family has just expanded fivefold.

Chapter Twenty-Seven

Jackie calls shortly after the New Year. "I need to ask a huge favor, and please say no if you think it's too much."

Intrigued, I say, "What is it?"

"I need to clean out Aaron's closet and drawers. I feel like I'm living in a shrine. Every time I come into my room, it feels like I'm entering some kind of mausoleum, filled with Aaron's things. His change jar. His clothes. Cuff links. I need them gone."

I sit on the edge of my bed, thinking of the file hidden in my own closet and wondering what might be hiding in Aaron's. Light filters through the curtains in my bedroom, and I can hear Miles watching TV in the living room. "Of course."

"Thank you," she says. "If Beverly helped, it would turn into another afternoon of tears and reminiscing, and I can't deal with that. I need to do it before she offers, and if I do it alone, you'll find me buried and wallowing under all of his clothes. You'll keep me on task. I need you to be ruthless."

"When do you want to do it?"

"This afternoon, if you can. The boys can watch a movie or something. I don't think it'll take more than a couple of hours. We'll load up some trash bags, and I can take them to Goodwill tomorrow."

I cringe at the idea of Aaron's belongings shoved into Hefty bags. But I can only imagine what it must be like for her to go to bed every night surrounded by his things.

"We can be there around two," I tell her, trying to quiet my racing thoughts.

Once we get the boys situated in front of a movie, I follow Jackie down the hall past a half-open door. An enormous desk with files stacked on top dominates the room, a paper shredder next to it, and bags of trash litter the floor.

Jackie catches me peeking. "Aaron's office. He's kept every piece of paper he's ever touched since the Clinton administration. I try to go through a few files every night, but it's slow going. Our attorney wants anything that might be important, so I have to read it all myself." She leans against the doorjamb, and I stand next to her, wondering if a file holding all the details of Aaron's sperm donation is in there somewhere.

I imagine the moment Jackie discovers the paperwork, alone in a small circle of lamplight, an empty wineglass next to her. She pulls out yet another file, expecting a receipt for a trip or a new appliance. She scans the top page—the same donor profile I have. As understanding clicks in, she turns the pages faster, until she reaches the end of the file with more questions than answers. Aaron's secrets laid bare, with no way to confront him or ask for an explanation. Selfishly, I worry how I'll react when she tells me. If I'll be able to feign surprise and keep from burdening Jackie with not only another secret but also another betrayal.

"If you want, I can help with that too." I try to keep my voice cool, as if it's no big deal. "I can spend some time this afternoon, after we're done. Give you a break."

"Thanks," Jackie says. "But I don't mind doing it; it's just time-consuming."

I drop it, though every instinct urges me to push her, to keep asking, to find a way to get into that room by myself. If I can intervene in time, Jackie will never have to know. I could save her this pain, at least. "If you change your mind, let me know."

I follow her down the hall to her bedroom and try to imagine Aaron there, living out his final few hours, tossing and turning while Jackie slept, worrying about a secret only he and I knew.

Jackie disappears into the walk-in closet, a box of trash bags tucked under her arm.

"Where do you want me to start?" I ask.

"In here."

She hands me the bags. "I've already set aside the things I want to keep, so let's do this quickly. I've limited myself to his favorite college sweatshirt and a sweater I bought for him our first Christmas together. Don't let me get sentimental. Don't let me talk myself into keeping anything else. I don't need it."

I look at the shelves of clothes, the hangers of golf shirts, pants, and button-downs. "Do Leonard or Beverly want to keep anything? Or Nick?" I ask.

"I have other things for Nick," she says. "Leonard and Beverly have the entire contents of his room, intact since he left for college. Trust me, they don't need any of this stuff."

I try to ignore the nagging sadness that Miles won't have anything, no small token of his father to remind him of the man he knew.

I tear open the box of garbage bags, pull one out, and snap it open, and Jackie begins emptying hangers and shelves, shoving clothes in with abandon, as if she's trying to stay one step ahead of her emotions. Every time something goes into the bag, a puff of air is displaced, and soon the entire closet smells like sandal-wood soap, like Aaron.

—

Jackie empties the last drawer, and we sit on the bed, shoulder to shoulder. She takes a deep breath. "Okay," she says, though it sounds more like she's talking to herself than to me. "I'm going to rearrange everything in here. New bedding, maybe some new furniture." Her eyes travel around the room, taking in the empty drawers that still hang open, the closet with bare shelves, all evidence of Aaron removed. "If this were happening to someone else, I'd think that sounded so cold, erasing him and starting over. But I'm terrified that if I don't deal with it now, I'll turn into someone who'll freak out if you move his toothbrush."

I give her a sad smile and reach out and squeeze her hand.

"Thanks for helping today," she says.

"I was glad to." I pull her up to standing. "C'mon," I say. "We deserve a drink."

We look around the room one last time before heading into the kitchen, and I cast one last glance down the hall and pray that Aaron destroyed whatever documentation he had from ACB a long time ago.

—

Later that evening, Rose and I are sitting in her kitchen drinking wine when Miles comes in with a question. "Josh is sleeping over at Grandma and Grandpa's tonight, and he invited me to go." He's bursting with excitement, bouncing on his toes. "So can I?"

I look at Rose for an explanation. "Mom and Dad want to

have one-on-one time with the kids. Day trips. Overnights." She shrugs, as if it's no big deal, but a weight descends, a realization that Miles and I are on the outside, looking in.

"I don't think so," I say. "It's Josh's night."

"But he invited me," Miles argues. "We already called Grandma, and she said it was fine."

Annoyance that he's done this without my permission zaps through me. "My answer is still no."

His face crumples in disappointment. "You never let me do anything."

I try to lighten the mood, to push past the topic by saying, "You're right. I'm the meanest mom in the world."

Miles just glares at me.

"I'm sorry," I tell him. "Not tonight."

"When?" he pushes. "When can I have *my* night with Grandma and Grandpa? I haven't had a sleepover with Grandma in months."

He hasn't slept over with my mom since my dad returned. Rose watches me, saying nothing. "Arguing with me isn't the best way to change my mind," I tell him. "It's not happening tonight. Call Grandma back and tell her you're not coming."

Rose intervenes. "Hold up, Miles. Go upstairs and play with Josh. I need your mom to help me with something. Don't call anyone just yet."

Miles clomps up the stairs, and Rose turns to me. "Can you come with me to the garden center to pick up some potting soil? I ordered seven bags and I want to get there before they close."

I look at the stairs, feeling whiplash at the change of topic. "Is this some kind of trick?" I ask, following her to the car.

"No trick," she says. "I need your help."

As we pull out of the driveway, Rose clicks on the radio.

NPR. North Korea. Israel. She flips the stations until she comes to ABBA singing "Waterloo."

I laugh. We used to dance to this song as kids, making up a routine that we'd perform in front of the mirror in my bedroom.

We both begin to sing, falling into the roles we had when we were younger. At a red light, right on cue, we turn and sing to each other, "'I feel like I win when I loooose.'"

We make our way through the entire song, moving our shoulders in sync, as if no time has passed. And it feels so good— to be here with Rose, driving and dancing and singing, as if we weren't constantly at odds with each other.

We pull up to the gardening center just as the song ends, and Rose cuts the engine. We sit, catching our breath, and I say, "I don't want to argue with you anymore."

"He's dying, Paige."

"I know." I look out the window at the large outdoor space, filled with a riot of color. Hanging plants, tabletops filled, extending all the way back to the edge of the store, where ceramic pots and trees line the back of the lot. Customers push large flatbed carts toward the entrance.

Rose turns to me. "You need to stop using Miles as a shield." I start to interrupt, but she holds her hand up. "This isn't about you. Or what Dad did to us. This is about how you're going to explain to Miles—one year, five years, ten years from now—why you refused to let him know his grandfather. And I promise you, all the reasons you think are so important right now won't matter. They will be empty and hollow and meaningless."

I look up at her. She's not yelling. She's not crying. She's just laying out the facts. And she's not wrong.

She reaches across the console and takes my hand. "You've been hiding behind science to justify your solitude. But you alone are not enough for Miles. *We* aren't enough for him anymore. His world is expanding, and you have to let it."

"And you think an overnight with Josh, Mom, and Dad will give him what he needs?"

"Of course not. It's an overnight. They'll watch movies and eat junk food and stay up too late. That's my point. It's harmless. You need to realize that every interaction with Dad isn't going to turn into a scene from *Invasion of the Body Snatchers*. He'll still be Miles in the morning."

I smile, and something inside me loosens. I can't keep banging against this wall.

Rose continues, "Time is short. This isn't about forgiving Dad or even having a relationship with him. It's about not hating him when he dies."

"Okay," I say, staring out the window. "Can we go home now?"

Rose opens her door and gets out. "No. I really need your help with this soil."

I follow her, grabbing a flatbed cart from a stand. It rattles over the concrete, sending vibrations up my arms, the loud sound eliminating any chance of further discussion, which is a relief.

———

I volunteer to pick the boys up the next morning. When I arrive at Mom's, I sit for a minute in my car, practicing my lines. I will be kind. I will smile and say, *Thank you for hosting the boys.* I will tell them we don't have time to linger; no, I don't have time for a cup of coffee, and we will leave.

I unbuckle my seat belt and head in.

Mom leads me to the back, where the boys have built an enormous pillow fort. She looks at me over her shoulder. "I told them they could sleep in there last night. They had the best time."

Pillows lean against the dining room table, blankets cascade over sections, and Miles's head pokes out of a small opening near the top. "Mom, check it out! This is my room."

"Cool," I say. "Where's Josh?"

Josh pokes his head out of a different section. "Hey, Aunt Paige. Can we get doughnuts on the way home?"

I smile. "We'll see. Are you guys ready to go? Where's Grandpa?"

"Here!" a voice calls from deep within the fort. "Hold on."

My father crawls out a side entrance and stands, carefully bracing himself on the table.

"Should he be doing that?" I ask my mother.

She looks at me sideways. "He has cancer, Paige. Not a broken leg."

The boys tumble out after him and hug him. "Grandpa slept in here with us," Miles says. "All night."

I watch them, three Robson boys, and I wonder what it would have been like to have had this version of my dad when I was growing up. What kind of holes it would have filled for me. The magic of having an adult build something with you, play in it with you, pretend in it with you. I never had that. And even though I'm glad Miles will have this memory of my dad, I feel cheated that I never got one for myself. Like a whisper, the realization creeps up on me. *It's not too late.*

I turn to them. "Get your things and meet me by the door."

They hustle out of the room, and I look at my parents—older, broken down by life and illness and regret. "Thanks for having them," I say, surprised by how easily the words come.

My mother turns away, tears in her eyes. My father offers a small salute. "Thank *you*," he says.

IMPRINTING

Several years ago, Rose and the kids were over for dinner when my refrigerator conked out. No light. No motor. With hamburgers sizzling on the stove, four kids chasing one another around in the backyard, and repair rates firmly in the *after hours* category, I went in search of my owner's manual, hoping to find something that would save a fridge full of groceries. But before I could even scan the index, Rose fixed it. *Reset button on your outlet,* she said. This is how it's always been. While I research answers, Rose simply knows them.

Imprinting is an irreversible brain mechanism controlled by biochemicals and genes, which occurs when an early experience becomes a permanent part of a young animal's mind. For example, if you want your child to be bilingual, it's best to speak to them in two languages from birth. Conversely, if you deprive a child of language and keep them in silence, no amount of instruction will allow them to acquire even the most rudimentary understanding of grammar and syntax. It will be too late.

What experiences recorded on my mind during my own childhood, between birth and age twelve, when the window for imprinting closes? Somewhere along the way, I must have learned that answers were to be found outside of myself. And Rose must have learned the opposite. Although we were raised in the same house, by the same person, and lived through the same disappointments, our approach to problem-solving—and to life—is completely different. I think about that evening often and how easily Rose understood that the problem wasn't the object, but the source.

Chapter Twenty-Eight

We've looked at Scott Sullivan's inhibitor gene from every one of his samples, and they're all identical—until shortly after Mara's death, when a single substitution appears on the Y chromosome. We believe this is attributed to the trauma of his wife's death. At this point, we have no choice but to officially release him from the oxytocin trial. I've scheduled a home visit with him to close out the paperwork for phase one and hopefully get him to agree to let us study what we think is happening to him. I'm also anxious to check in on Sophie and confirm that what Jenna says is true, that she's doing okay and Scott has things under control.

Their street looks the same as it did on my last visit, five years ago. Mara was frazzled that day, the top half of her blouse unbuttoned and her hair looking like it hadn't been washed in days. Scott, however, looked showered and rested, ready to begin our interview.

When I knock on the door today, an older and heavier Scott answers. The TV is blaring, and a dish towel hangs over one shoulder. "Dr. Robson, come in. It's good to see you."

"Thanks for taking the time to meet me today," I say.

"No problem." He leads me into the house. A layer of dust covers every surface, shoes litter the floor by the door, and a pile of laundry has tumbled sideways outside the master bedroom. "Sorry about the mess."

In the kitchen, Sophie sits at the counter, swinging her legs and drawing a picture. A pot of spaghetti sauce bubbles on the stove, the strong smell of garlic and oregano inviting. Almost cozy.

"Hi, Sophie. I'm Dr. Robson. The last time I saw you, you were a baby."

Sophie looks at me for a moment. "Did you know my mom?"

I study her, the shape of her face so similar to Mara's. "I did. I liked her a lot."

Sophie nods once and resumes her work.

"I'm going to talk to Dr. Robson in the dining room, okay, Soph?"

"Sure, Daddy," she says, not looking up from her drawing.

Evidence of Mara is everywhere—photographs dot the surfaces, Mara in mid-laugh, Mara with an infant Sophie, Mara and Scott on their wedding day. I compare the mess and clutter around me to Jackie's pristine house. But she's always run their home. Here, Scott has gone from doing nothing to doing everything. And if my suspicions are correct, the change is showing up in his DNA.

"How are you adjusting?" I ask. I need the anecdotal data if I'm going to close out the file.

Scott sighs as we sit in chairs across from each other. "At first I was totally overwhelmed. Sophie cried all the time. There wasn't anything I could do to console her. Truthfully," he lowers his voice, "I could barely function. All I wanted to do was run away."

This doesn't surprise me.

"I had no idea how much Mara did—the meals, the scheduling, the homework, and school events. It was crazy. One time, I forgot to go grocery shopping. I had nothing to put in Sophie's lunch, so I tossed in four chocolate puddings and a spoon and prayed the school wouldn't call."

I laugh. "We've all been there."

Scott smiles, reassured. "I'm doing better now. I've got a system. A schedule."

"Schedules are good."

He looks down at his hands, folded on the table in front of us. "It's still hard to think about how much Mara's missing. It's not fair that she doesn't get any more days with Sophie, or get to see these milestones." He looks back at me. "Sophie lost her first tooth a couple of weeks ago. I knew enough to tell her to put it under the pillow for the tooth fairy. When she was asleep, I slipped her a twenty-dollar bill. The next day I found out no one gives more than a dollar. Everyone seems to know this stuff except me."

"We all have moments when we feel clueless," I tell him.

"What's crazy is that sometimes I look at Sophie, and she'll have an expression on her face or she'll say something, and it'll be *so much* like Mara. How could she have learned that from her in such a short time?"

I set my pen down. "Fifty percent of Sophie's genes came from Mara, that's how. Some things, the learned behaviors, will fade over time, while others, the things she inherited directly from Mara, will sharpen."

Scott leans forward. "Seriously?"

I explain mtDNA, and his eyes grow hopeful.

"If Sophie has a daughter, she'll pass it on to her children too. A whole history of Mara, of her mother before her, lives inside of Sophie."

"You're kidding me," he says. "So you mean I could be a

ninety-year-old grandfather and see a flash of Mara in my grandchildren?"

"Not only is it possible," I tell him. "It's likely. Mara's mitochondrial DNA will be present, unchanged, in every cell of your grandchildren's bodies. So in essence, Mara will be there too."

He looks across the dining room to a picture of Mara, her hair swept up in the wind and laughing. "Incredible," he whispers.

I flip open the file in front of me. "I want to thank you for finishing phase one, but I also came to talk to you about the phase two trials starting in the fall."

"Sure," he says. "You got my paperwork, right?"

I pull out his latest labs and say, "Well, there's a problem with your levels."

Scott looks concerned. "What problem?"

I point to the line measuring oxytocin. "See these numbers here? How they're increasing?"

He looks confused. I push the lab work toward him. "We think the gene that inhibits the release of oxytocin has been methylated."

Scott traces the line of numbers with his finger, from left to right. He looks up, worry spreading across his face. "Is that a problem? Is it dangerous?"

"No, not at all." I explain how methylation works and how life events can trigger a change. "In this instance, the methylation is actually allowing your body to do what it's supposed to do." I slip the labs back in the folder and look at him. "But we don't know if it will continue until the oxytocin inhibitor is completely dormant or if it will halt here, so we'd like to continue working with you and study the gene itself."

He looks at the picture of Mara, then back at me. "What would I have to do?"

"Pretty much what you're already doing. Blood draws, home visits. You'll even keep working with Jenna, who's going to spearhead it."

"Can I think about it and get back to you?"

"Of course."

Just then, Sophie yells hysterically from the kitchen. "Dad! Come quick!"

Scott jumps, his body on alert. "What is it, Soph?" he calls.

"I spilled."

He relaxes and stands. "This will only take a minute."

"No worries. We're all done here," I tell him, packing up my things. "I can let myself out. It was good to see you."

"You too. Thanks for talking with me. It helps."

I smile. "I'm glad."

I linger by the door, listening to Scott and Sophie in the kitchen behind me, and when Sophie lets out a deep belly laugh, my final traces of worry dissipate. Sophie and Scott will be fine.

—

Jackie calls me a few days later. "What are you doing for lunch?"

"The usual. An apple and a bagel while I read reports."

"I'm bringing you lunch then," she says. "I need to get out of this house for a little while."

I look out the window toward the quad, recent sunshine and warmer temperatures making the idea appealing. "Okay. Can you come around one o'clock? I need to wrap a few things up."

"No problem."

We meet in a sunny corner within sight of my office window and settle on a bench shoulder to shoulder. She unpacks two large bags of food—fries, soda, and hamburgers from In-N-Out—and my mouth begins to water. She catches me looking at her and says, "What, did you think I was going to bring you a salad?"

I take a bite of my burger and close my eyes, focusing on the warmth of the sun on my shoulders. As always, the shadow of my secret sits between us. But I don't want to worry about what might happen, or could happen, or will happen. I just want to enjoy a sunny afternoon eating a hamburger with my best friend.

"Hey, Dr. Robson." Rebecca, from my Bio 101 class last fall, approaches us. I haven't seen her since last semester.

"Rebecca. How are you?"

She stands in front of us, squinting into the sun. "Good," she says. "I wanted to tell you I took your advice. I sent off for one of those DNA tests and got it back. No major genetic mutations, though I need to be careful about high blood pressure."

I smile. "You and everyone else in the world."

"And no biological relative hits. Yet," she adds. "Anyhow, I wanted to tell you that your class was my favorite last semester."

I smile and take a sip of my Coke. "Thanks. It's always nice to hear that."

"Seriously," she says, shifting her backpack to her other shoulder. "You made science seem real. Relevant to what's happening now. I've got Dr. Rivas this semester for organic chemistry, and it's everything I can do not to fall asleep."

"Organic chemistry will do that. Be careful though. I hear Dr. Rivas is famous for pop quizzes."

"We've already had three," she says. "I wish you taught more than just Bio 101."

Jackie follows our conversation, a smile curling the edges of her mouth.

"Anyway. Thanks. See you around."

"Stick with the science, Rebecca," I call after her. "I'd love to see you in my lab someday."

Rebecca turns and grins. "I'd love that too."

When Rebecca's gone, Jackie says, "That was nice."

I take another bite of my burger. "She's a great kid. That's why I love teaching. You've got a captive audience who think they have to laugh at your jokes in order to get an A."

Jackie shakes her head. "No. That's not a student sucking up. That's someone whose life was changed by you."

I squint across the quad. "I taught her biology. I doubt that was life-changing."

Jackie rummages in her bag for some napkins and hands me one. "I'm not saying the biology was life-changing," she says. "I'm saying *you* were. You have a way with people. You inspire me to want more from my own life, to seek something that's just for me, separate from being a mother and a wife."

She takes a sip of her soda and puts the cup on the bench next to her. Two of my grad students wander by, and one of them says, "Hey, Dr. Robson, good to see you know how to find your way out of the lab."

I wave, acknowledging that maybe I don't get out very much.

Jackie looks at me with a raised eyebrow. "See?"

I've always focused on my research. That's where I've put the bulk of my energy—and, to be honest, my ego. The teaching is fun, but it's not something I spend a lot of time thinking about.

I must look like I don't believe her, because she continues, "I don't know why you paint yourself as this closed-off, unforgiving person."

I shrug. "Because I am. I lost Liam because of it. I've always been that way."

Jackie shakes her head and stares across the quad. "I don't

agree, and I don't think your students would either. You lost Liam because you were afraid." She looks at me. "That's not a personality flaw. That's just being human."

"How do I stop then?" I ask.

Jackie tucks a flyaway piece of hair behind her ear and eats a french fry. "I don't know," she says.

I laugh. "Thanks a lot. You're so helpful."

She smiles. "At some point, you'll get tired of running," she says. "I just want you to see that you're worth it. You're funny and warm and generous. It's obvious to me why Liam loved you. I think it's likely he still does."

Once again, Jackie has shined a light into my life, showing me a better version of myself. One I never really saw, until she came along.

She bumps her shoulder into mine. "Finish your lunch, Dr. Robson."

THE SCIENCE OF FRIENDS

Neuroscientist Moran Cerf of Northwestern University has found scientific evidence to prove that long-term happiness depends on who you're friends with. He says that when two people are together, their brain waves will sync, becoming nearly identical. "The more we study engagement, we see time and again that just being next to certain people aligns your brain with them. This means the people you hang out with actually have an impact on your engagement with reality, beyond what you can explain. And one of the effects is you become alike."

Cerf concludes that if you want to lead a happy life, you should surround yourself with people who have traits you'd like to have yourself. Over time, you will begin to absorb them and exhibit them on your own.

Chapter Twenty-Nine

"Thanks so much for picking up Nick," Jackie says. I'm maneuvering through traffic, trying to hear her voice through my earpiece while the boys argue in the back seat.

"Be quiet, you guys. I can't hear." To Jackie I say, "No problem. We can stay as long as you need us to."

"Just until Beverly gets there. She shouldn't be more than twenty minutes behind you."

"Okay." I try to keep my tone light. Remembering how Beverly stared at Miles at the funeral, I'd prefer to keep my distance from her.

"I've got to go," Jackie says. "They're calling me in." This is the third interview Jackie's been on in as many weeks, all of them for small marketing positions she's overqualified for. She doesn't need the money—Aaron's life insurance will more than take care of them—but she needs something to keep her mind occupied when Nick is in school. *I'm going crazy, spending my days wandering around the house, half expecting my dead husband to call or walk through the door.*

"Good luck."

I glance in the rearview mirror at the boys. "Ms. Denny emailed earlier today about the science fair project due in a couple of weeks. We'd better get started on it tonight, Miles, or we won't have enough time." Normally we spend at least a month on it, and I'm embarrassed I've let the project go this long. The scientist's son will be the only one with a cookie-cutter project this year.

"It's almost done already," Miles says.

"What? How?"

"Liam and I have been working on it at Aunt Rose's for like a month."

"Great," I say, trying to keep the shock and hurt out of my voice. "What's it about?"

"We built a solar-powered heat lamp that can be used for an indoor garden."

I nearly crash into the car in front of me and slam on the brakes. "You what?"

"We built a solar-powered—" He starts again, but I cut him off.

"Why didn't you tell me?" What I've wanted to happen for so long—for the two of them to be friends—has been happening without my knowledge, and it cuts through me, this idea that maybe I was the problem. Not Liam. Not Miles. But me.

Nick's eyes shift between us. A horn honks, and I face forward again, accelerating through the last intersection before turning onto Nick's street.

"Are you mad?" Miles asks in a small voice.

"Of course not," I say. "I'm glad Liam's been helping you. I'm just sorry I haven't asked about it before now." I smile, as if to prove it.

—

When we get to Jackie's, I let us in with the key Jackie told me was hidden under the flowerpot next to the porch rail. The house is quiet, and the boys head to Nick's room.

"Don't get too busy with something," I call after them. "We're leaving as soon as Nick's grandma gets here."

I slide the key back under the pot and close the front door, unsure what to do with myself. I glance down the hall, tempted to peek into Aaron's study again, to see if I can find anything in the short amount of time I've got.

Just as I'm weighing the pros against the risk of being caught—by Beverly, no less—my phone rings. It's Rose.

"Thank God," I say. "You just saved me from myself."

"You're welcome," she says "What's going on?"

I fill her in on where I am and what I was about to do.

"Jesus, Paige. You need to get out of there."

I wander back toward the kitchen so the boys don't overhear me. "Beverly will be here soon."

"Beverly?" Her voice carries through the phone, so loud I have to hold it away from my ear.

"Shh," I say. I step into the powder room—the same one I found Aaron's blood-soaked towel in not so long ago, though it feels like an eternity. I close the door most of the way, leaving it open a crack so I can hear the boys.

"Look," she says. "I get why you stuck with Jackie after Aaron died. You're a good friend. But the longer you let this go on, the bigger the consequences. Enough already. You need to back away."

I lean against the counter, my back toward the mirror. "We've been over this, Rose, and I don't think you're wrong. But Aaron was Miles's father. The boys are brothers. And while Miles may not know that outright, he knows it on a subconscious level. He needs them, so I'm going to have to risk it."

Behind me, the bathroom door swings open, and Beverly stands there, her face a mask of shock and accusation.

I feel my legs go weak. "I need to go," I manage to say, and hang up the phone.

We stand there, staring at each other, until Beverly says, "I think you'd better explain yourself."

I start to slip past her, but she stops me, her hand strong and forceful, holding me in place. I gesture toward the living room. "Maybe we should sit."

"No," she says. "You can tell me right here. And then you'll leave this house and never return." Her voice is like steel, and I falter.

"It's not what you think," I start, but the rage on her face pulls me up short. "Please," I say. "I'll tell you everything, and if you still want us to leave, we will."

Beverly nods once and steps aside so I can exit the bathroom. She follows me down the hall, and we settle in the living room. I twist my hands in my lap, feeling sick to my stomach and unsure where to start.

"You said Aaron was your son's father," she says. "I'd like to know how that's possible. He was a good man who loved his wife and son."

"He was," I say. "He did. He didn't do anything wrong. In fact, it's the opposite."

And then I tell her, starting with my desire for a child and all I'd hoped to give him. And how that wasn't enough, until Aaron and Nick came along. As I talk, Beverly's expression begins to soften. Several times, she glances down the hall, where we can hear the low murmur of the boys' voices and an occasional laugh.

"Did Aaron know who you were?"

I think about that afternoon on the porch, of the rage that pushed me to tell Aaron, the words flying out of my mouth with no concern for anything other than punishing him with the truth.

"He did."

"What proof do you have?" she asks. "Did you run a paternity test?"

I think about the DNA test, but I'm unwilling to admit that to Beverly. Not when she's still so angry at me. "Aaron knew it was true," I tell her. "If you don't believe me, I can show you the baby picture that came with his donor profile. But I know you see the resemblance. I saw how you looked at Miles at the funeral."

Beverly's eyes dart toward the hallway and back again, so I continue, "I didn't go looking for him, if that's what you think. And I don't want anything . . . I signed something at the clinic. You don't have to worry about me coming after their money. I only want Miles and Nick to know each other. To know you, Leonard, and Jackie. I would never do anything to hurt her, or Nick. I have more to lose than gain if it were to come out."

Beverly stares out the window. "Does Miles know?"

"No."

She nods, as if this confirms something, but her face is unreadable. I imagine the death of your only child will do that to you. Leech out every ounce of feeling you have, leaving only a gaping emptiness behind.

"At the funeral," she says, her voice just barely above a whisper. "I couldn't stop looking at your son's eyes. At their shape, and the tilt of his head. That funny piece of hair that sticks out over his ear. Aaron had the exact same one. I thought my eyes were playing tricks on me, that I was losing my mind."

I take a deep breath and look up at the portrait of Aaron, Jackie, and Nick that hangs over the fireplace, the three of them smiling and happy, no clue what tragedy lay ahead, and ask Beverly the question I haven't been able to ask Jackie: "On the day Aaron died, was Jackie able to request a genetic test for Huntington's?"

Beverly shakes her head, her shoulders slumping. "She didn't. It didn't occur to any of us."

I let out a long, slow exhale. It's what I suspected all along. "Of course it didn't."

We sit in silence for a few minutes, lost in the memory of Aaron's last day. "You must be terrified," she says, and our eyes meet across the room.

"I am," I say.

Just then, Miles comes into the room. "Can we stay during Nick's piano lesson so I can keep working on the robot? Nick says it's only a half an hour. It'll take me at least that long to build the base."

He stands just a couple of feet away from Beverly, and her hand reaches out, as if to smooth his hair, but then lowers to his shoulder, where she pulls an invisible piece of lint off his shirt.

He turns to her and smiles. "Hi," he says. "You're Nick's grandma, right?"

Beverly nods, unable to tear her eyes from his face, and it's everything I can do to hold myself together. "We need to go," I say to him.

I start to stand, but Miles slips away, calling over his shoulder, "Okay, just five more minutes."

I sink back down, looking at my hands and giving Beverly a chance to compose herself. "You can get to know Miles if you want," I tell her.

Beverly's eyes drop to her lap. "As much as I'd like that, it's probably not the best idea." She looks up at me, her eyes distant. "I wonder if it's wise to let the boys be as close as they are."

"Please don't suggest that," I say.

"I have to protect Jackie and Nick," she says. But her words are flat. "I know you don't want to hurt Jackie, but you can't possibly think she won't find out. Miles looks exactly like Aaron. If she doesn't recognize it now, she will as he gets older."

"The boys need each other. They're best friends." *They're brothers.*

Beverly closes her eyes, as if she's fighting an internal battle. When she opens them again, she says, "I know your friendship means a lot to Jackie, but if she were to discover the truth, it would destroy her and taint any memories she has of my son. Aaron decided not to tell her, and we have to respect that."

"What didn't Aaron tell me?"

Our heads snap around. Jackie is standing in the doorway, the piano teacher hovering behind her.

Beverly and I glance at each other, horror mirrored on our faces.

"Nick," Jackie calls over her shoulder. "Mrs. Snyder is here."

She stands in the entryway, her eyes darting between me and Beverly.

Beverly looks at me, wide-eyed.

"Paige," Jackie says. "Tell me what's going on."

Nick passes behind her on his way to the back of the house, and soon the sound of melodic scales fills the air.

"Mom?" Miles appears in the doorway next to Jackie. "I thought you said we were leaving."

My throat closes up, and I swallow hard. "You said you wanted to work on that robot base. Give us five minutes."

After he's gone, Jackie says, "You guys are scaring me." She's still standing in the entryway, her coat on, purse gripped tightly in her hand. "What's going on?"

Beverly shakes her head, begging me to stay quiet. My mind

is blank, any believable lie outside of my reach. I press my lips together, wishing I had left when I had the chance, wishing I had convinced Jackie to cancel the piano lesson and let Nick come home with us instead. But we would have arrived at this moment eventually. If not today, then some other day.

"Paige, just say it," Jackie says.

I look at Beverly again, but she refuses to catch my eye. I don't have a choice. "Aaron was Miles's biological father."

Confusion flits across Jackie's face, and she shakes her head. "That's impossible. You used a sperm donor." Her eyes shift from me to Beverly. "Right?"

"I did. Aaron was the donor."

Jackie bursts out laughing, sinking into a chair. "Impossible," she declares. "Aaron never donated sperm. I would have known. He would have told me. Beverly?"

Beverly stares at her hands, folded in her lap, not looking up.

Piano music swirls around the room.

When it's clear Beverly isn't going to tell her I'm wrong, Jackie whispers, "Are you serious?" The confident facade slips off her face, replaced by horror. She looks at me. "Did you . . ." She trails off. "Did you come looking for him?"

"No. I found out by accident."

"When?" Her voice is faint, shadowed with fear. "Did he know?"

I nod, unable to admit my betrayal aloud. "After the Turner House beach party."

Shocked, she looks between me and Beverly, as if she's hoping one of us will break down and tell her it's all a joke. "You've known since November? Why didn't he tell me?"

"He said he was going to."

I can see her mind running through the events of those last

weeks and her realization that he didn't have time to tell her. She buries her face in her arms. I make a move, but her hand shoots out to stop me. "I need you to leave."

"Jackie," I start, but she interrupts me, her voice shrill.

"I need you to leave."

Beverly speaks. "Sweetheart, he never meant to deceive you."

Jackie barks a laugh. "Really, Beverly? Seems to me he had ten years to bring it up." She glares at me, and I shrink away. "When you told me you'd used a donor, I kept that to myself. It was your business, and it wasn't my place to tell anyone—not even Aaron." She gives a bitter laugh. "And all this time, you knew my husband was the father of your child." She shakes her head. "I can't believe how fucking stupid I've been." She pinches the bridge of her nose. *"Dammit!"* she yells.

The piano notes stop.

"Jackie, listen. I had no idea when I met you." I fight back tears, desperate to make her understand. "He was worried about having the Huntington's gene. He asked me what his ethical obligation was in relation to the clinic and what it meant for any kids conceived with his sperm. I only put it together because he donated to the same clinic I used."

She explodes off her chair. "Get out of my house!"

I can hear Mrs. Snyder murmur something to Nick, and he resumes playing, jumbled and off-key.

"Both of you," Jackie roars. "Get out!"

"Mom?" Miles stands in the doorway to Nick's room, his voice scared and uncertain.

Jackie looks toward him, then at me, her eyes cold.

"Go to the car, honey," I say, trying to sound normal, but my words are strangled. I can't leave until I can make Jackie see that I never meant to hurt her.

Beverly's cool hand lands on my arm. "Come on," she says. "She needs some time."

She guides me away from Jackie. Miles stands at the front door, waiting, and Beverly falters. She looks like she wants to hug Miles, but then glances at Jackie and steps away.

"Why is Jackie yelling like that?" he asks.

"She's just sad," I tell him.

"I'll stay with her and try to talk to her," Beverly says. "She'll be okay."

I glance back through the arch that connects the entry and the living room, where Jackie is slumped over, sobbing into her hands, her coat still on and her purse spilled open at her feet.

"Give me your number," Beverly says. "I'll call you."

I search my bag for a card and hand it to her.

"I'll be in touch," Beverly says, opening the door and ushering us out.

Outside, the sun is bright, and I have to squint. Nick's piano lesson fades away as we walk to our car, the distance between Jackie and me growing with every step.

———

The next day, despite a full day in the lab, teaching a class, and preparation for phase two, nothing can quiet the echo of Jackie screaming at me to get out of her house. I know Beverly said she needed time, but I can't focus on work while Jackie is out there, hating me. I have to fix this. I slip out and drive back to her house.

The curtains are drawn. Either she's not home or she's hiding.

I ring the doorbell, straining to hear any sound from inside. I knock, softly at first, then louder. Finally, I hear shuffling and step back as the door opens. Jackie peeks out at me, her red-rimmed eyes squinting in the light.

"Go away." She swings the door closed.

I hold my hand against it, pushing it back toward her. "We need to talk," I say.

She lets out a bark of laughter that might also be a sob. "*Now* you want to talk about it? You kept this enormous secret from me, allowed our friendship to grow around it. You intended to hide it from me forever. But now you want to talk." She swings the door wide-open and gestures with her hand. "Fine. Come in. *Let's talk.*"

She's wearing dingy socks and a long T-shirt that hangs to her knees. She glares at me, challenging me to say something as she curls her legs under her on the couch. I stare at my knuckles, turning white in my lap, searching for something to say that will fix this.

"Well?" she asks. "You begged to talk, so talk."

"I'm so sorry," I whisper, the words slipping out.

Her eyes are hard. "Just tell me. When you figured it out, why didn't you walk away?"

I came here to fix things, but all I can offer are slippery excuses. "I should have. But you're my best friend. The boys are best friends." I'm crying now. "I should have walked away, but I couldn't. I didn't want to lose you. I didn't want Miles to lose the only friend he's ever had." I press my fingers over my eyes, trying to compose myself. "Jackie, please just let me—"

"What?" Her voice is harsh. "Think for a minute what has just happened to me. To my child. My husband lied to us—for years. He left me to discover, in the most horrific way possible, that he had a child with another woman. Many other women, actually." Her voice cracks, and I try to jump in, explain that he never had a child *with* me. But she keeps talking, louder now so that any words I might say wouldn't be heard. "I wanted more kids. I craved them. And to discover my husband has them, just not with me—" She wipes away the tears falling down her cheeks. "You can say what you want about how it all happened, that you picked him from a database and how the rest was just coincidence, but it doesn't erase the fact that *you have a child with my husband*. It doesn't undo the fact that he kept this from me, hid it like a dirty little secret. And now you want to talk about it, to figure things out so that everything will be okay." She laughs. "Paige, this will never be okay."

"It has to be," I plead. "Miles and I need you."

She looks at me with pity. "I found his ACB file, you know. I made a call to the clinic. He fathered nine children. *Nine*. Miles isn't the only one." She shakes her head in disbelief. "And now *I* have to be the one to clean up the mess." Tears tumble down her cheeks, and I want to go to her, hug her, but I'm frozen in my chair.

Jackie closes her eyes. "Aaron is ours. Mine and Nick's. He's supposed to belong to *us*. But now he belongs to nine others."

She's right. Miles, Nick, and those other eight children all share Aaron's genetic code. Jackie has nothing.

I can see her shutting down, but I can't let the conversation end until she understands. "It's my fault Aaron didn't tell you. I was angry that he refused to get tested, and I threw it in his face. It was unfair to tell him that way, with no warning, no context. He was stunned. But his first concern was you." I think about the conversation on the side of the hill at Nan's party and the way he smiled when I talked about Miles. I take a ragged breath. "Go ahead and be angry with me, but please don't shut us out." In a softer voice I say, "The boys are brothers. Don't punish them for a decision Aaron made."

"Get out," she says in a low voice. This isn't the hysterical yelling of yesterday. This is a woman who has reached her limit. Her anger rolls over me, and I step sideways, trying to stay strong.

Desperate, I say, "You said you'd have forgiven Aaron anything."

Jackie's expression is hard and uncompromising. "I forgive *him*. I don't forgive you."

Her words pierce me, slicing through any hope I had. "I was just trying to protect you," I whisper.

She stares at me, saying nothing, and I have no choice but to leave.

Two days later, she's pulled Nick out of school and disappeared.

PHYSICAL SYMPTOMS IN THE LAST TWO TO THREE MONTHS OF LIFE

Fatigue: Try to balance rest with activity. Only undertake activity if you're feeling up for it or if it's very important. Remember, your energy gets spent more quickly and takes longer to build up.

Pain: Stay on top of your pain medications and be as specific as you can with your doctor about where you're feeling pain, how severe it is, and what makes it feel better.

Appetite changes: You're moving less, and probably eating less too. You will get full faster, and your body will not get the complete benefits of nutrients because your healthy cells are competing with the cancer cells for important resources.

Problems breathing: Sometimes you will feel like you can't get a full breath or that your lungs have fluid in them. Try sitting up with pillows propped behind you. Sometimes a fan blowing in your face helps make you feel like you're getting more air. Breathing and relaxation exercises also help.

Chapter Thirty

Bruno has kicked me out of the lab. *Figure your shit out*, he said. *Stay on email, and I'll do the rest*. I learned a long time ago that it's pointless to argue with him.

Ever since Jackie left a week ago, I've been useless. She just took off. No goodbye. She unenrolled Nick from school and disappeared. Miles is devastated and spending recess alone again. When I try to engage him in conversation, he tires quickly, slipping back into one-word answers. Gone is my curious child who would talk for the entire ride home, barely pausing for breath. I blame Jackie, but most of all I blame myself.

The only ray of hope is what Rose tells me is happening at her house. "He and Liam work on the solar-powered lamp together. They don't talk," she clarifies. "Just work. But I think Miles is going to be okay." I want to be grateful that my son is finding comfort in spending time with Liam, but it's left me feeling stranded and alone. "And what about Dad?" I'd asked, and she shrugged. "It's dinner. Dad mostly just watches the kids play. They don't pay much attention to him."

I twirl my empty Danish plate in a circle and curse Bruno again for forcing me to do my job from a coffee shop. The soft clatter of cutlery and conversation swirls around me as I try to focus on work.

I hear the door open and close but don't look up until I feel someone's presence next to my table.

My dad.

"Hey," I say.

"May I join you again?"

I think about how I felt after the sleepover—jealous and left out. "Sure." I clear away my computer and files.

He slips into the seat across from me, wincing as his body settles.

"How are you feeling?" He doesn't look well. I haven't seen him in several weeks, and it really hits me that his time is slipping away.

"Not too bad." He grimaces, adjusting himself in his seat. "Not great though," he admits when he looks up at me.

"Do you want anything to eat?" I ask.

He shakes his head. "Not much of an appetite these days. My morning toast can carry me all the way through lunch."

"What are the doctors doing for you?"

"Keeping me comfortable," he says. "Though to be honest, it's been a long time since I've felt anything like comfort."

"Can they do anything else?"

"Not without hospitalizing me, and I don't want that." He signals the waitress and orders tea. "So. Trying to clear your head again?"

"Something like that," I say.

He arranges his silverware next to him.

"Sometimes, it helps to get an outside opinion," he offers.

I think about what's happened, how much I've lost. At the root of it all stands my father and his choices. And because I have nothing left to lose, I tell him about Aaron and Nick, and Jackie leaving town.

"You can't blame her for going," he says.

I sit back in my seat and stare at him. "Of course *you* wouldn't."

He shrugs. "It's a lot to look at every day, that's all. People only want to live with lies of their own creation."

His tea arrives, and he carefully doctors it with cream and sugar. "My father used to say the way a person took their tea was an important litmus test for their personality." He spends a few more moments, stirring and pausing, stirring and pausing.

"What did he think about the way you do it?" I ask, feeling bad that I know almost nothing about his own father, other than what he told us at Thanksgiving.

My father shrugs. "I don't know. I was never invited to have tea with him." He taps his spoon against the side of the cup and sets it in the saucer. His hands tremble as he lifts the cup to his mouth, and for the first time in my life, I see him as a person with his own story, an accumulation of joy and pain and life experiences that have defined him. If pressed, I don't think I could tell you a single one of them.

"Tell me more about your parents," I say.

He sets his tea down again. "My father worked and drank. My mother was emotionally unavailable. They taught me to be self-sufficient and essentially left me alone."

"That must have been hard." I try to imagine him as a lonely little boy instead of the man who derailed my childhood.

"I don't remember thinking much of it. It was just normal."

I've never asked my father why he left us, afraid of what he might say, convincing myself that it wouldn't change anything anyway. But now I realize time is slipping away and soon I'll never have the chance to find out.

"So if your own father was so awful, why didn't you do a better job?"

He looks across the café, through the scattered customers in various stages of their meals, their conversations low and steady. "I wanted to be different," he says. "But I didn't know how. I couldn't trust myself not to become my father."

"But in not trying, you did just that."

He takes another sip of tea. "It's interesting, isn't it, that despite our very focused efforts, we end up like our parents anyway."

"I wouldn't say I'm like Mom."

He gives a short raspy laugh, which evolves into a cough. Once he's recovered, he says, "Rose has turned into your mother. You, though, have turned into me."

I nearly leap out of my seat. "Hardly," I say, trying to keep my temper in check. "I haven't abandoned my child."

"You're the opposite side of the same coin." When he sees I'm about to argue, he holds up his hand. "I mean no offense. I understand why you don't want to be compared to me. You're certainly a better parent than I was. But look at how you isolate yourself."

"What the hell are you talking about?"

"You don't trust yourself to let people in. You don't want them to see that you're flawed. You think they'll only love you if you're perfect." He holds my gaze, and I can't look away.

"Maybe I'm afraid they'll get up and walk out on me," I say, and my father has the grace to flinch. I shouldn't have to explain myself to him, of all people. But it's disconcerting that a man I barely know has such a handle on me, and that makes me worry that maybe we are more similar than I'd like to admit.

He takes a sip of tea before continuing. "Fear kept me from parenting you girls. Fear I would ruin you. Break you. And yet, that's exactly what I did. You can't protect people from pain. It's inevitable."

This is what everyone's been telling me. First Liam and Rose, then Jackie, and now my father. "So now what?"

He gives me a wry smile. "You keep trying." He drinks the last of his tea. "You keep coming back."

His cell phone buzzes, and he pushes his cup to the center of the table and slides to the end of the booth. "If you'll excuse me, my Uber driver's here. But I know you'll sort this out. You've always been resourceful."

In the span of twenty-five minutes, my father has explained why he left us and informed me that I've grown into my own version of him. I watch him walk toward the door, his words echoing in my head. *You keep coming back.* Is that what he was doing every time he returned? Trying again to make a place for himself in his family?

I never thought about what it cost him to return again and again, always wondering if this time it would stick or if he would be rejected once and for all.

———

Over the next couple of weeks, my father becomes the most consistent thing in my life. I return to the café every morning and set up my laptop, telling myself I'm getting out of the office so I can think, when really I'm hoping my dad will show up for his tea and Danish.

I don't know if he comes looking for me or if it's a routine he's developed and I happened to slip into it. We don't discuss it, and I try not to think too much about why I keep showing up. Mostly, we talk about unimportant things.

"Tell me the worst thing you ever did as a kid," I say one morning.

He laughs. "What kind of a question is that?" he asks.

"Just tell me a great story," I say. "I want to know what kind of a kid you were."

My dad stirs his tea, thinking. "I once stole my dad's car and took it all the way to Mexico with John Spencer." He sets his spoon down and takes a drink. "When we got back, our fathers were waiting on the front porch."

"What'd they do?"

"Took us into the garage and beat us with a belt."

I wince. "Gina Ferrar and I did the same thing when Mom and Rose went to Florida for a cheerleading competition."

"You're kidding me," he says, a grin spreading across his face.

"Nope. But Mom never found out."

"Clever girl," he says.

Clever girl. His words shoot straight to my center, glowing like warm embers.

Another time, we talk about his older brother, my uncle Paul, who died when my dad was six.

"My father was never the same after that. Nothing pleased him. I could never work hard enough or get good enough grades. Everything I did was a reminder of something Paul never got to do. After a while, I just stopped trying." He looks at his hands, decades older than Paul's would ever grow. "The thing is, no one ever thought it might have been hard on me. That I lost something important too."

Another morning, we talk about Miles. "He's an extraordinary child," my father tells me. "You're a terrific mother. Miles is kind and funny and smarter than any kid I've ever met. You're doing an incredible job with him."

Tears spring to my eyes, and I blink them away. What my father thinks of my parenting shouldn't matter. But it does. I'm rais-

ing this amazing child all by myself, and it's rare for anyone to stop
and acknowledge it. Sure, my mother comments on how hard it
is every now and then, or Rose will say she doesn't know how I
do it, but no one has ever spelled it out for me in quite this way.
Leave it to my father to be the one who finally gives that to me.

"Thanks, Dad."

The best conversations are when my father talks about things
I have no memory of. "Do you remember when I took you and
your sister to the circus?" he asks one day.

"You never took us anywhere," I tell him.

"Not true."

"You took us to a bar once," I say, and he flinches, chuckling.

"Well, one time I took you girls to the circus. You wanted to
see the elephants. The problem was, the clowns came out first,
and you got so scared you hid beneath the bleachers and missed
the entire thing."

This makes me wonder what else happened, what other things
my father did right that have been shoved aside and lost forever.

Sometimes I think of how he might describe what we're
doing right now, in the coffee shop. *Remember how we'd meet every
morning in the coffee shop to talk? It was our secret,* he would say. *Just
the two of us. I remember, I was dying of cancer at the time.*

The more time I spend with my father, the more I can see how
sick he is. We don't talk about it though. We only tell stories about
ourselves, laying them like stones on a pathway so we can find our
way back to each other again. And I feel lighter. When you spend
your life carrying anger around like a backpack, an extraordinary
thing happens when you finally set it down. The world becomes
brighter and easier. It was scary to take the risk, but in doing so
I've reclaimed some of that bravery Rose swears I used to have.
And maybe, with enough time, I'll learn how to use it again.

But one morning, about three weeks after our first conversation, he doesn't show up. I wait, drinking tea and flipping through my files, which are nothing more than props at this point. I check my phone and realize with a lurch I've turned it off. "Shit," I whisper, hoping I haven't missed a call from Bruno or Miles's school.

When it turns on, I see I've missed a string of texts and several calls from Rose. But there's only one voice mail from an hour ago.

It's Dad. You need to come.

The drive to my mom's is a blur, and I somehow manage not to get pulled over. Despite his absence throughout my life, my father has been a constant shadow, a visible lack of light. And it wasn't until recently, when I finally gave him space in my life, that I realized how much I still need from him. I want more of his steady, calm demeanor, an antidote to my own manic anxiety and overthinking. *You keep coming back.* That sentence has somehow come to define him. To define us. I fight the thought that it might be too late, that I might have unknowingly already said my last goodbye.

When I get there, Henry opens the door, and I fall into his hug. "They're in your mom's room," he says, gently nudging me down the hall. I find her and Rose huddled together on a chair, my father asleep in her bed, and an enormous, tattooed man in scrubs taking his blood pressure. My mother looks exhausted, and guilt scorches through me for not supporting her as I should have. Rose holds her hand and leans her head on my mother's shoulder. I hesitate in the doorway, unsure whether I belong here. As far as they know, I've had nothing to do with my father since his return. We both protected our time together, like an artifact, afraid too much attention might shatter it.

But when my mother sees me, she cries out, holding her arms open, forgiving as always of my hard heart. I sink into them, letting her comfort me. I begin to cry, softly at first, but harder as she holds me, murmuring that she loves me.

I pull myself together and ask, "How is he?"

My mother takes a tissue from her sleeve and wipes her eyes. "He's in and out of consciousness. Oscar thinks he has hours, at most."

At the mention of his name, the man turns toward me and offers a kind smile. "It's good you're here," he says. "Even though he's asleep, he can still hear your voice. It's important to say goodbye to him. It will help him transition better."

"What happened?" I want to say he seemed fine yesterday, that he was still able to get around, still able to talk. I thought he had at least another month. But I don't say anything. I want to hoard for myself all the small things we discussed, his stories, his expressions. They belong to me.

"When he woke up this morning, he was incoherent," Rose says. "He was growing bloated and jaundiced, and we knew his liver wasn't working anymore. But the confusion, the inability to stand and talk . . ." She reaches out and takes my mom's hand.

Hepatic encephalopathy. It's irreversible. I've wasted so much time and given him so little, even after I let him in. But then anger surges through me. However much time I wasted, he wasted more. Decades. His advice now seems self-serving.

You keep coming back. I want to add, *When it suits you.*

"Can I have a minute alone with him?" I ask.

This request sends my mother into a fresh round of tears. "Of course, honey," she says, her voice strained and thick. "We'll be right outside." Rose squeezes my hand as they walk out.

I stand over my father, unsure of what to do. I look over at Oscar, who's wrapping the cord around the blood pressure machine. He looks at me with gentle eyes that have probably watched this scene play out a hundred times. "Just talk to him," he says. "He'll hear you. I promise."

I nod, and Oscar leaves, closing the door softly behind him.

My father sleeps, emaciated and small, though his stomach looks as if he's six months pregnant. Whatever anger I felt toward him a moment ago fled as quickly as it came. There's still so much I need him to tell me. He figured out a way to come back. I need him to tell me how to do that with Jackie and Liam.

I whisper, "Dad?"

He doesn't respond. I can barely detect the rise and fall of his chest.

I can't even begin to wrap my mind around the fact that this will be my last conversation with him, that I will no longer be waiting for the next time he rolls into town. He will leave, and this time he won't come back.

"Dad?" I say again. When I don't get a response, I sit on the edge of the bed and take his hand. My tears come fast and hot, and I lean down, pressing my ear against his chest. His heart beats a steady rhythm, and it comforts me. He's not gone yet. If his heart still beats, he can still hear me.

"I'm glad you came back," I say.

His hand tightens against mine, and I sit up again, squeezing back. Rose's words float back to me. *This isn't about forgiving Dad . . . It's about not hating him when he dies.*

And I realize I do forgive him. He's a different person. I saw it with Miles. I experienced it myself. It's just too bad that it happened so late, that we lost so much time. I think back to the man he was just three short months ago, walking into Rose's kitchen and saying *Hello, Peanut.* My naivety is like a kick in the gut.

"I forgive you," I whisper.

His eyes open to slits. I consider calling my mom and Rose back into the room. But I don't know how long this moment of clarity will last, and I don't want to miss it.

He struggles to find words, and when he does, they come out slurred, as if he's drunk. "I need you to understand something," he says.

"Shh," I tell him. "Don't talk."

He shakes his head. "No," he rasps. I worry he'll wear himself out and lean closer so he doesn't have to speak louder than a whisper. I smooth what's left of his hair across his forehead, and those familiar blue eyes linger on mine. "I went looking for you."

I wonder if the painkillers are making him confused. "What?"

"In the coffee shop," he whispers. "I knew you'd be there." He coughs, and I wait. When he catches his breath, he says, "I knew you were never going to find your way back to me, so I had to find my way back to you." He closes his eyes and smiles. "I wasn't sure it was going to happen," he tells me. "But you were worth the wait."

He closes his eyes, and soon he's asleep again. I sit there, tears streaming down my cheeks, and hold tight to his hand, savoring the warmth and willing the blood to keep pumping, the heart to keep beating. I'm not ready to let him go. But as always, I don't get a say.

When it's clear he's gone deeper into sleep, I whisper, "Goodbye, Daddy. I love you."

I leave him, seeking the comfort of my mother and sister, who wait for me in the living room. Forty-five minutes later, my father's gone.

MEMORY

There are about seventeen genes that are crucial to laying down memories. When you learn something, a gene in your brain is activated, and your synapses create a memory.

Most people assume memories build up over the course of a lifetime and then disappear with death. I think of all the memories my father never got to share with me. What were his school years like? Who was his first love, his first heartbreak? New research is showing that some memories can pass through generations. Certain experiences can embed themselves in our genes, causing a methylation, a change in our genetic makeup, which then gets passed on to offspring. This accounts for why some people have phobias or stress disorders without a specific trigger.

When we learn something, it becomes a memory that we can access to inform future decisions and behaviors. Repeated enough, that learning becomes instinct—the accumulation of memories passed down through the generations. Instinct is the dog biting a child who tries to take its food. It's the zip of adrenaline when someone follows us down a dark alley. It's the monarch butterfly, traveling tens of thousands of miles with nothing to guide it but a whispered memory embedded in its genes.

Chapter Thirty-One

After Dad died, Mom didn't want to be alone in her house, so we all reassembled at Henry and Rose's, where we talked about Dad late into the night. I stayed quiet and listened to their stories about outings with the kids, funny things he said, or habits he had that I never knew about. I expected to feel a sharp pain at all I missed, but I just felt numb. I kept the last few weeks we spent together to myself, unwilling to share, ashamed of how few memories I had.

Now I sit in my pajamas, nursing a cup of coffee while the rest of the house sleeps, thinking of my father's last words: *You were worth the wait.* In the end, he didn't abandon me. He showed up, one last time, and rewrote the story.

And now it's my turn to rewrite mine. Voices echo in my head—the voices of people who love me, trying to tell me what I refused to believe—that if I take a risk on them, they'll be there for me. There's Bruno, telling me if I continue to treat Liam as an acquaintance, that's all he'll be. And Rose, who tried to tell me that the resolution I fought so hard to give Miles was actually the one I needed for myself. My mother, who told me I was afraid to see my father had changed, because then I'd have to do something about it. Jackie showed me I was lovable, and my father showed me I was worth it. And then there was Liam, who tried to make me see how hard I worked to keep him out of my life, while he worked so hard to stay in it.

Fear. It's exhausting.

With no clear plan of what I'll say, I reach for my phone and dial Liam's number. When he answers with his familiar *Hey*, my heart melts. *Hey*. What he used to say in the morning, after nights Miles slept at Rose's. Liam, on the pillow next to me, hair messy, eyes half-closed, and smiling. *Hey*. What he used to say when I'd open the door and find him leaning against the frame, head tilted and that smile he reserved just for me. *Hey*.

I fall apart, deep sobs stealing my voice.

"Paige?" he asks, panicked. "What's wrong? Are you okay? Is it Miles?"

"We're okay," I manage to say. "My dad died last night."

He sighs. "I'm so sorry," he says.

The silence stretches between us, thin and tenuous. I think about how my father sought me out, putting himself in my path so I couldn't avoid or ignore him.

"Will there be a service?" Liam asks.

"He didn't want one." I fight the instinct to gloss over the pain and appear strong. "I miss you," I blurt out.

There's a long pause before Liam says, "I miss you too."

I push forward, equal parts terrified and exhilarated, as if I were stepping onto a high wire, with nothing below me except sharp rocks. And maybe sharks. "I don't expect you to forgive me, but do you think we could start spending time together again?"

He hesitates, and I cringe, realizing that yet again, I'm holding myself back and not asking for what I want. But I also know I can't do this over the phone. I need to be able to see his face, to look in his eyes when I ask him to come back.

I hurry to clarify before he can say no. "I just . . . would love to see you. Not in passing, not as part of a larger gathering, but just the two of us."

"I'd like that," he finally says, and I release the breath I'd been holding. "Call me when things settle down."

It's a start.

———

"Paige, right? Miles's mom?"

I turn away from the barista who just took my coffee order, to the woman in line behind me. She's petite with short blond hair pulled into a tight ponytail. She looks vaguely familiar.

"Isabella," she says. "Trevor's mom from karate."

I smile and step out of the crowd of people until my order is ready. "Right," I say.

"Decaf, black," she says to the barista and then she joins me. "Does you son go to school around here?"

"He's at Elmwood. How about Trevor?"

She accepts her coffee from the barista with a smile. "He's at Saint Anthony's."

I reach across the counter for my drink, and Isabella says, "Have time to sit? I'm trying to make more time for myself these days. It's always go-go-go. But it won't kill me to take a few minutes, sit down, and enjoy my coffee before I get back to it." She pulls out a chair and gestures to the one across the table. "Please."

Since Jackie left and my dad died, I've slipped into ten-hour days, as comfortable as an old shoe, trying not to think about how much I miss Jackie's texts and calls, or the black cloud of my father's absence that hovers over me. I haven't had the nerve to call Liam again, afraid to seem too eager too soon. But if Jackie taught me one thing, it was to get out of my head. To be more of a human and less of a machine. "Sure," I say. Maybe I can make a new friend. Find someone to fill the hole that Jackie's left.

I sit across from her and take a sip of my coffee, suddenly feeling awkward. Was this what it was like at first with Jackie? Me fumbling around for something to talk about? I flash back to the school picnic, to how nervous I was, and think, *Yes. That's exactly what it was like.*

Isabella smiles, and I smile back, fighting the urge to check my watch and make my exit. I need to do this.

"So Trevor just loves Miles," she says.

I'm trying to think of a time when Miles has given Trevor anything more than a cursory glance, but I can't. "Same," I say, wishing I'd ordered a smaller coffee so I could finish it and be gone.

"Trev's taking karate to help with his anxiety," Isabella says, dumping a packet of sugar into her coffee and stirring it. "His therapist recommended it. Though his father thinks that's all in my imagination, but you know how it is. Your baby! You want them to be happy. Is Miles your only one?"

"Yes," I say.

"Then you know how it is! You only have one chance to get it right. Actually, I've got a meeting with Trev's teacher, about some incident." She looks incredulous. "They say he clogged a toilet yesterday when he was supposed to be in class. But I'm sorry, I feel like there has to be more to the story, you know? Like who was with him? Who gave him the idea? I can't imagine Trevor woke up yesterday and thought, *You know, I think today I'm going to vandalize the bathroom.* It's ridiculous."

I nod and try to imagine Jackie at the table with me. The way she'd probably press her knee up against mine, the way she'd roll her eyes at Isabella's obvious blind spot about Trevor, who is most certainly playing her for a fool. And all of a sudden, I feel the loss again, fresh and burning, and I need to get away.

I check my phone. "Oh gosh, I didn't realize it was so late," I say, grabbing my cup. Isabella looks up at me from the table, confused by my sudden departure. "I'm sorry. I have to get across town for a meeting. Good luck with Trevor. I'm sure it was a misunderstanding."

"Thanks," she says. "See you at karate."

I wave and push my way out the door and onto the sidewalk. I can't believe this is my life now.

———

I've gotten it into my head that before I can go any further with Liam, I need to make things right with Jackie. I don't want to tell him everything that happened until I can also tell him that Jackie's forgiven me. I call Beverly, hoping she can help.

"She asked that I not tell you where they went," Beverly says, though I can tell she disagrees. "I'm sorry, Paige, but I have to protect my relationship with them. I hope you understand."

"I do," I tell her. "It's just that Miles misses Nick so much. If they could at least be in touch—emails, phone calls." But I know I'm pleading my case to the wrong person.

"I wish I could help," she says.

"I do too." I stay on the line a few more seconds, wondering if she'll give me a hint, a little clue as to where to look. But she hangs up softly, as if she doesn't even trust herself to say goodbye.

Jackie must have gone home. She'd have to put Nick in school somewhere, and home is the most logical place for her to take refuge and regroup. I dredge up what she said about her mother, from that long-ago night over dinner. *She's reinvented herself. She's the head children's librarian at the Rockaway public library.* Long Island.

A quick Google search reveals the Rockaway public library's main branch website, and I find a name listed under *Head Children's Librarian.*

Marilyn Miller.

I pick up the phone and dial, checking the time to make sure it's not too late. But it's three o'clock on the East Coast, and Jackie's mother should be at work.

After navigating through the automated phone system, I get connected to the children's department. "May I please speak to Marilyn Miller?"

"This is Marilyn," the voice says. It's warm, like Jackie's.

"You don't know me, but I'm a friend of your daughter Jackie's, and I'm trying to reach her."

"What is your name, please?" Her voice is now guarded, the warmth gone. Of course, she knows about me.

"My name is Paige Robson, and I'm sure Jackie's told you all about me. I'm sorry to intrude on you at work, but I'd like to send Jackie a letter. Can you tell me your address so I can send it to her?"

Marilyn doesn't say anything for a few seconds, and I wonder whether we've been disconnected. Finally she says, "You can mail it to me here at the library. I'll give it to her, but I can't promise she'll read it." She gives me the library's address, and I quickly take it down.

"Thank you." It's not much, but I'll take it.

"Good luck, Paige. My daughter seems resolute in keeping you out of her life."

"I understand. Thanks again." I hang up and stare at the wall, fighting the urge to give up.

I address the envelope, checking and double-checking the address she gave me with the one on the website. When I'm done, I reread the letter, hoping it will work.

Dear Jackie,

I don't think I did a very good job of explaining myself to you. I understand why you're angry, and you have every right. I kept an enormous secret from you. But I thought I was doing what was best for Miles, just as you're doing for Nick now.

Before you knew us, Miles was a different kid—withdrawn and lonely. I worried about him constantly, and I had no idea how to help him. I wondered if knowing his father would make him more comfortable in the world, but there was no way for me to find him. I hoped someday our donor would contact us through the agency, but there was no guarantee. And then you and Aaron and Nick landed in our lives, and my child woke up.

I'm so very grateful to have known Aaron. He was a good man, so funny and smart and kind. In the short time Miles knew him, he blossomed. Aaron had the gift of intuiting what Miles needed, and he gave it to him. I can only imagine the tremendous loss you and Nick feel every day, and my heart breaks for both of you.

When Miles is older, I'm going to tell him the truth. He deserves to know he has a brother he already loves. You can make your own decisions, and until I hear from you, Miles will know to respect that boundary. But the boys share a history, a connection to one special person. I can understand your desire to maintain that connection for Nick alone, but genetics isn't something you can hoard. Each of the boys is his own unique version of Aaron, and they deserve to know their father through each other.

We both share the worry that one or both of the boys will carry the Huntington's gene. Your fear is my fear, and someday it will be the boys' decision to address it. Think about how much easier that will be for them to navigate with each other's support. Please don't make them go through it alone. At the end of the day, it's not about me, or you, or even Aaron. It's about Aaron's legacy that lives on through them. I hope someday you'll realize how lucky they are to have found each other.

The secrets I kept may seem unforgivable, but I was never trying to deceive you, only to protect you. I know I violated your trust and will understand if you want to cut me out of your life. But please don't punish the boys for something out of their control.

Despite everything, I have no regrets. I had the chance to know you, and that has been a gift.

Love,
Paige

I seal the envelope and decide to walk it to the mailbox in the student union. If I put it in our outgoing mail bin, there's no guarantee I won't lose my nerve and pull it out again.

The cold air bites through my thin sweater, and I hug my arms across my chest as I cut across the quad, past small clumps of students. "Hey, Dr. Robson," someone calls.

I think again of what Jackie gave me and of that day in the quad when she helped me see a better version of myself. When I reach the mailbox, I hesitate for a moment. But I shove the letter in and close the lid with a loud clang that vibrates up my arm. It's done. And I'm surprised by how powerless I still feel.

ANCESTRY

It used to be, if we wanted to know our ancestry, we had to rely upon the fuzzy memories of our grandparents, supported or disproven with family records and a bit of luck. Today, the study of ancestry has collided with science, allowing us to learn secrets our forbearers assumed would die with them—ethnicity, religion, paternity. Traces of the past are hidden in our genes, the remnants of our ancestors, alive and well inside of us.

Chapter Thirty-Two

Since calling him the morning after my dad died, I've been thinking about Liam on an endless loop. I break things down to their smallest parts, my mind working out the details the same way I do at the lab. Analyzing, cataloging, trying out different ideas until I hit on one I think might work. Liam complained that I always kept him on one side of the line, shielding him from the messy parts of my life. I thought I was protecting Liam from the chaos and Miles from having to adjust to an uncomfortable transition. But I was only protecting myself. And in the end, I still lost everything.

"I need to fix this," I tell Rose.

Rose looks at me from across her kitchen island, where she's decorating green cookies for Hannah's Saint Patrick's Day party at school next week. "Fix what?" She wipes her frosting-covered hands on a towel.

"Things with Liam."

Rose suppresses a smile. "It's about time," she says. "Do you want me to help?"

I give her an amused look. "I'm afraid to ask."

"I was thinking I could stand outside his office with a sandwich board and bell. *Please forgive Paige!*" She pretends to consult her calendar. "I could probably give you a couple of hours next Tuesday."

I laugh and steal a cookie. "No, thanks. Although I don't know how anyone could resist a middle-aged woman in a sandwich board."

"And a bell," she reminds me, snatching the cookie back.

—

I call him late at night, after Miles has gone to bed, my nerves jangling and pulling my thoughts in too many directions.

"Hey," he says.

"Hi." I take a deep breath and deliver the line I've rehearsed. "Sorry for calling out of the blue, but the Asian fusion cooking class is this Saturday." The words tumble out, too fast.

When the email reminder showed up in my in-box, I knew this was how I would approach Liam. Directly, with an invitation to spend time together. Just a few months ago, we'd both been looking forward to this class, and I'm hoping he'll still want to go.

"I know it's last minute," I continue. "But I checked the website, and the class is nonrefundable and nontransferable. I'm fine skipping it," I add, "if that's what you want to do. But I thought I'd ask."

"No. Um, wait. Thanks."

Something inside me shifts, filling me with relief when the refusal I expected doesn't materialize.

"Okay, sure. Let's do it." Liam's voice is cautiously happy. "I'm looking forward to *A Night of Asian Fusion*." He laughs, and I let the sound fill me. "Should I pick you up around six?" he asks.

My insides flutter. *I'm going to see Liam.* "That sounds good," I say. "See you then."

I hang up and stare out the window, wondering what he'll think when I tell him all that's happened, and remind myself that the mess was what he wanted all along.

—

When I open the door on Saturday and see Liam leaning on my doorframe, I go soft. I haven't seen him since before Christmas, and I'm reminded of how tall he is and how deeply the corners of his eyes crinkle when he smiles. "Hey," he says, and I have to fight the urge to fall into his arms.

"Hi." When he passes me, I can see the back of his hair, still damp from his shower and curling up at the ends. I want to run my fingers through it.

"*River Monsters,*" Liam says, walking straight to the couch where Miles is sprawled, watching TV. "Cool. Have you seen the episode about the monster that's been eating villagers in India for the past fifty years?"

Miles peeks over the top of the couch and asks, "Is that the one where it started out attacking the local dogs?"

My eyes dart between them, finally observing what I've only heard from Rose. A subtle ease threads between them, the high tension from last fall almost gone now.

"Yeah." Liam sits on the arm of the couch facing the TV. The narrator is talking about twelve rows of razor-sharp teeth, strong enough to rip out the bottom of a boat.

I edge forward. "I thought this show was about fishing."

Liam and Miles exchange a look, and then Liam says, "Fishing for monsters, maybe. The creatures on this show are insane."

"Like sharks?" I grimace, making Liam and Miles laugh at me.

Gemini wanders into the living room, a can of Diet Coke in her hand, her straw-colored hair pulled back into a tight ponytail. "Hey, Liam," she says. "Haven't seen you in a while."

Liam gives me a quick glance. "How are things at the gallery?" he asks her.

"Pretty good. We're featuring a show on abstract puzzles right now. You should check it out."

"That reminds me." Liam turns to Miles, reaches into his coat pocket, and tosses a colorful cube to him. "I brought this for you."

"What is it?" Miles sits up, turning it over in his hands.

"It's a Rubik's Cube. Here, let me show you."

Liam slides down onto the couch next to Miles and begins twisting and turning it, scrambling the colors into a hodgepodge. "You have to manipulate the squares so that all six sides are the same color again." His large hands move the pieces around, and I step closer to get a better look. Miles watches, riveted. I can see his mind waking up, cataloging every move Liam's hands make. His own hands twitch, and I can tell he wants to give it a try.

Liam holds out the cube, yellow side complete. "Getting one side is easy. The trick is getting all the sides without messing anything up. It's harder than it looks. When I was a kid, I was pretty fast. My personal record was three hours."

Gemini stands behind me and mutters, "Challenge extended."

I look at her, and she smirks, settling into a chair to read.

"Thanks." Miles turns the cube over in his hands, studying it from every angle.

"We'd better go," Liam says. "*Asian Fusion* awaits."

I lean over and kiss Miles. "We'll be back in a couple of hours."

"Have fun," Gemini says from behind her book.

Miles doesn't look up. He's completely absorbed in the Rubik's Cube.

———

We park a few blocks away, and Liam feeds a couple of coins into the parking meter.

"I'm glad we decided to do this," he says. His hands are shoved deep into his pockets, and gusts of wind from cars racing down the street blow my hair around my face. I wonder what he means. Glad we're spending time together or glad we're going to the class? Things with Liam were never confusing, but now I'm unbalanced, trying to figure out what he's saying.

"I'm glad too," I say, hoping he'll say more, but he doesn't.

We walk without touching, which is unnerving. Liam always made a point of holding my hand or wrapping his arm around me. Without that, I feel I might float away, like a balloon into the sky, and he would just watch me, eyes turned upward, hands still shoved into his pockets, letting me go.

Inside Culinary Masters is a giant industrial kitchen for demonstrations, and scattered around it are eight separate islands, each with a sink, cooktop, and assorted knives and chopping boards. Liam and I choose a space near the back and watch the other stations fill up with laughing groups out for a night of fun and food.

When it looks like everyone's arrived, a tiny man with jet-black hair and a white chef's coat enters and says, "Welcome to *Asian Fusion*. My name is Neil." His booming voice ricochets around the space. He shouts the words in the same way we've been shouting them, and I glance at Liam, who is trying to suppress a laugh.

"Well, we've been pronouncing it right," he whispers.

I press my lips together, trying to keep a straight face.

Neil points toward the ingredients and a list of instructions written on a large board in the front and continues to shout. "Asian fusion is a blend of Chinese, Thai, Indonesian, and Indian influences. Tonight we'll be making lettuce wraps."

"Does he have to shout?" I whisper.

"Shh," Liam says, his face serious. "I can't hear."

I almost dissolve in a fit of laughter.

Neil reviews the directions, but I keep eyeing Liam, who is turned toward Neil and pretending to listen intently, all the while stealing sideways glances at me and wiggling his eyebrows. No matter what happens later tonight, at least I'll have one final memory of us laughing together and having fun.

"Begin!" Neil shouts, making us both jump.

"What do I do?" I ask.

"Shred the carrots. I'll chop the garlic and ginger," Liam says, pulling a huge knife out of the block.

Neil wanders by and says, "Smaller pieces," directly into Liam's ear, startling him. He looks up at me and grins.

"You should be thinking about browning your beef!" Neil yells.

Liam grabs a skillet and heats up the peanut oil. He drops in the garlic and ginger, and a sweet fragrance surrounds us. I take a deep and steadying breath. Liam adds the beef to the sizzling pan. "Hand me that hoisin sauce?" he asks. "Wait." He squints up at the board. "I need five tablespoons of hoisin and one tablespoon of soy."

I measure each into a glass bowl and hand it to him. Our fingers touch, and I feel a warm fizz, making me want to inch closer to him.

But Liam seems unfazed. "Get started on the water chestnuts." He glances around at the other workstations. "I know this isn't a race, but I think we're winning."

I choose a knife and begin to chop. The salty scent of the beef is overwhelming, and my mouth waters.

Liam washes the lettuce and pats it dry with paper towels, and I crush the peanuts with the side of my knife. We don't talk much, just work in companionable silence. I find myself forgetting the last several months, like we skipped over everything—the camping store, Aaron and Jackie, our breakup—and landed here instead.

Soon we're assembling the wraps, piling a small mountain of the beef mixture on top of the lettuce leaves and topping it with shredded carrots, peanuts, and green onion. Liam clears a space on the counter, and we face each other and bite into our wraps.

"Oh my god," Liam moans.

Flavors explode in my mouth—salty and sweet with a hint of garlic and ginger. "Try to enjoy the fruits of your labor!" Neil shouts from behind us, causing me to nearly choke and Liam to almost spit his wrap out.

When Neil moves to the other side of the room, I ask, "How's work?"

"Pretty good," he says. "We're designing a new game that has a completely different consumer interface module."

"Which means?" I ask, taking another bite.

He smiles. "Basically, it's how the customer plays the game."

"Why can't you just say that?" I ask, laughing.

"We can, if we want to charge fifty percent less."

He holds up the last lettuce wrap and looks at me expectantly, and I nod, grabbing it. I was too nervous to eat today, and I'm starving.

"How are Jackie and Nick doing?"

"They're back east." I bite my tongue, trying not to dwell on this half-truth. This isn't the time or the place to explain things.

Liam wipes his mouth with a napkin. "How's Miles surviving that?"

"Not well. I'm surprised he hasn't mentioned it to you."

"We don't really talk much. I help him sometimes with his homework if I'm over at Henry and Rose's and he's there. I tell him about games I'm working on." He shrugs. "It's pretty one-sided."

"Thanks for helping him on his science fair project," I say. I pop the last of the wrap into my mouth and look around for a napkin.

Liam hands me one and says, "We're taking it slow."

I hesitate, thinking I've found my opening. But Liam reaches for the skillet, turns on the water, and starts to scrub, and my words dry up, fluttering away like leaves in the wind.

—

As we walk back to the car, Liam bumps his shoulder into mine. "I had a good time. I'm thinking about going to their Italian night so I can learn how to make pasta."

"Sounds fun," I say.

I wait to see if he'll invite me. But he's just making conversation, and my stomach sinks.

He unlocks the car and holds the passenger door open for me. I slide in, tucking myself in the corner of the seat. The ease I felt earlier has vanished, leaving only the minutes ticking down toward the evening's end, our time together nearly gone.

"Thanks for coming," I say.

"Thanks for inviting me." He looks at me with a half smile that reminds me of sleepy mornings and hot coffee and a time when it was easy to be in love.

—

When Liam pulls up in front of my house, I say, "Can you come in for a little bit? I need to talk with you about something."

A look of uncertainty passes over his face, as if he's not sure he wants to risk it.

"Please," I say. "I just need you to hear me out."

He cuts the engine and follows me to the front door.

I pay Gemini and thank her for staying with Miles. "Do you want something to drink?" I ask Liam when we're alone again, hovering in the door of the kitchen. "Beer? Water?"

"I'm good, thanks." He stays perched on the edge of the sofa, as if he might pop up and leave as soon as possible. I walk past the spot next to him that I wish I could take, to the chair opposite him. As I lower myself, my knee accidentally knocks a pile of mail off the coffee table and onto the floor.

I'd tossed the stack there earlier, not giving it more than a cursory glance. I'd been too excited at the prospect of seeing Liam to look through it. But when I pick it up off the floor now, one envelope catches my attention, or rather the postmark *on* the envelope catches my attention. Rockaway, Long Island. Jackie.

I flip it over, but there's no return address, so I tear it open just as Liam says, "I'm glad you invited me in. It's fun to watch you open your mail." I look up, relieved to see a smirk on his face.

"Hold on," I say. "I think this is from Jackie."

Liam watches as I pull out what looks like a photocopy of a genetic test. My eyes leap to the top, where I read Aaron's name.

"Oh my god," I say. I quickly scan the results. There at the bottom are the words: *less than 27 CAG repeats, negative.*

Negative. Aaron did not inherit the Huntington's gene from his father, and with less than twenty-seven repeats, Miles is safe too.

"What is it?" Liam asks.

Relief surges through me as I look up at him, tears welling in my eyes. "A gift."

Confusion flashes across his face. "What are you talking about?"

The worry that's been following me floats away, as if it was no more than a bubble. I can see the path in front of me now. Once I break down the wall, I'll finally be free to tell the story. Because that's all it is. A story, with a beginning, middle, and now, an end.

"Aaron was Miles's donor."

Liam recoils, clearly not expecting that. "What? How do you know?"

"I found out by accident." I tell him how Aaron sought me out for advice about Huntington's and his desire to keep his past a secret from Jackie.

"Wait, Huntington's?" Liam asks. His eyes dart toward Miles's room, and I hold up the genetic test.

"Aaron didn't have the gene," I say.

Liam looks confused. "I think I need you to start at the beginning."

I take a deep breath and tell him everything, from the chemistry between Miles and Nick through Jackie's discovery and departure. I even tell him about the DNA test I ran. If I want things to be different, there can't be a penalty box. Or any box at all.

When I'm done, Liam looks at me, the warm glow of the

table lamp illuminating his tired eyes. "Why didn't you tell me any of this when it was happening?" he asks.

This is the moment, the one in which I either step forward and let him all the way in, show him my uncertainty and fear, or I continue to pretend I have everything under control, with all the answers in my pocket.

Which is it, Paige? my father's voice asks.

"I didn't learn most of it until after we broke up. But the truth is, I was scared." I curl the genetic test between my fingers, unable to see the judgment—or rejection—in his eyes. "I never wanted you to think I didn't know what to do."

"You didn't trust me." His words are flat, which worries me more than if they were infused with anger.

"I *couldn't* trust you." My voice cracks, but I push on. "I didn't know how."

Liam shakes his head. "So why now? What's changed?"

I set the paper on the coffee table and look down at my empty hands. "Everything," I say. "Who I am. How I see myself. And how I see you. I know it might be too late, and maybe you don't want to put yourself through this again. But I'm done pushing you away, pretending I always know the answers. I'm tired." *He's not going to believe me. He's going to lecture me and then get up and leave.*

He shakes his head, frustrated. "What does that even mean?"

I don't have an answer. "My dad told me the best thing I can do is keep coming back. So that's what I'm doing."

I hold my breath, knowing it will crush me if he walks away.

"Your dad?" he repeats.

"I was able to get to know him, and learn some things."

"Like?"

I shift in my chair, itching to touch him, so I move to the

couch and sit next to him. "I hung on so hard to the belief that he could never change, which made me think that I couldn't either. That my flaws were something I had to live with, no matter the cost to you or to me. But I don't want to believe that anymore."

His voice grows softer, the anger ebbing away, replaced with regret. "How do I know that the next time things get hard, you won't turn away from me again?"

"You don't." My voice is no more than a whisper. "But I want the chance to show you." I study his face, the planes of it so familiar I want to run my fingers along them. "We can make a timeline," I continue. "Sit down with Miles and explain that we're going to do more together, that you're going to be a permanent part of our lives—if that's what you still want."

Liam gives an impatient sigh. "Don't do this because it's something I want," he says. "It has to be what you want too."

"It is," I insist, taking his hand and squeezing, hoping he'll believe me.

He shakes his head and pulls away. "You've said these things before, Paige, and then nothing's changed."

"This time will be different," I say. "I promise." I think back to the call I made the other day and what I've been avoiding since that first disastrous therapist at age sixteen. "If there's one thing these past several months have shown me, it's that I need to make peace with my past. The time with my dad made me realize it's not enough to box up the pain and shove it into a corner and consider it *dealt with* simply because it stopped muddying up my everyday life. I've found a therapist who specializes in childhood trauma, which is what I think happened to me. I have my first appointment next Tuesday."

I steal a glance, relieved to see his expression soften. "I think that's a good first step. And it's not that I don't want to believe you; it's that I can't. Not yet." Liam looks across the room, his eyes catching on something, and walks over to get a closer look. "Look at this," he says, bringing it back to me.

It's the Rubik's Cube, solved. I take it from him and turn it around, and he sits on the couch next to me again. The fact that he's just inches away from me makes all my nerve endings tingle.

We sit there in silence, my mind pinging through one topic after another—anything to keep him there a little longer. "I'm sorry I messed things up," I say. "I was afraid. I'm *still* afraid. But I'm going to stop running."

Liam takes the Rubik's Cube from me and places it on the coffee table, on top of Aaron's genetic test. He looks at me, and I search his face for any hint that he's forgiven me. But there is none. Maybe a softening in the eyes. And perhaps he sits a little closer on the couch. But I've said my part. I've laid everything down in front of him, and the only thing between us now is my honesty. I hope it's enough. I have to believe that it will be.

————

After he leaves, I pick up the printout again, reading it slowly and savoring the words. My eyes snag on the date of administration, and my breath catches in my throat. *November 10.* The day Aaron died. Did he schedule the appointment early in the morning? I imagine him in a sterile waiting room somewhere, anxious about what the test would reveal about his future, maybe worried about getting to work on time. If only he knew none of it mattered. That just a few hours later, he'd be gone.

A sob escapes me for everything we've lost and for Aaron's

final gift to us all. Miles won't have to face the horrific reality of Huntington's, and neither will Nick.

"Thank you," I whisper, and hope somehow he can hear me.

I search the envelope for a note from Jackie, some explanation why results that should have come weeks ago are only now arriving. Did she withhold them from me? But then I think back to that morning in November, the beginning of a nightmarish two months, culminating in Jackie's abrupt departure. I imagine somewhere in there, an anonymous envelope arriving and sitting in a large pile of mail, waiting to be sorted and forwarded. Or an email sitting in Aaron's now-defunct in-box. Regardless, I'm grateful she had the courtesy to let me know.

But her message is clear. With a negative result, neither of the boys carry the Huntington's gene and therefore won't need to rely on each other. Not now or at any time in the future.

Jackie is leaving everything in the past, including Miles and me.

I carry the envelope and test results into my bedroom and pull out my ACB file. I flip through it one last time, tucking Aaron's genetic test in the back and pushing the folder far into the corner of the closet shelf, where it belongs.

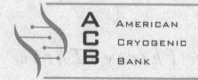

A
C
B

AMERICAN
CRYOGENIC
BANK

INTEROFFICE MEMO

From: Dale Whipple, CEO American Cryogenic Bank
To: All ACB staff
Re: New Client Protocol

With the advent and accessibility of direct-to-consumer genetic testing, we can no longer guarantee anonymity to our sperm and egg donors. Please make sure all participants understand this ***during their intake meeting*** and continue to reinforce it throughout the screening process. A waiver will be added to the donor paperwork. ***Please make sure it's signed and dated.***

Likewise, make sure parents using donor conception fully understand that their children's DNA will identify that they are not the biological parents, and they should ***strongly consider*** disclosing the use of a donor as early as possible.

Please direct them to our website for resources on talking to children about gamete donation, which should answer any questions they might have.

Chapter Thirty-Three

Five Months Later

I sit across from Bruno and Jenna in the student union, cups of coffee between us and students filtering around us.

I turn to Jenna. "Are you ready?"

She looks nervous. I remember that feeling well, the terrifying leap into publication, throwing my name out there for peer review, which could result in either a parade or a bloodbath. "Relax," I tell her. "You've done the work. Your findings are solid."

We're publishing what's happened with Scott Sullivan's inhibitor gene. Or rather, Jenna's publishing it, and I'm mentoring her through the process.

"It's just a first draft." She pushes a folder toward me.

"I'll read it and get back to you soon." I tuck it into my bag and stand, gathering my trash. "I've got to pick Miles up from his new friend Eli's house. Tonight, we're going to his first concert at the Hollywood Bowl for his birthday."

Bruno looks impressed. "Who are you seeing?"

"The LA Symphony performing *Star Wars*." When Bruno raises an eyebrow, I say, "What did you expect, Justin Bieber? Miles is still Miles."

Bruno cringes. "'Justin Bieber'? You're embarrassing yourself."

The day of Miles's birthday party is a typical late summer day, bright and hot. I haven't heard from Jackie since she mailed me the copy of Aaron's genetic test, but that doesn't surprise me. I'd mailed her an invitation to the party several weeks ago, addressed to her mother at the library. We never got a response. Every couple of weeks I drive past their house to see if they're back or to make sure she hasn't put it on the market. But it's always locked up, curtains drawn, unoccupied. I'm trying to practice acceptance. There may be nothing I can do about it now, but I'll never stop hoping.

I stand on Rose's back porch and survey the madness. Ten boys, in various stages of undress, tear around the yard, some in shorts and T-shirts, some shirtless in bathing suits, others wearing rash guards to protect against the hot sun. I find it incredible that Miles even *has* ten friends. Nick did this for him. And Liam. Their friendship has continued to develop, and Liam has given Miles opportunities to reach out to other kids in his class—surf lessons or video game previews at our house— slowly helping him develop the friendships that eluded him for so long.

And I've learned how to include Liam—to truly incorporate him into our lives instead of keeping him separate. It was slow going at first, both of us picking our way carefully through the wreckage and back to each other. But Liam is now a fixture in our lives—and our home—and at the end of the month, he's going to give notice on his cottage and move in with us.

Rose corrals some of the shirtless kids over to a table to apply liberal amounts of sunscreen. They wiggle, impatient to return to the game. Hannah and Mikey have disappeared with friends, claiming to be *too old* for a water balloon party, but they'll be joining us for a family dinner later. Miles screeches and laughs and careens around the yard, filled with joy.

I'm relieved to see him so happy. This morning, he'd mentioned how nice it would be if Nick could come today. I wish I could fix this for him, but I'm learning that I have to let life happen for Miles, including hurt and disappointment.

But for now, Nick seems forgotten. The last of the mothers have left, and I heave a sigh of relief. I'd specifically said *drop off* on the invitation, and my mind flits again to Jackie, imagining her here, drinking the sangria Rose mixed up for the adults, making snarky comments about some of the other mothers and their perfectly pressed yoga outfits that have never seen the inside of a studio. My therapist, Dr. Sheffield, wants me to start making more of an effort with the other moms, to widen my circle. And while I'll probably not embrace Trevor's mom, Isabella, as my new best friend, there are a few others from Miles's karate class I think might become friends. But I'm nervous, the way I would have been at age twelve, to approach them about socializing outside of class. A part of me wishes it could be as easy as it was with Jackie, that effortless connection that seemed to drive itself. But I also understand friendships like that are rare. There's no guarantee I'll find another one, and I'm going to have to be okay with that.

The boys are so loud that I almost miss the sound of the doorbell ringing. I do another head count—ten—and my stomach lurches.

When I open the door, Jackie and Nick stand on the porch. She looks the same, but Nick seems to have grown a foot. He grins and pushes past me. "Hey, Paige," he calls over his shoulder, rushing toward the sound of the kids laughing outside. I hear Miles scream his name and smile as I imagine their reunion. I'm certain it's better than the one I'm having on the porch.

Jackie stands, rooted to the spot. She doesn't smile, and her eyes remain covered by sunglasses. She holds a rectangular present in her arms, which she shoves toward me.

I want to grab her by the shoulders and hug her, but her posture is stiff and uninviting. "I'm glad you could make it," I manage to say.

She forces a smile. "Nick really wanted to come."

I wait to see if she'll say anything more. "Would you like to come in?" I step sideways, hoping she'll walk through the door. *Just come inside,* I silently beg her. *Please.*

She shakes her head. "I can't. I have a lot to do. We just got back yesterday."

"You're staying?" I ask, unable to keep the hope from my voice.

"For now. Look, I've got to run. I'll be back to pick him up by four." She gestures toward the package and says, "That's not really a birthday present. Nick has a gift card for Miles. That's . . ." She trails off. "You should open it alone." She turns toward her car and starts walking away.

I slip the gift onto the hall table and follow her to her car. When I get there, we stand, facing each other. Jackie wraps her arms around herself.

"I've missed you," I say.

She looks down the street and then back at me. "Look. I'm sorry, but I'm still not ready." I start to say something, but she interrupts me. "I know this isn't your fault. You're not the one who did this to me. But you're the one who's here. You're the one

who's going to make me think about it, every time I see you."
She sighs. "I'm not angry anymore. And I forgive you. But I can't
pretend it never happened."

"What made you come back?" I ask.

She leans against the car, her posture softening a little bit.
"Running away didn't fix anything," she says. "No matter where
I go, this will follow me. Leonard and Beverly need me. They
need Nick. And Nick needs that connection to Aaron."

"And where do I fit in?"

She looks down. "I don't know. Maybe someday we'll have
a different kind of friendship. But I'm not sure if it can ever go
back to how it was."

I nod, unable to speak. I get it. I'm just glad she doesn't hate
me anymore.

She continues, "I understand that I can't control the decisions
you make as a parent, but I'd like to ask that you not tell Miles
who his father was until the boys are older."

"Of course," I say. "Can the boys still be friends?"

She gives a sad smile. "As if we could stop them." She pushes
off the car and digs in her purse for her keys. "I'll be back at
four."

I stand at the curb and watch her car until it rounds the corner, out of sight.

—

Back inside, I take the present and head up the stairs, settling
myself in the spare bedroom.

I sit on the bed and unfold the corners, pulling the wrapping
away to find a leather-bound photo album. Taped to the cover is
a note written in Jackie's slanted, angular handwriting.

I hope someday Miles will gather understanding and comfort from
this. It was hard for me to assemble, but it was healing as well.
Thank you for being such a great friend.

Love,
Jackie

I open the album, expecting to see photographs of Miles and Nick, a chronicle of their friendship, but instead there are photographs of a baby and a house I don't recognize, with furnishings that look like they're from the seventies. I flip a few pages and see a young boy on a bike, then the same boy climbing a tree. A few more pages, I see him dressed up for a dance, then running shirtless through a sprinkler.

"Oh my god," I whisper. Jackie has gifted us a photographic journey of Aaron's life. She's given my son his father.

Tears stream down my cheeks as I continue to study the boy as he grows into a teenager, a young adult, and finally a man. Aaron, holding his own son, tears of joy in his eyes as he smiles at the camera. He looks so happy, and for a moment it's impossible to believe he's not still here. Miles will never have a photograph of that moment with his father, though I know he'll understand why his story is different. And thanks to Jackie, he'll have more than I ever thought possible. I realize she must have gotten many of these pictures from Beverly, and I make a mental note to call her and thank her for facilitating this.

I flip to the next page, but it's empty. I turn back to the beginning and scour the book again, studying Aaron's face and his expressions, seeing so much of Miles in him. I find a photo of him at about the same age Miles is now, grinning and leaning over the handlebars of a bike. He looks like he's about to laugh or say something, the street behind him empty except for anonymous lawns and seventies-era cars. Beverly was right. They're identical. I trace the outline of Aaron's face, wondering what thought lived inside his head at that exact moment and what he did immediately afterward. What he had for dinner. What he looked like, asleep and sweaty on his pillow that night. And the thousands of days that followed it, all the way until the last one.

I keep turning pages, slowly recounting his life in pictures. When I reach the end, I close it and place it on the dresser, then walk to the window and look down into the yard. The kids have divided into two teams and are attacking one another with the water balloons. I find Miles and Nick, hiding behind a large planter, their backs arched identically as they huddle together, waiting for the perfect moment to ambush their friends. My eyes travel over to the corner of the house, where Liam and Henry stand with a hose, filling balloons and piling them into tubs. Liam laughs at something Henry says, and the sound carries up and into my heart.

It's not how I imagined it would be, but life rarely ever is. Jackie left the door open to something new, a different kind of friendship. And I latch on to that for now. Because so much of what I thought would be impossible has happened in this past year. Why not this?

Miles and Nick emerge from their hiding place and move toward Rose in a planned attack. She screams and ducks, but a water balloon hits her between her shoulders. Liam and Henry roar with laughter as the boys make a hasty retreat.

"Paige!" she yells. "Get out here!"

"Coming!" I head down the stairs, into the messy chaos that is my family.

EPIGENETIC INHERITANCE

Epigenetic inheritance is the idea that a parent's experiences can be passed down to future generations. It means that events in your grandfather's life may have shaped the way you experience events in your own.

Studies have been done, on mice all the way up to humans, and the results are the same—trauma can lodge itself in your cells and transmit the effects across generations. The phrase *I felt it in every cell of my body* has some scientific truth to it. Everything we experience shapes our genes. These experiences are transferred to our tissues and into our cells through biochemicals. Win the lottery? It's recorded. Survive an acrimonious divorce? That experience becomes a part of your genetic code and could be traced generations from now.

In one such study, pregnant mice were subjected to a physical stressor accompanied by a specific odor. Two generations later, offspring of the affected rodents had a significantly higher biological and behavioral response to that odor than offspring of nonaffected mice. A more recent study using worms has measured that impact through fourteen generations. If we translate that to our own life span, it would be approximately 350 years.

It's harder to measure in humans. But we know that descendants of Holocaust survivors are three times more likely to develop a stress disorder, even when they never knew their surviving ancestor. And pregnant women who survived September 11 have significantly lower cortisol levels, as do their children. Epigenetic stress can cross generations, and we are only just beginning to understand how long the effects can last.

When someone survives a traumatic experience, they often say, *That changed me. I'm not the same person I was before*. And they're right. You might think your experience is wholly yours, formed by your DNA and unique life experiences. But epigenetic inheritance tells us you're wrong.

My father's childhood trauma exists somewhere in me, and it also lives in Miles's genetic code. It will impact the decisions he makes, though he will only know it as *intuition*, that small voice that lives inside of him, guiding him toward his own truth.

Sophie Sullivan's children will carry epigenetic markers of the loss of Mara, just as losing Aaron will manifest itself in Nick's children. Miles will carry it too, though for him it will be different, the loss of a man still mostly unknown. This theory is being proven in labs across the world.

When someone dies, you can't help but think in terms of *last times*. The last time you talked with them, the last time you held their hand, the last time you kissed them. But we're learning that we never really lose those last times. They embed themselves in our genes to be carried forward, a quiet memory of people long since forgotten.

I often wonder what my father would say about Jackie's return, about the life I'm building with Liam. But if I'm still and I listen hard, he's here, in the silent rush of blood through my veins, telling me what I need to know.

Author's Note

I didn't start out writing a book about genetics. Truthfully, I knew almost nothing about genetics, and when I realized Paige was going to be a geneticist and there was going to be a genetic subplot, I was terrified. So I did what I tell my own children and students to do when they don't know the answer to something—read a lot of books and ask an expert a lot of questions. *The Invisible History of the Human Race* by Christine Kenneally was invaluable in planting the seed ideas for my genetics chapters. The book is a wonderful primer on how DNA and inheritance work and how the past can manifest itself in the present.

I was also lucky enough to be able to connect with geneticist Dr. James West of Vanderbilt University. Dr. West has been incredibly generous with his time, patiently answering my questions and forwarding me articles over the course of the past two years. It was from Dr. West that I first heard about oxytocin production in new fathers—which got me thinking about the men in the world who aren't good fathers and that perhaps it isn't a conscious choice to be a bad parent, but rather a genetic one. From there the oxytocin inhibitor gene was born. I've done my best to stay true to the way Dr. West described labs, DNA tests, and research studies and how they're funded, though I've taken some license with procedures and how Paige's study is structured. And of course, all errors—scientific and otherwise—are entirely mine.

I am fortunate to know several families who conceived their children using an anonymous donor. But Miles and Paige are entirely my own invention, not based on any one mother or any one child. It is true that the United States lags far behind in anonymous donor policies. More and more sperm banks are offering *open donor programs*, an opportunity for donor-conceived children to have access to biological information and contact with their donors once they turn eighteen. But that doesn't address the larger need of millions of donor-conceived children who cannot access their donor records. Websites such as the Donor Sibling Registry offer these children forums, workshops, and support groups, as well as a database that allows them to search for biological siblings and parents. Founded in 2000 by Wendy and Ryan Kramer, the DSR's mission is to help people who were conceived via sperm, egg, or embryo donation find genetic relatives. The DSR also works to fight for an individual's right to their biological history. For more information, you can go to www.donorsiblingregistry.com.

For many years, my route to work took me past my great-aunt Edna's old apartment. She, along with my grandparents, are long gone, but every time I'd pass, I'd feel a sense of loss for all the things I'll never know about them simply because I never asked: my aunt's heartbreaking affair with a married man or the scandal surrounding my own grandparents' marriage. No one knows the details anymore. They are just faded memories that have traveled down through the generations, like legends, landing at my feet and making me wonder what dramas in my own life will someday be lost to time. So learning about epigenetic inheritance—that experiences from their lives can manifest in mine and that my own might somehow shape my children and grandchildren—resonated with me.

What I've learned through writing this book is that genetics isn't static. Our environment, our emotions, even the people we choose to spend time with are all recorded in our cells, shaping who we will become. Whether we like it or not—be it a cancer mutation or the methylation of the oxytocin inhibitor—the control we think we have is limited to what we see in front of us, the moment we're living right now.

Acknowledgments

Thank you to my agent, Mollie Glick. From day one, working with you has been a joy. You're fierce and funny and so incredibly smart. I'm grateful every day that I get to have you on my team, and I look forward to working on many more books together. And a thank-you to Joy Fowlkes and Emily Westcott, for keeping all of the moving parts running smoothly.

Thank you to my editor, Lauren McKenna. You took Paige and instantly turned her into *our girl*. You are such a force in the publishing industry and helped to make this book better than I'd ever dreamed it would be. And thank you to the entire Gallery team: Jen Bergstrom, Abby Zidle, Diana Velasquez, Lisa Litwack, Christine Masters, Erica Ferguson, Sara Quaranta, Michelle Podberezniak, and Mackenzie Hickey.

I have some very talented writers in my life who also happen to be great friends. First, a tremendous thank-you to Brenda Drake, Karma Brown, and Susan Bishop Crispell. I would not be here without you. Thank you to Aimee Molloy and Liz Kay— you are not only brilliant critique partners, but hilarious as well. You held my hand and kept me laughing through this process. And, Aimee, I am forever grateful to debut alongside you. It's made everything ten times more fun than doing it alone. Now go get your sandwich board and bell ready.

Thank you also to Dedi Felman, for putting me through my paces early on, and to Alexandra Alessandri, for urging me to stick with this book when I wanted to give up.

A huge thank-you to Dr. James West (and his wife, Mary Beth) for answering every one of my questions—no matter how basic—with patience and enthusiasm for this project. There would be no genetic subplot without you! And my deepest appreciation to Wendy Kramer, founder of the Donor Sibling Registry, for allowing me to share its mission and history with my readers.

Thank you to the many early readers willing to take a chance and sit down with a very rough version: Lori Sawyer, Carey Madill, Magda Pecsenye, Kristina ElSayed, and Susan Jackson.

My parents, Joyce and Bob, have supported me in everything I've ever done in life—enthusiastically and without reservation—for the past forty-plus years and counting. I love you both.

And finally, to my boys, Alex and Ben, who have lived alongside this book for so many years. You are, and will always be, the two brightest lights in my life, and my two greatest creations. I love you both more than the entire world—north, south, east, west, up, down, and all around.

The Ones We Choose

Julie Clark

This reading group guide for The Ones We Choose *includes an introduction, discussion questions, ideas for enhancing your book club, and a Q&A with author Julie Clark. The suggested questions are intended to help your reading group find new and interesting angles and topics for your discussion. We hope that these ideas will enrich your conversation and increase your enjoyment of the book.*

Introduction

Abandoned by her father when she was young, geneticist Paige Robson has dedicated her life to pulling apart the science of his choice—discovering a gene that explains why some men stay while others leave. So when she decides she wants a child of her own, she turns to an anonymous sperm donor who will never complicate their lives. Now, nine years later, Paige loves Liam, a man with a big heart and a steadiness that makes her want to set aside her past and build a family of three with him.

But moving forward is more complicated than she expected. Her son, Miles, is desperate to know his biological father and views Liam as nothing more than a stand-in for the real thing. Paige feels trapped, unable to make either of them completely happy.

When fate thrusts Miles's donor into their lives, Paige is shocked to discover he's already connected to them in ways she couldn't have anticipated. Paige fears that revealing his true identity may do more harm than good and decides to say nothing. But when tragedy strikes, she must face the consequences of keeping a secret only she knows.

Topics and Questions
for Discussion

1. When Paige tries to get Miles to go on the dads' campout with Liam, Miles expresses his desire to know his biological father. Up until this point, Paige has been able to handle her son's questions about his conception. What has changed? Is it just the campout? Or is the development of Miles's desires something Paige didn't anticipate?

2. Paige meets Jackie and Aaron at parents' night at Miles's school. Paige says the PTA mothers make her feel inadequate. What is different about Jackie? Paige is always worried about Miles having a friend, but why is it important that she also have one?

3. Paige feels torn between giving Liam what he wants and making sure Miles is happy. Is that a dichotomy of her own construction? When Liam breaks up with her, he tells her Miles is "never going to let me in because you've taught him *he doesn't have to*." Is that a fair point? Or, since Liam knew Paige's history with her father, could he have approached her fears in a different way?

4. The reader is put in Paige's shoes when her father doesn't show up to have lunch with her and Rose. Does this make you more understanding of her position that neither she nor Miles will have anything to do with him, despite the fact that he is dying? She takes a harsh line that only Jackie supports; is it a fair reaction to someone responsible for a lot of emotional damage?

5. Both Paige's mother and sister want Paige to have contact with her father before he dies. Her mother wants Paige to grant him forgiveness, saying it "doesn't mean forgetting. . . . It means understanding what happened, looking beyond your version of the past and seeing things from someone else's perspective." What events lead to Paige finding this version of forgiveness?

6. Rose is blunter with Paige. She says, "This isn't about forgiving Dad or even having a relationship with him. It's about not hating him when he dies." Is this different from what their mother was trying to say? Why is finding this place so important for Paige as a daughter, mother, and possible life partner?

7. Paige's father is the one to show her how similar they are to each other. Do you think her work on the genetics of emotional detachment has blinded her to the power of learned behavior?

8. Bruno understands why this gene study is important to Paige both professionally and personally. He calls her out when she

asks Jenna to make extra visits to Scott, which could compromise their work. Were you surprised she then took an even bigger risk by using her lab to test Aaron's DNA? She says the mother in her won out over the scientist. Were you comfortable with this justification?

9. Paige does not mean to tell Aaron he is Miles's father, but blurts it out in her frustration that he won't get tested for Huntington's. Do her rights as a mother trump his rights as the actual owner of his genes? What emotional consequences does her revelation have? How are they compounded by Aaron's death?

10. How do you feel about Paige's decision not to share her secret with Jackie? When Jackie does find out, does Paige's explanation seem reasonable? Does her letter to Jackie do a better job of explaining all of her motives? Do you understand why Jackie cannot forgive her?

11. Although Liam decides to give Paige a second chance, it's hard earned. Liam says, "It's not that I don't want to believe you; it's that I can't. Not yet." Is this a satisfying response? Is it true to their characters?

12. When Paige visits her father's deathbed, she sees her mother and feels guilty that she hasn't been a more supportive daughter. According to Rose, Paige used to be the bravest person she knew. What changed for Paige after she became a mother herself? Do you think motherhood makes you more brave or less?

13. The chapters are preceded by short informational pieces about genetics. The final two pages are about epigenetic inheritance, and they note that even if we don't get to hear family stories, our ancestors are genetically "carried forward, a quiet memory of people long since forgotten." Why is it so important that Paige and Miles understand both their fathers' genetics *and* their stories?

Enhance Your Book Club

1. Has anyone in your group used the websites 23andme.com or ancestry.com? If so, have members share what they gained from the experience. If not, consider using one after reading this book. Ancestry.com offers but does not require DNA testing; 23andme.com is based entirely on genetic information. Does Paige's story affect your preference for using one or the other?

2. Although Jackie does not forgive Paige, she gives her the beautiful gift of a photo album of Aaron's childhood. As the child of a sperm donor, Miles will have this very unique connection to his genetic father. Does it make you feel any differently about the photo albums you might currently have of your family? Create a photo album of your own dedicated to connecting the generations and share it with the group.

3. Paige uses *A Night of Asian Fusion* to reconnect with Liam. This worked well for the characters, so why not try it with your club? Find a cooking class in your area and sign up with members of your group. If a class on Asian food does not appeal to you, try one on creating desserts or another specialty, such as Indian cooking or pizza making.

A Conversation
with Julie Clark

This is your debut novel! Was the writing and publishing process what you expected? If not, how was it different? Is there anything you wish you had known before you started?

I am one of those fortunate writers who have had a wonderful debut experience . . . all the way from my agent to my editor to the entire team at Gallery Books. No one knows what to expect, and you sometimes hear horror stories. I'm so fortunate to have such a solid team behind me and *The Ones We Choose*. I think the one thing I wish I'd known beforehand is that it takes a long time. When I started pursuing publication seriously, I really needed money to help pay for my boys' preschool tuition. They will be twelve and nine at the time of publication, so the joke's on me.

You are a fifth grade teacher. Are there any skills you developed as a teacher that helped you write *The Ones We Choose*? What made you decide to become an author?

Too many to count! There is nothing more instructive than taking apart a middle grade novel with my students and studying plot, character, and theme . . . and then going home and applying those lessons to my own work. Even though I write adult fiction, the framework remains the same and can sometimes be easier to see in a middle grade novel that is shorter, with fewer subplots and POVs. Another advantage is my front row seat to kids who are just a little bit older than Miles is in *The Ones We Choose*. I admit to listening in on their conversations and paying attention to the rhythm of their words. The back-and-forth of a conversation between ten-year-olds is different than it is between adults. Writing dialogue between children is hard. You have to get it *just right* in order for it to be believable.

I've always wanted to be an author. Ever since my early twenties, when I worked at Berkeley and could take creative writing classes at a steep discount, I knew writing was something I would someday do. But then life got in the way, and I set it aside for a little while (actually, twenty-five years). In 2012 I lost one of my best friends to breast cancer, and I realized that if I wanted to pursue my dream of being a published author, I couldn't wait. It took me three years and two manuscripts to get here, and I'm very excited about what's next. I'm lucky in that I get to do two jobs I love—write and teach children. Every day!

You have two young sons. Did they serve as inspiration for Paige and Miles's relationship? Did any of the scenes in *The Ones We Choose* happen in real life with your boys? I parent my boys very much the way Paige parents Miles. I'd say people who know us will hear my voice very clearly when Paige and Miles are together on the page, though Paige and Miles's relationship is uniquely theirs. Like Miles, my boys are obsessed with robots and LEGO building and *Star Wars*. In the scene at the pizza place, where Miles and Nick are arguing about *Star Wars*, I originally had them arguing about a book their teacher read in class. My editor wanted me to change it to something about *Star Wars*, so I asked my oldest, "What might two kids debate about *Star Wars*?" thinking he would give me something really great. But he never got back to me about it, so I ended up having to Google it.

Can you tell us a little bit about your writing process? How do you map out a book? Did you know how Paige and Miles's story was going to end when you began writing, or did it come to you as you wrote?

Every book is different. This is the sad news, but it's also the exciting news because the process is always fresh and thrilling (and frustrating). The first book I ever wrote, I just sat down and wrote it. I didn't map anything out, just let it take me where it wanted to go. Obviously it was awful. With *The Ones We Choose*, I was a bit more thoughtful about plotting out the general character arcs. But it still went through some insane permutations . . . including one version that had Paige tracking the donor down and orchestrating a meeting before she chose him. I also knew how it would end from a very early stage. I knew I wanted this to be a story about female friendship, and I knew Jackie would gift Paige a photo album at the end, all the while still not fully forgiving her.

With my next book, I've got an entire wall of note cards outlining the chapters and twists and reveals. But to be honest, I'm not sure how useful that will be, as I'm already starting to move in a different direction. I think the one thing that's consistent every time is that I have to give myself space to think. To try things out, throw them away, and come at a story from twenty different directions before I figure out what it's supposed to be. I don't know if I'll ever be someone who has a tight outline that she writes from religiously. But I'll keep trying!

You describe your characters so vividly. How did they come to you? How did you name them? Are they based on real people?

My characters are the result of many years of living with them every day. Making them talk to one another, fight with one another, joke around with one another. They're not based on real people . . . but I try to study people I enjoy being around and pinpoint what it is about them that makes them so likable. And then I try to put some of those qualities into my characters. But characters evolve over time, just like friendships do. In the book I'm working on right now, I'm struggling to figure out my two main characters: how to get them to go where I want them to go, learn what I want them to learn. I don't know them as well as I know Paige, Rose, and Jackie. By the time my editor and I were doing our final revisions on *The Ones We Choose*, it was almost effortless to put them into new scenes. I'm finding it a lot harder now, with new people I don't know as well. But the only way to get past that is to keep writing them.

I'm terrible at naming characters. Really awful. My writing partners often annotate my drafts with the comment "This is an awful name. You need to change this." In early drafts of *The Ones We Choose*, Paige's name was Gerda, and Aaron's name was Bryon. I sometimes still use these names by accident.

One of my favorite things about the book is the interstitial chapters on genetics and the Donor Sibling Registry. How did you become interested in genetics? What kind of research did you conduct while writing? What was the biggest takeaway from what you learned?

In an early draft of *The Ones We Choose*, Paige was the manager of a dog rescue, and she had a funny assistant named Bruno.

None of it was working. I needed something that would drive Paige's motivation. After talking with a close friend and editor about it, we landed on genetics. Paige's reliance on science and facts was a critical part of figuring out who she was, and ultimately dictated the direction of the entire book. The genetic subplot unlocked everything. Which was alarming because I teach fifth grade and don't know anything about genetics. So I put out a call on one of the many Facebook groups I'm in, asking if anyone knew a geneticist who might be willing to answer some questions. My friend Mary Beth wrote and said, "My husband, James, is a geneticist! He'd love to talk to you!" And from there, Dr. James West became my sounding board for all things genetics. He was so generous with his time, and we even spoke on the phone a few times as I was hammering out the oxytocin inhibitor gene. I absolutely love the interstitial chapters. Making sure I got the science right, making sure Paige was believable as a geneticist, was very important to me. I hope I've done Dr. West justice.

My genetics research confirmed for me something I already suspected—that our life experiences impact our cells, and can change our DNA. What I found most exciting was the newest research about epigenetic inheritance and how we can pass our experiences on to others. In 2015 I was diagnosed with cancer, even though I had no family history and no genetic markers. What caused my cells to mutate? Was it a perfect storm of circumstance and biology? Some studies are beginning to find a correlation between stress and certain types of cancer. There's so much we don't understand, but incredible discoveries are happening every day. It's an exciting time to be alive.

Is there anything you've found particularly rewarding about writing and publishing *The Ones We Choose*? If so, what?

Without a doubt, all the people I've met. Writers are some of the most generous people in the world. They are always willing to offer help or advice. Publishing, in general, is filled with truly wonderful people.

What is your favorite way to procrastinate? What's your best trick for overcoming a creative block?

I'm not much of a procrastinator when it comes to my writing. But when I'm stuck, I step out of the manuscript and journal things out longhand. I don't try to write the book . . . I just try to write *about* the book. What's stumping me about a character? What's bothering me about a certain line or chapter? I give myself permission to stop trying to fix it in the manuscript, and give myself the space to really talk it through with myself. I sometimes do this with my writing partners, but I tend to forget things, so having a written record—even if it's just a conversation I'm having with myself on paper—allows me the freedom to think without worrying about whether I'll remember it later.

What is your favorite book of all time? Do you find yourself more interested in plot-driven or character-driven works?

My favorite book of all time is probably *The Time Traveler's Wife*. I also love *A Discovery of Witches* and *Where'd You Go, Bernadette*. I enjoy both plot-driven books and character-driven books, depending on my mood. I have a deep love of historical fiction, although I don't think I could ever write it.

What other authors are you friends with, and how do they help you grow as a writer?

My writing partners first and foremost—Aimee Molloy and Liz Kay. Nothing we write gets sent to editors or agents without first passing through the group. It helps to have people you can count on to read something and tell you whether you're on the right track or not. I have a lot of other writing friends who are my greatest cheerleaders and commiserators, which makes the journey a lot less lonely.

***The Ones We Choose* is such an emotional book, and it delves deep into intricate relationship dynamics and familial bonds. Do you find it easier or more difficult to write an emotionally charged scene? Why? What was your most difficult scene to write?**

Once I know the characters, writing them in emotional scenes happens pretty naturally because I know what they'll probably say or not say. Or say wrong. It's when I'm still trying to figure out who they are and what they really care about that I find it hard to write them in tense, emotional scenes. I think my first chapters are always the hardest to write. Because you have to get those pages *just right*. There's so much riding on them. I've probably written and rewritten the first chapter of *The Ones We Choose* a hundred times, in a hundred different ways. The big emotional scenes that come later in the book weren't as hard because I was in the middle of the story. I knew what my characters wanted and what was standing in their way. But first pages are *hard*. So much needs to be communicated in a very nuanced way.

How do you prepare yourself to be creative? Do you have a ritual or a time or place that is most conducive to work-

ing? What one element is absolutely necessary for your process?

I write every day first thing in the morning. Monday through Friday I wake up at 3:45 in the morning and write until 6:00. On weekends I let myself sleep in and then get right to work. My best thinking happens when my brain is still soft from sleep, with a giant pot of hot coffee next to me. But during the week, my writing time is usually over by 6:00. After that, I have to get the kids up, get lunches packed, get out the door, and teach a full day. There isn't room to write on top of all that. If I'm on a deadline, I'll put in a couple more hours in the evenings, but I try to save evenings for reading and relaxing. I always say . . . you can write a whole book in just two hours a day!

Follow Julie Clark on social media to find out what she's working on next!

Twitter: @jclarkab
Instagram: julieclarkauthor
Facebook: julieclarkbooks